CHASING TRUTH AND REDEMPTION

DETECTIVE CARLA MCBRIDE CHRONICLES
BOOK 3

NICK LEWIS

ROUGH
EDGES
PRESS

Rough Edges Press
An Imprint of Wolfpack Publishing
9850 S. Maryland Parkway, Suite A-5 #323
Las Vegas, Nevada 89183

roughedgespress.com

Paperback ISBN 978-1-68549-221-2
eBook ISBN 978-1-68549-220-5

For Scott, Andrea, and Cynthia, my three children who have grown up into successful adults. I am immensely proud of them and extremely honored to be their father.

CHASING TRUTH AND REDEMPTION

CHAPTER 1

JUNE 23, 1997 5:30 PM

Officers McBride and Picetti's afternoon shift began like any other day, quiet and uneventful. Oakmont's west end, an old-established neighborhood of craftsman style houses with welcoming front porches, had one of the lowest crime rates in the city, making their job easier than other beats. The residents, known as Westenders, were just honest working people from all walks of life. While watching out for each other and their homes, they paid particular attention to keeping all the kids in the neighborhood safe.

Carla McBride, out of the police academy for just a few months, was Irish all the way. With fiery-red hair, she had a hot-headed temper to go with it. Cocky, aggressive, and fearless, her work behavior and personality rocked in the male-dominated police force. Tony Picetti, her training officer, was a ten-year veteran with many accolades. He was the ideal mentor for hot-shot rookies, like McBride, who wanted to put a stamp on their rising careers quickly.

After cruising up and down the west end for several hours, their patrol car rested proudly in the middle of Monroe Avenue. It was another typical boring shift for them, and McBride, more than Picetti, was itching for some real action. Observing the neighborhood children playing in their front yards brought happiness to them on this carefree summer day. Tag and hide-and-seek seemed to be the favorite activity this sunny afternoon. Sounds of "you're it" and "one-two-three, here I come" took McBride back to her childhood days. As she continued to watch the kids playing, Picetti's thoughts drifted to his two boys, Owen and Evan, and how much he loved them.

"Squelch...squelch!"

That annoying sound interrupted his daydream of them playing soccer in the backyard. With deer-in-the-headlight eyes, mouth in awe-and-shock mode, McBride's face lit up like a Christmas tree. A blueish vein on her left temple pulsated faster and faster. Her best ready-for-action grin met Picetti's pale and stoic face. He had seen that look before. Shaking his head back-and-forth, he wondered whether that expression was now taught in the police academy. With anticipation rising, palms sweating, McBride waited impatiently for dispatch to bark out their orders.

"Car 37, 10-57, 407 Washington Avenue, copy?"

Ready-for-action glared all over McBride's rosy face. "Umm, Picetti. We finally get to see some action, right, partner?"

A questioning frown met her ready-for-action pose. Picetti's years of mentoring and experience kicked in. "Be careful what you wish for, McBride. We have a missing person, and knowing the neighborhood as I do, it's probably a child. And you might not like how this plays out."

Silently, McBride sarcastically laughed at him. "Yeah, I know what a 10-57 is. I believe I can handle what we might find." Scowling, Picetti rolled his eyes, shook his head back-and-forth, pointing at the mic as dispatch barked out the command once more.

The moment she prayed and prepared for had arrived. Like a seasoned officer, she snatched the mic off the magnetic clip with ease, responding vigorously.

"Copy that, dispatch. En route to 407 Washington Avenue."

"10-4, Car 37."

For McBride, that simple command was like hearing the "start-your-engine" command at the Indy 500. As McBride delivered her best ready-for-action grin once more, Picetti rolled his eyes and shook his head back-and-forth. While knowing the drill, the engine growled. Picetti whipped it in gear and hit the gas pedal. McBride's face lit up like a Christmas tree once more. With respiration heavy, pulse thumping, and adrenaline in control, her head jerked back against the headrest as the tires squealed. As the cruiser fishtailed around the corner, her head hit the passenger door window. A broad smile beamed across her face; her moment of truth was near.

Within minutes, 407 Washington Avenue, the fourth house on the right, sent McBride's pulse into overdrive. Her first real action was in front of her. A man and a woman stood nervously holding hands on the porch, fear and uncertainty plastered on their faces. Pulling in front of the house, the man and woman rushed toward the cruiser as McBride and Picetti exited. Tears streaming down the lady's face said it all; this situation was not good. McBride's ready-for-action face quickly soured. Angry butterflies dusted her heartstrings, and queasiness welled-up in her throat as Picetti's comment, "be careful what you wish for," resonated in her soul.

A broken emotional voice cried out, "Officers, umm, our only child, uh, is missing. When we, we called her for dinner, umm, she didn't answer. We searched every-where, but we couldn't find her."

Picetti said, "Sir, please take a deep breath and calm down. What's your name? What's your daughter's name?"

"I'm, uh, Jack Miracle, and this is my wife, Sandy. Umm, our daughter's name is Penny."

While handling it like the seasoned veteran that he was, Picetti calmed Mr. Miracle down and continued. "Okay, may we go inside? We don't want to create any more of a scene out here than we have to." Once inside, he continued in a caring and calming tone. "Please tell us everything you can, so we can find your daughter."

Wiping away tears, Jack nodded. "It was a normal day. Penny was playing with her friends throughout the day, especially Zoe, who lives two houses down the street. Late this afternoon, Zoe, Mason, and Scotty were walking to Davenport's Grocery just around the corner to get candy. Penny wanted to go. We gave, uh, her permis-sion, and I handed her two dollars to buy a Snicker's candy bar and some bubble gum. We told her, umm, to come straight back, umm, which she did."

Visibly shaken, eyes glistening, Jack hyperventilated and stuttered his words. McBride recognized he needed calming down again presented her with the opportunity to taste her first real action. Interrupting Jack at the disdain of Picetti, she interjected, "Mr. Miracle, please slow down, and take deep breaths. We'll find her, okay?" Jack nodded as Picetti's stare attempted to wipe off the bright gleam across McBride's face to no avail.

After a short pause, Jack continued. "I went upstairs to take a shower before dinner. Sandy asked Penny to pick the perfect tomato from the garden for dinner. She took forever, but that's not unusual for her. Sandy, who was setting the dining room table, hollered that dinner was ready. She went back to the kitchen, and the tomato Penny picked was on the counter, but she wasn't there. Sandy yelled for her, but she didn't answer. Looking out in the backyard, she was not there either. We called her friends; no one had seen her. By then, we were terrified and called you guys."

"Has she ever done this before?" Picetti asked. "You know, disappeared for a short time, then shown up later."

Calm enough now to answer a question, Sandy, in a defensive tone, frantically responded, "Never! She's a good girl, umm, always obeying us, or she knew the consequences."

"Mrs. Miracle, what was she wearing?" McBride asked.

"A pair of white cut-off shorts, a pink tank-top, and yellow flip-flops."

Panic slowly crept inside McBride's curious psyche; a swarm of butterflies attacked her gut, pollinating seeds of anxiety. Breathing deeply, she tried her best to quiet their angry wings. Although Penny had been missing a half hour now, McBride realized what her partner told her was coming true. Instinct told her this situation was escalating quickly; every minute wasted could seal Penny's fate.

Adrenaline in control, McBride stepped out on the porch, radioing dispatch for help. When she returned inside the house, Picetti passed out wallet-sized photos of Penny. McBride immediately noticed Penny was a beautiful young girl mature beyond her years; blonde hair and almost-thirteen-going-on-twenty best described her striking features. As Jack and Sandy embraced and cried as one, a hundred different emotions crowded McBride's vulnerable psyche. Picetti's comment, "be careful what you wish for," repeatedly screamed in her soul.

Bernie Kowalski, who recently achieved detective status, arrived with additional officers to help in the search. As the lead detective on this case, he met with the officers and assigned Picetti to coordinate the search. Welcoming front porches morphed into ones of concern, uncertainty, and gossip. Kowalski remained with Penny's parents to question them further and keep them as calm as possible. He assigned McBride to visit Zoe Pendergast, Penny's best friend, who lived two houses down the street.

As McBride approached the house where Zoe lived, it wasn't much different from the one she just left. An old craftsman style house with a welcoming front porch greeted her. A pair of white wooden rocking chairs flanked a white wooden table, while at the other end of the porch, a white wooden swing hung from the tongue-in-groove ceiling. Realizing the peacefulness on the porch, the thought of disrupting the tranquility inside the house sucker-punched her in the gut. As she knocked on the door, goosebumps speckled her arms, sending her pulse faster. McBride searched for calmness and courage; her defining moment had arrived. A lady, presumably

Zoe's mother, appeared through the full-length screened storm door.

"Ms. Pendergast?"

"Yes, how may I help you?"

"I'm Officer McBride with the Oakmont Police Department. I have some disturbing news. May I come in?" Opening the door, she motioned McBride to sit on the sofa. After they were both seated, McBride continued, "Jack and Sandy Miracle reported Penny missing this evening."

"Oh, my heavens, please, Lord, not Penny…she's like a second daughter to me."

Remembering her training, McBride calmly and confidently continued, "I'm afraid so. I understand your daughter and Penny are best friends and were together this afternoon. May I ask her a few questions?"

"Of course. I'll go get her."

Walking up the stairs to Zoe's bedroom, McBride heard Judy explain to Zoe the situation. Within minutes, Zoe and her mother came down the stairs and entered the living room. Zoe's eyes glistened. "Honey, this is Officer McBride I told you about. She wants to ask you some questions about this afternoon with Penny."

Tears streamed down the cheeks of a frightened young girl. Training in high gear, although Officer McBride was childless, her maternal instincts took over. "Ah, sweetheart, everything will be okay. Will you answer a few questions for me? It may help us find her." Zoe nodded. "I understand you and your friends walked with Penny to the grocery store this afternoon. Will you tell me about it? Did you see anyone strange this afternoon?"

"Well, when Penny and I played this morning in her

backyard, a car stopped in the alley, rolled down the window, a man waved at us, and tossed out some wrapped candy, then he left. Penny said his name was Tommy and he was her friend." McBride nodded as memories of a similar incident when she was thirteen-going-on-twenty flashed before her eyes.

"Can you tell me what he looked like?" Sniffling, she shook her head, back-and-forth erratically. "That's okay, sweetheart, anything else you can tell me?"

Zoe nodded and continued. "Hmm, then this afternoon, Mason, Scotty, and I stopped at her house. She came out, and we walked to Davenport's Grocery. Once we got there, she took forever to pick out her candy like always. We walked back. When we were in front of her house, we stopped and watched her go inside, and then I came home. Mason and Scotty watched me go into my house, and they left. That's the last time I saw her."

Although Judy was trying her best not to alarm her daughter, the emotional toll of Penny missing seized her face. After seeing the concern on her mom's face, Zoe's emotions erupted. Hugging Zoe, she kissed her on the forehead and whispered reassuring words in her ear. Remembering from her training never to show your feelings, McBride glanced out the window, regaining her composure. Peering into the eyes of the scared twelve-year-old girl, McBride smiled. "Zoe, everything will be okay. I will find your best friend. I promise you, okay?" With more reassurance from her mother, Zoe nodded.

While walking back to the Miracles' house, McBride pulled out the photo of Penny, realizing that she, amazingly, looked a lot like Zoe. Both pretty, blonde hair, and blue eyes. Zoe looked her age; however, Penny did not, and it was clear why teenage boys or older men were attracted to her. Penny's physical maturity reminded her of when she was blossoming and the issues she had to deal with when she was almost-thirteen-going-on-twenty. Reaching Penny's house, angry butterflies vigorously fluttered in her gut. She had just made a promise to a frightened little girl she knew would be difficult, maybe impossible, to keep.

Standing on the porch, Detective Kowalski scanned the street with panic-stricken eyes. Welcoming porches became a spectacle of concern; random gossip chattered up and down the avenue. At the bottom of the steps, the fear on Kowalski's face matched the helplessness in his soul. "Any news?" Kowalski shook his head back-and-forth. "I got nothing from Zoe. She's a frightened young child that just had her best friend in the world vanish. How are they holding up?" Shaking his head back-and-forth again answered her question.

Through the big picture window, Jack and Sandy held each other, sobbing and praying for a real miracle. Wiping her tears away, McBride wondered what she could say to them that could make things better and give them hope. Unfortunately, those words were impossible to find. With their hearts ripped apart, thoughts swirled throughout her mind of what they were feeling at this moment. The pain inside Jack and Sandy had to be excruciating, life-altering, she thought. If one day she were fortunate to have a child, she hoped she would never have to endure the pain and hopelessness displayed in that living room of despair.

CHAPTER 2

FIFTEEN YEARS LATER

Naked and shivering from head to toe, Beth Pendergast observed her reflection in the bathroom mirror. After letting out a big sigh, a frazzled and lonely young woman's reflection stared back and shrugged her shoulders.

Beth mumbled, "What a day, right?" Her reflection nodded. "Yeah, my first day as a forensic psychologist and profiler was a real bitch, if you know what I mean."

Silence echoed off the walls as Beth's reflection shrugged her shoulders again. "I wonder what tomorrow will bring, whether I'm ready for my first case." Staring at her reflection, she asked, "Do you think I am?"

Her reflection smiled and nodded. "Great, that's what I thought. You think I could use a drink to unwind, to ease the tension holding my body hostage?"

Her reflection nodded and smiled once more. "Now that's exactly the answer I wanted to hear."

After a quick shower, she slipped on her favorite lounging top—her ex-boyfriend's long-sleeve white shirt. Scott's bittersweet scent still lingered throughout it, while memories of the last time they made passionate and magical love flashed in her mind. She still loved him dearly; however, he wasn't ready to commit to 'till death do us part,' and they parted ways.

Pinot Grigio called her name. Retreating to the kitchen, she poured a glass, hoping it would ease the tension and sorrow wearing on her soul. The first sip didn't quite measure up. A second sip, a much longer one, lingered on her palate, tasting much better. The third taste began to ease the tension inside her body, slowly replacing some of the emptiness in her life.

Walking back to the bedroom with her wine, she turned on the television to the local news. Immediately, the big story about a missing twelve-year-old girl seized her attention. She remembered that fateful day fifteen-years-ago when her best friend, Penny Miracle, disappeared. Tears of sadness began to trickle down her cheeks. She wiped them away, while another sip of wine tried to calm her surging anxiety. As the big story ended, her guilt-ridden complexion spoke. "I'm sorry, Penny, so very, very sorry."

With her wine on the bedside table, darkness captured the room. Within minutes, a deep sleep controlled her body and soul. Happy dreams flooded her subconscious reality until being squashed by a haunting childish-like voice echoing throughout her room. Subconsciously, she replied to the voice, "I will find you, I promise."

Rising quickly, she hugged her knees tightly, letting out a big calming sigh. Yellowish muted light filled the room. With squinted eyes, she scanned her bedroom, and Penny wasn't there. "Where are you?" she whispered. Eyes fully open and focused, she breathed deeply to calm her nerves and raging pulse. Cold sweat cooled the embers smoldering inside her body.

Her unfinished wine called her name once more. While draining it in one swallow, its fruity flavors helped release the tension still ravaging her body. "Ugh," she mumbled as her head crashed hard on her pillow. Vivid colors of darkness painted the walls as her mind delved deeper and deeper, searching for answers.

A short time later, Penny's voice spoke once more; however, this time, it was in an almost laughingly, creepy-helium-like tone you'd hear in a haunted house on Halloween. Anxiety punished Beth's body, while fear grabbed her soul. Her subconscious mind finally lost control as she screamed out, "Why do you interrupt my sleep almost every night? You say the same damn thing, in that same haunting childish tone, repeating it, over and over—why? You know, I never told anyone about that promise, so, how the hell do you know about it? And dammit, why won't you ever answer me?" An eerie silence bounced from wall to wall as her eyes searched for any resemblance of Penny.

Eventually, peaceful darkness crept in and smothered the room. For the remainder of the night, silence blessed the far recesses of her subconsciousness. As morning broke, bright rays of a sunny morning replaced the peaceful muted darkness surrounding her. Shielding her eyes, she squinted at her bedside clock: 6:30 AM was rearing its ugly head back at her. "Ugh," she groaned. While lying motionless, her blank stare drilled holes in the ceiling as she tried to make sense of last night's disturbing subconscious episodes of guilt and denial.

Rolling out of bed, she slowly sauntered to the bathroom. As she splashed cold water on her face at the bathroom vanity, the reflection in the mirror lashed out at her. "Zoe Elizabeth Pendergast, what the hell is going on with you?" As she stared at her reflection in the mirror, she whimpered, "Hmm, you know, uh, I wish I knew."

After a quick shower and breakfast, she felt prepared for her second day as the forensic psychologist and profiler for the Oakmont Police Department. Anticipation gripped her as she entered the police station; however, she was most excited about getting her feet wet and solving her first case. Police Chief Brock Evans continued making rounds with her throughout the department, introducing her to the staff. She was confident and professional as she interacted with officers, detectives, and administrative personnel.

In Beth's peripheral vision, a pretty lady whom she had yet to meet stared at her relentlessly, a stare that was haunting in an oddly kind of way. The woman's eyes looked familiar, and for some odd reason, Beth could not fight off the woman's stare. With fiery-red hair and stunning looks, that woman walked directly toward her. Locked in on her, Beth thought she recognized her but couldn't quite remember where that might have been.

Before Beth knew it, the lady approached her, extending her hand out. "Hi, I'm Detective Carla McBride."

Chief Brock Evans quickly interjected, "Carla, meet Beth Pendergast, our new forensic psychologist, and profiler. She will be assisting us in our cases, especially the cold ones."

"Nice to meet you, Detective McBride. Have we met before?"

Casually, Carla replied, "Not that I recall."

"Then maybe I'm mistaking you for someone else. Anyway, I look forward to working with you."

"Likewise. If I can be of any assistance, please don't hesitate to ask."

Beth acknowledged her and followed Chief Evans as he continued introducing her to the rest of the employees. After Carla returned to her desk, she pulled out a huge file folder, gave it a thorough review, and closed it. Noticing that Beth had returned to her workstation, Carla approached her carrying a folder. Suddenly, a loud thud startled Beth. She gave Carla a strange glare. After Beth returned her gaze to the bulging manila folder on her desk, her pulse skyrocketed. In big, bold black letters, Penny Miracle—June 23, 1997, bored holes in her soul.

Pointing at the file, Carla quietly but forcefully said, "Open it, Zoe. That was your childhood name, wasn't it?"

While glancing at Carla, a stone-cold expression of guilt met her eyes. Returning her gaze to the file, Beth opened it, sending a strangeness throughout her body she'd never felt before. After a short pause and exhaling, Beth murmured something under her breath. She closed the file and remembered where she had met Carla; tears trickled down her pale rosy cheeks. As she wiped tears of sadness away, a familiar haunting voice, which only she could hear, came to life inside her mind. Her face tensed up, her lips quivered, and tears trickled down her cheek once more. She wiped them away and silently said to herself, "I will find you; I promise." She opened the file folder again; an old tattered wallet-sized photo of Penny immediately captured her eyes. It appeared Penny's eyes followed Beth's every move, sending chills up and down her spine. Tears resurfaced, but Beth quickly wiped them away. Glancing at Carla, a teary-eyed guilt-ridden detective was doing her best to keep her emotions at bay.

Beth reached in her purse and pulled out her wallet. Fumbling around, she finally found what she was looking for. An identical photo of Penny was neatly tucked away behind other pictures. The message written on the back of the photograph brought back bittersweet memories followed by tears. Beth handed the photo to Carla; she turned it over, silently reading the fifteen-year-old personal message from Penny... *To my best friend Zoe, in the whole-wide-world, love Penny...* She returned the photo to Beth, wiped a tear away, and smiled. Beth reopened the file folder and paper-clipped it right beside the picture attached in the file. Closing the file folder, she handed it back to Carla, waiting for the next move.

Carla took a deep breath and exhaled, "This is how I know you, maybe why you felt you knew me or at least had a connection to me. This was my first real case after joining the police force, and I couldn't solve it. An innocent young girl went missing that day, and it was something I never forgot. As a young child, I was almost a victim of an abduction myself, but my father came out of the house just in time and saved me. You see, that's one of the reasons it's personal to me as well. The other reason is on that day, I made a promise to you that I would find Penny, and I wasn't able to keep it."

"Is that why you kept that folder in your desk all these years?"

"Yeah. You know, I reviewed it every month hoping something new would surface, but every time something did, it led to a dead end. You know, I made a promise to myself that I would never give up on this case until I found out what happened to Penny."

"That makes two of us. Where do we start?"

"Chief Evans. Follow me."

In the eerie silence of the hallway, they walked side by side to his office. In the past, Carla would have just barged in; however, after one embarrassing incident, she learned that wasn't such a good idea anymore. She gently knocked on his partially open door and peeked in. Chief Evans motioned them in. After entering, he gave them a strange look and motioned them to take a seat. Before Chief Evans could get a word in edgewise, a large file folder landed on his desk. Giving them a questioning glance, he stared at it for a brief moment before breaking the silence captivating his office. "What the hell is this, Carla?"

"Chief, just open the damn file, okay?"

After opening it, he glanced up at Carla and then returned his gaze to the file. Penny's picture stared back at him, following his every movement. He remembered her and the case. Continuing to scan the documents, he stopped on page three. Looking up at them, he returned his gaze to the folder for a brief moment. Silence filled the room once more until Carla locked eyes with him and spoke.

"Chief, you remember this case, don't you?"

"Hell yeah, I do. Your first case, shortly after you joined the force. If I remember correctly, it affected you personally and emotionally. That's why I removed you from it. I don't think you ever forgave me for that."

"You got that right, chief, and I never will."

"So, why bring this case up now?"

"Page four."

He flipped through the file again, and after he reached page four, he scanned the page until his eyes flew wide open. He looked up at Carla, then Beth. Beth smiled as he continued reading page four. After he closed the file, his face grew tense. He rubbed his forehead and temples as an eerie silence swallowed the fresh air in his office.

"Carla, is this that Zoe?"

"The one and only, Zoe…Elizabeth…Pendergast, Penny's best friend until she disappeared that day. Chief, you need to read the message on the back of the first picture."

Reopening the file, he flipped the picture over, reading Penny's note to Zoe. After closing the file folder, he locked eyes with both of them. He rubbed his hands through his hair until his face became flushed and beads of sweat dotted his forehead. Wiping the sweat away, he stared at Carla with questioning eyes.

"Carla, why now after all these years?"

"I think it's time we find out what happened to Penny. Umm, it was my first case. Bernie Kowalski was the lead detective on it, and the investigation involved Beth as a young child, and we both made a promise to ourselves to find out what happened. We need to do that, get closure. Chief, you know what I mean, right?"

He studied them for a while, picked up the file, and handed it to Beth. "Yeah, I know. Let's do it. It's not going to be easy, and you may discover things you don't like or wished you never knew. There was always something bizarre about this case, but Bernie couldn't quite nail it down. So, good luck, be careful, and keep me abreast of your progress, got it, Carla?" She nodded. As they got up to leave, he said, "Carla, play fair and by the rules, okay?"

"Don't I always?"

Chief Evans rolled his eyes, rubbed his forehead, and replied in an overly sarcastic tone, "Right, now get the hell out my hair."

CHAPTER 3

Returning to the police station's common area, Beth asked Carla what that conversation was all about. Carla informed her it was a love-hate thing between them. The longer she worked there, the more she'd understand it. Arriving back at Beth's desk, she handed Carla the file. She opened it, paused for a moment and closed it quickly, tossing it down on Beth's desk.

"You keep it. I've had it long enough."

"Okay, Detective McBride, where do we start?"

"Just call me Carla, and we will get along just fine, got it?

"Sure. Carla, it is. Now, where do we start?"

"McGruder's for lunch. I'm starved. Is that okay with you?"

"Favorite place, let's go."

"My partner, Bernie Kowalski, will meet us there. Hope you don't mind."

"Not at all. Since he was the lead detective on the

case fifteen years ago, we need his help to solve this case."

"Great, and after lunch, we will take a ride."

"Where?"

"Don't be so impatient. You'll know when we get there."

Arriving at McGruder's, Bernie already had a booth for them at the front of the pub. Carla and Bernie hadn't been partners very long, and in their early years, they didn't like each other all that much as well. They were like oil and water. Carla always felt Bernie gave up too quickly on the Penny Miracle case, and she never forgave him for that.

However, Chief Evans put them together to solve The Black Rose case. Out of that, a trusting partnership formed. Returning from medical leave, Bernie was still on desk duty until Chief Evans cleared him to fight crime on the streets.

Sliding into the booth across from him, Bernie chastised them. "Ladies, where have you been? I'm hungry."

"Bite me, dickhead," Carla said. "Then why haven't you ordered?"

"That's my girl. Order lunch without you, well, wouldn't that be rude?"

"Hasn't stopped you before, has it?"

As a quick indiscreet bird flew her way, she responded with a smirky grin. With a shocked look on her face, Beth quickly figured out this was typical behavior between them. Bantering continued for a moment or two, annoying Beth. Clearing her throat and coughing, Beth said, "Enough, guys. Let's get something to eat, and please be nice to each other in my presence, okay?"

Bernie was a little taken aback by Beth's directness, while Carla shot her a look that said, "Hey bitch, I'm the one in charge here, and don't forget it." As things settled down in the booth, Sam, their go-to waitress at McGruder's, finally came to greet them. "Well, if it isn't Detectives McBride and Kowalski. Nice to see you both. Want the usual?" They nodded. "Who's that with you?"

"Meet Beth Pendergast, our forensic psychologist and profiler at the police department."

"Wow, pretty heavy stuff. Nice to meet you. What may I get you?"

"Likewise. Rueben, fries, and water with lemon, please."

"You got it. Good luck with these two. They'll drive you crazy if you let them."

"Yeah, I know, but I can handle them both."

After a double thumbs-up gesture, Sam put in their lunch orders. While waiting on their food to arrive, Carla informed Beth how Sam got mixed up with some very dangerous men in The Gold Fedora Case. She faked her disappearance and chose a safe-haven with a distant cousin in Canada. After things settled down, and with John Dickerson securely in prison, Sam returned to Oakmont and McGruder's.

Lunches arrived, and the Rueben and fries looked exceptionally good today. The fish and chips with tartar sauce nestled together in a red plastic basket were just as delectable. Silence blocked out the muted chatter around them. While picking at his fish and chips, a quiet disposition infiltrated Bernie's body. With Beth and Carla oblivious to his uneasiness, Bernie cleared his throat ever so slightly, interrupting their girly talk.

"Carla, there is scuttlebutt going on in the station that

you two are reopening the Penny Miracle case. That was fifteen years ago. What makes you think you can solve it now?"

"I have new evidence."

"Right, and what may that be, McBride?"

"Meet Zoe Elizabeth Pendergast, Penny's best friend back then. She's all grown up and goes by Beth now."

After a single thump to his chest, he swallowed hard. Grabbing the sweet tea, he washed the cod down. Breathing hard, his temples, and brow felt the roughness of his weathered fingers. A cringe found his lips. Remembering the events of that day sent his pulse racing. Carla's eyes zeroed in on him. He wiped his sweaty palm on his sleeve as he glanced at Beth's grown-up smile. Moving his fish and chips around, bittersweet memories about the case swelled in his mind. Elbows on the table, his cupped hands met his chin as though he was asking God for guidance and forgiveness. Although he never expressed it to anyone, this case still bothered him.

Carla and Beth had resumed their girly talk ignoring his changing disposition. Blocking out their chatter, he thought more about the case, one he couldn't solve. Now it was being reopened, and his every note scrutinized once more. Bernie and Carla were partners now. When Carla was a rookie officer, he had just made detective. Carla looked up to him as a rookie officer, and Bernie failed her on the Penny Miracle case.

As the lead detective on that case fifteen years ago, he was also the one to end it when all leads went nowhere. As the only African-American on the force in 1997, he was always under the microscope. He had something to prove back then, and it didn't pan out as he imagined it would. He could never forget the grief on the faces of Sandy and Jack Miracle the day their daughter disappeared forever.

While picking at the cod, the fries had grown cold, and he pushed them aside. Carla and Beth continued their girly bonding, oblivious to the personal dilemma building inside him. His glass of ice became a drum, his fork, a drumstick. While keeping beat to the music blaring from the ceiling-mounted speakers, their useless chatter continued. Frustration found his brow as they continued ignoring him. With an intentional slight of the hand, ice slid across the table with the lemon leading the way. Girly laughing ushered in silence as melting ice trekked toward them.

Quickly, a napkin stopped the flow. "Jeez, Bernie, are you okay?" Angry stares battled silence as Beth wiped the melting ice into his glass. His internal struggles covered his face as a scowl found his lips. "What's going on, partner?"

With silence tormenting the booth, cupped hands found his brow and his thumbs massaged the tension bulging in his temples. His face, in full view, revealed a man struggling with physical and mental anguish. "Hell no, I'm not okay, McBride. Meeting Beth, finding out she was that young child I interviewed many times was like a dagger penetrating my soul. It's like a ghost coming back to haunt me if you know what I mean?" As Carla reached for his hand, he jerked it away. His stare was like a bullet of disdain heading straight for her brain.

"Listen, Bernie, I get that. If it makes you feel any better, I feel the same way. We'll solve this, finally get redemption and closure."

"I'm glad you feel that way. What about you, Beth? How do you feel?"

Apparently in a state of confusion, Beth's eyes moved beyond his stare, battling his angry eyes. As the silence continued, his eyes searched for respect. A nudge jolted Beth's arm, and Beth met Bernie's scowl.

"What about you, Beth…are you ready for this, reliving that day and its aftermath?"

As her chest moved in and out, her lips quivered. "Uh, me, ready as I'll ever be. I was twelve, well almost thirteen, and I remember bits and pieces of the investigation. However, it's becoming a little clearer now that our paths have crossed. I'm sure as we get further into this case, more will surface." Eyes closed, she swallowed hard. "Every time I hear Penny's haunting voice, I've become more determined to find out what happened regardless of what we may discover."

Cupped hands quickly found his brow; his eyes met her stoic expression. "Voices, seriously. What the hell does she say?" His eyes grew darker, waiting for a response. "Well, what does she say?"

"Bernie, this is not the time or place to discuss this."

"The hell it's not, McBride."

"Carla, it's okay. I made a promise the day Penny went missing that I would one day find out what happened to her. Back then, it may have been a simple wish, but now it's real. In my dreams and subconscious mind, she visits me about every night, reminds me of that promise. To this day, except for Carla, no one else, not even my mother, knew I made that promise. I'm not sure what is going on. However, it's time to honor that promise. I will find out what happened to her with or without you." A battle of wills and personal struggles clashed; heavy breathing silenced the stares in the booth. "Well, are you in or not, Bernie?"

As a crooked smile cracked his face, he extended his fist toward Beth. She smiled as her fist met his. Within seconds, Carla joined them, extending her fist. As they planned their strategy, Sam observed them from behind the bar. Carla glanced in her direction and gave Sam a slight wave of the hand. Within a minute, their check arrived. As they walked out the door as a team, the resurrection of the Penny Miracle case took center stage.

CHAPTER 4

The west end of Oakmont had changed little since Penny Miracle disappeared. The massive oak and maple trees loomed over the streets as they did on that fateful day. While Beth remembered the majestic colors of Autumn, bittersweet memories growing up in the west end of town flooded her mind. Riding shotgun, Beth took in everything as they turned onto Washington Avenue. She hadn't been back to her childhood home in many, many years. At first, butterflies danced in her stomach, like an experience very similar from high school and college, as she stood at center court ready for the referee to blow the whistle and toss up the basketball. After the game started, the butterflies in her gut subsided. However, these butterflies were much different. Anxiety and tension churned as she scanned the street of her childhood innocence, pointing out where Penny, Scotty, and Mason lived.

Beth's childhood home looked a little different from when she grew up in it. New paint and accents gave the old craftsman style home new life. An older couple sat on the porch enjoying lemonade, and Beth wondered how long they had lived there. After stopping in front of her childhood home, the couple paid no attention to them. In the car, Beth sat quietly, trying to put the butterflies to sleep, while Carla watched her go through breathing exercises to relax the anxiety in her body.

Standing on the porch, the woman caught her gaze through the passenger door window. After a deep breath, the passenger door opened, startling Carla. As Beth stood forty feet from her childhood memories, Carla joined her. The man and woman gave them a friendly wave, and Beth and Carla reciprocated as they walked down the street. In fifty yards, Penny's house would be upon them; silence crossed every step they took. With thirty yards left, Carla felt as though she was all alone. Turning around, Beth was walking in the other direction. Catching up with her, Carla grabbed her arm. With a determined expression on her face, Beth jerked away, continuing back toward her childhood home. As the couple sat sipping on the lemonade, they were oblivious to what was playing out in front of them. Finally, Carla caught up with Beth in front of her childhood home. "Beth, what is going on? Are you ready for this?"

Forty feet away, anxiety, bitterness, paranoia, and fear were just ahead. "Yeah, I'm ready. Follow me."

After several steps toward the porch, Carla grabbed Beth's arm again, locking eyes with her. "What is going on, Beth? We came here to walk the neighborhood and talk about Penny's disappearance, not intrude on anyone."

"I've got to do this, so trust me on this. We both need this. Something is pulling me toward the house, and I can't explain it."

Releasing her arm, Beth approached the porch. Carla was a few steps behind her. By now, the couple was fully aware of them. The couple rose to greet them. "You look lost, may I help you?"

"Sir, I'm Beth Pendergast, this is Detective Carla McBride with the Oakmont Police Department. Although it may seem strange, I have a special favor to ask you, but please sit back down before I continue, okay?" Stunned, Carla was beside herself. She questioned herself for bringing Beth back here. Seeing the determined expression on Beth's face, it would not do any good to fight her on this.

The couple returned to their rockers. Harold and Charlene Anderson owned the house now, Beth's child-hood home. Casual chit-chat filled the air as Harold poured them each a glass of lemonade, returned to his rocker, and asked, "What brings you to the west end today, detectives?"

An outgoing person, Beth light-heartedly responded, "Oh, she's the detective, I'm just a forensic psychologist. We're reopening a fifteen-year-old cold case about a young girl from this neighborhood that disappeared without a trace."

"I see, but how may we help you? We've only lived here for about ten years. I understand the young girl you are referring to was Penny Miracle, but I still don't know how we can help you."

"I was Penny's best friend, and I grew up in this house. Well, your home now." Harold and Charlene glanced at each other. "I moved away after I finished sixth grade. My mom took a job in Cincinnati, and we settled in Northern Kentucky, where I excelled in basket-ball. I returned to Oakmont when I received an athletic scholarship to play basketball at the university. Now, I'm a forensic psychologist trying to find out what happened to Penny. Ironic, isn't it?"

"Yes, it is, but how may we help you?"

"Would you allow us to go in your home? I grew up in this home, and Penny was here just about every day. I'm hoping something stands out that may help me remember more about my life here. I'm hoping it will also jog some memories for Detective McBride since she interviewed me several times when she was a rookie police officer investigating the case."

With a quizzical look on her face, Charlene shot a glance at her husband, who nodded. Considering Beth's request for a moment, Beth looked up and down the porch, as memories flooded her mind. Lost in her memories, Carla tugged her arm and pointed. An open door invited them in. The living room, although painted a different shade of green, looked the same. Other pictures hung on the walls and accented the mantel framing the fireplace. The memory of Zoe following her mother down the steps was bittersweet. Carla wiped her glassy eyes. A grandfather clock nestled in the corner chimed loudly, interrupting the bittersweet memories bouncing around in her mind.

After glancing at Beth, silent emotions exploded in their souls as the room swirled around them. Charlene beckoned them toward the kitchen. Cabinets were different, the appliances modern, and a tiled floor replaced the linoleum Beth used to scuff up as a child. The back door was new, with a full view of the backyard. A vegetable garden was where her swing-set once was. Visions of she and Penny swinging brought tears to her eyes. Back then, a cinder alleyway ran between the houses on Washington

and Adams Avenue. Today, hot black asphalt covered the
alley.

"What else do you want to see?"

"My old bedroom, if that is possible."

"Be my guest. I will let you have some privacy."

"Thank you. We will just be a few minutes."

Up the stairs, turn left, ten steps down a short hallway, and her old bedroom loomed on the right. With the
door open, a silent voice called her name. Happy butterflies fluttered in her gut as she entered. Childhood memories rushed out from her subconscious; smiles about the
good times she and Penny had in the room. Pictures of
Charlene's family replaced posters of teenage heartthrobs
that plastered the walls years ago. A framed diploma
hung proudly over an antique roll-top desk. Charlene's
degree in accounting from Altmont Community College
met her gaze. As Carla observed Beth's bittersweet trip
through her childhood, she wondered what was going
through her mind. A church calendar hung on the closet
door. Tears trickled down Beth's cheeks as the closet
contained more memories, some good, some not so good.
Tears wiped away, the crystal doorknob felt cold to her,
sending a shiver throughout her body.

"Beth, are you okay?"

Turning to face Carla, she nodded. "Yeah, it's just
that the memories are so real." The doorknob squeaked
as Beth turned it. On the right, winter clothes hung from
a steel rod waiting for cold weather to arrive—Charlene's
she assumed. Although it was not a big closet, two adults
could squeeze inside it with the door closed. The wall
behind the door was where Beth's most treasured childhood secrets lived. Although the closet was a different
color than when she lived there, indentions survived

several coats of paint. Her fingers slowly traced her most treasured childhood pledge. "Friends forever, Zoe and Penny. Carla, I can't believe it's still here after all these years."

"You must have been close."

"Yeah, we were more like sisters than best friends. My mom used to tell me that a lot. She even said we had similar characteristics, but as far as I know, we weren't related. Let's get out of here."

Returning downstairs, Charlene was in the living room waiting for them. They walked together to the front porch, where Charlene settled back in her rocker, sipping on her lemonade. Beth's eyes moved around the porch and shifted toward the street. While standing at the bottom of the steps, Beth expressed her gratitude for the necessary intrusion. Harold and Charlene nodded. As Beth and Carla took a few steps, a voice of wisdom turned them around.

Charlene said, "Not sure what you are looking for, but I hope you find it." Beth nodded. "You know, ladies; sometimes, it's better to leave well enough alone."

Carla responded, "Yeah, what do you mean?"

"We all want to find clues from our past, you know, the dark secrets. Everyone has them. When we discover them, lives are never the same. That's something to consider before you open Pandora's Box."

Carla replied, "Hmm, we'll keep that in mind. Thanks again. Have a nice afternoon."

As they turned to walk down the street, Harold said, "Honey, now that was weird, wasn't it?"

Throwing him the look, she replied, "Yeah, but you know what was really weird is that I felt a connection to Beth. Not sure what it could have been, maybe just knowing she grew up here. Do you want a refill on the lemonade?"

After Harold nodded, she left and returned with their glasses full of ice. Pouring the lemonade, she sat in her rocker, moving back and forth as the strange feeling about Beth lingered throughout her soul.

CHAPTER 5

Two houses separated Beth's childhood home from Penny's. Pausing in front of each home, Beth studied each one, taxing her memory about who lived there. The Archer family lived next door to them, she recalled. Frank and Mary, a middle-aged couple that had a daughter named Kelly who was in high school. Between the Archer family and Penny's house, the Simms family lived. Kathy and Steve, a young couple with a newborn named Cheryl.

Pausing in front of Penny's house, it had changed little other than showing its age. A woman looking out a full-length screen door gazed at them. Stepping out on the porch, the woman retrieved her mail and gave them a friendly wave. They acknowledge the woman, she entered, closed the door, and disappeared out of sight.

"Beth, did you know her?"

"Nah. She's beautiful, isn't she?"

"Yeah, probably early forties. Now what were you saying?"

"Yeah, I remember before I moved, a couple by the name of Finley's lived there. Penny's parents moved away after Penny disappeared. I believed they moved to somewhere in West Virginia. Her dad got transferred. After that, I don't know where they ended up. They may still be there for all I know."

"How do you remember all that stuff?"

"My mom told me. She kept in touch with them for a while, but the distance and pain of losing Penny were too much for them to handle. Starting fresh somewhere was the best for them, and eventually, for my mom and me as well."

Several steps later, Beth wasn't beside Carla any longer. She turned around to find Beth fixated on Penny's house. A thought entered her mind—not again. Motioning Beth to catch up with her, Beth ignored her. Still fixated on the house, a tap on the shoulder startled Beth. "What's going on? I hope it's not what I'm thinking."

"Follow me."

"Seriously, are you out of your mind? That woman will not let us in her home."

"We'll never know if we don't try, right?"

"What do you think you'll find?"

"Not sure. I spent many days and nights there growing up. However, I was never in that house ever again after she disappeared, but I imagine you were, right?"

"Well, yeah, so was Bernie. I was there several times before they moved."

"We need to do this, so trust me on this."

"I hope you are right."

After approaching the porch, a few steps put them at

the door. Chimes rang out from inside the house; two minutes went by, and a meow from a nearby window brought a smile from Beth. The albino feline's strange, mysterious stare reminded Beth of her mother's cat, Aliyah. Another meow, then silence. Ready to push the doorbell again, the door swung open. The lady partially opened the storm door, greeting them.

"Hi, I'm Beth Pendergast, and this is Carla McBride. We're with the Oakmont Police Department and reopening a cold case involving a young girl that disappeared fifteen years ago. Her name was Penny Miracle, my best friend, and she lived in this house."

"Yeah, I remember the realtor informed me about that. May I see some identification, please?"

"Of course, here's mine." Carla flashed her badge as the lady studied Beth's identification card for a moment and handed it back to her.

"Ms.?"

"Ali Sandy. How may I help you?"

"Hi, nice to meet you. As crazy as it might seem, would you allow us to come in for a moment, and if possible, may I visit Penny's old bedroom. I know where it is."

"What do you think you will find? It's been about fifteen years, and at least one other family, maybe two families lived here before me. So, I don't know what good it will do."

"I understand, but sometimes looking around, even though a lot has changed, something may jog our memory, helping us solve the mystery of her disappearance. We will take just a few minutes, then we will be on our way."

Pausing for a moment, Ali opened the storm door,

motioning them in. Although different, a modern sofa, coffee table, and two chairs set perpendicular to the fireplace as they did fifteen years ago. Carla remembered Jack and Sandy Miracle seated on the couch, praying. She remembered their heartbreak and pain. Carla felt a strange presence in the room as more memories flooded her mind.

Like Beth's childhood home, a large arched opening led to the kitchen. Beth had been in the kitchen many times as a child, eating lunch at a dinette table that was no longer there. A butcher-block portable island filled the space now. Memories of peanut butter and jelly sandwiches with Kool-Aid flashed in Beth's mind. Bittersweet smiles found her face. A vision of a ripened tomato appeared on the counter. As Carla blinked, the tomato vanished from her mind.

Opening the door, Beth stepped out to a covered porch overlooking the backyard. A swing swayed back-and-forth from the wind, and memories of she and Penny giggling flashed in her mind. The giant oak tree was their favorite place for a picnic; a stump was all that remained now. The vegetable garden that she and Penny planted tomatoes in had been replaced by a two-car garage. Beyond the garage was the same asphalt alleyway behind her old childhood home. Memories of the horrific day surfaced. While staring at the gate at the end of the yard, guilt painted her face. As Beth murmured something under her breath, her lips quivered and tears surfaced on her cheeks. Taking a big breath, she wiped them away and returned to the kitchen with Carla following her.

"Beth, what did you say out there? I'm a good lip reader, and it sure looked like you said, Penny, who is that? What's that about?"

"It was nothing. Just a flashback. Mrs. Sandy, would it be possible to visit Penny's old bedroom for just a moment? I know which one it was."

"Well, I guess it couldn't hurt. I use it as an office now."

Virtually in the same place as Beth's room at her old house, the door to Penny's bedroom was on the right, a few steps away. Standing in the doorway, Beth paused for a moment, then entered. A large wooden desk on a Persian rug was where Penny's bed was fifteen years ago. Pencils rested randomly on a legal pad to the right of Mrs. Sandy's laptop, while her framed diploma from Western Kentucky University hung proudly on the wall. Happy memories of sleepovers brought a big smile to Beth's face. A bittersweet memory of their last sleepover brought tears, washing her smiles away.

To her right, the closet door was closed. Opening the door, shelving holding books and other supplies lined the back wall. Beth moved a few books around and smiled. The same indention had survived several coats of paint; she traced the pledge with her fingers. Closing the closet door, Beth scanned the room for the last time. Raw emotions surfaced. She wiped them away, quickly leaving the room. Carla paused for a moment, remembering that Sandy Miracle showed her Penny's bedroom after her disappearance and gave her clothes for DNA purposes. Memories of that jump-started her emotions. Wiping them away, she joined Beth in the hallway at the top of the stairs. At the bottom of the steps, Mrs. Sandy and her albino furry feline, Fiver, watched them leave the upstairs. As they reached the bottom landing, she asked, "Did you find anything helpful?"

Beth said, "Just bittersweet memories. We will be on our way now. Thank you so much."

"You're welcome. So, it's been fifteen years since that little girl disappeared. I hope you find out what happened and get closure. So, this neighborhood can get closure. The people haven't forgotten her. I hear her name mentioned from time to time. If there is anything else I can help you with, please don't hesitate to contact me."

Carla said, "Hmm, thank you. I see a lot of university stuff here. Do you work there?

"Oh no, my husband does. He is an assistant football coach. We moved about seven times, but it goes with the territory of being married to a football coach. We met at Western Kentucky University, where he played football. Ironic, isn't it, my husband coaching for his bitter rival? I majored in English and Journalism, and that's why I chose to write mystery novels. That way, I wouldn't have to find a new job every time we moved. I publish under the pen name Annie Nicole. Maybe you've heard of me?"

Neither Beth nor Carla read many novels, so they shook their heads back-and-forth. After leaving the porch and reaching the sidewalk, Beth turned around, facing the house. Mrs. Sandy was still standing at the door watching them.

"Carla, if you don't mind, let's call it a day. Visiting these two houses where I spent much of my childhood has jogged so many memories—some happy, some bittersweet, and some I'd like to forget again. What about you?"

"You know, I agree. However, all my memories of

that day I'd like to forget, but we must find out what happened to Penny. It's time to answer all the questions we both have. What do you say, let's go have a drink and call it a day?"

"Where?"

"Whisman's okay?"

"Never been there."

"It's close to here. It's an old-style local neighborhood joint, one of a kind. You'll love it, trust me."

Within several minutes, they pulled into the empty parking lot at Whisman's. Entering the bar, a booth on the left side of the building was perfect for some special bonding. Gabe Whisman, who had just finished waiting on Rufus, approached them, placing drink napkins on the table. "Detective McBride, right?"

"Good memory, Gabe. Meet Beth Pendergast. We work together in the police department."

"Nice to meet you. What can I get you lovely ladies?"

"Jameson on the rocks for me, Pinot Grigio for her."

While waiting for their drinks, Carla asked, "What do you have going on this weekend?"

"Hmm, I'll probably go visit my mom. It's been a while since I was there, and I can use some mother-daughter time after my first week. I never expected my first case would be the most horrible memory from my childhood. I need to decompress. Reading the file has worn me out, mentally and physically."

"Yeah, me too. However, I've read that file so many times, I feel like I know every word forward and backward if you know what I mean?"

"Yeah, I get it. Hmm, how are you going to relax this weekend?"

"I'll be hanging out with my boyfriend, Chris, and my best girlfriend and her husband. Maybe some golf, and definitely more Jameson."

Gabe arrived and sat their drinks in front of them. Beth looked at Carla's glass and commented, "So that's Irish whiskey…um, never had it before."

"Well, try it." Beth took a little sip. A sour look took over her face, and she coughed as it went down. "Not bad, huh?"

Beth frowned and replied, "I'll stick to wine for now."

"It's an acquired taste. You have a love interest in your life?"

"Not any longer. Scott Carlson and I broke up a few months back. He ended it. I was ready for a long-term commitment, and well, uh, he wasn't. I still love him, though. However, I'm not sure he feels the same way. I'm fairly sure our relationship is over for good."

"I'm sorry to hear that. Relationships can be hell. I had many failed ones until I finally realized Chris was my soulmate. Most of our relationship was like a brother-sister one until I really needed him one night in my darkest hour. Over a drink one day, I'll tell you more about The Black Rose case."

"Okay. You know, Scott was the same Scotty that went with Penny, Mason, and I to Davenport's Grocery the day Penny disappeared. We reconnected in graduate school. He is now with the FBI. Well, enough about him. We should probably leave now. I need to get on the road."

Carla dropped off Beth at the police station by her car. As Beth exited, Carla said, "Drive safely, and see you on Monday."

"You bet. Thanks for everything this week."

As Beth opened her car door, Carla left the parking lot drained from the resurging emotions from today's emotional roller coaster ride.

CHAPTER 6

Having about a two-hour drive to her mother's home in Northern Kentucky, across from Cincinnati, listening to an audiobook would help Beth pass the time away. After meeting the lady that now lived in Penny's house, Beth inquired at the library, reserving the only audio copy by Annie Nicole. After picking it up, she removed the audio CD from the case and inserted it. Annie Nicole gave a brief introduction to the novel. Three minutes later, she switched her radio back to Sirius XM. Once she was on the interstate, she would resume listening to the book.

The entrance ramp off Oakmont's by-pass merged onto the interstate heading north; traffic was moderate. By reading the summary on the case, the book was about a husband-wife private investigation team. Hal and Haley Cruse specialized in domestic disputes. Their current case involved a wife that allegedly was cheating on her husband. While staking out the wife, Hal disappeared without a trace. Pushing the CD icon on the screen, Annie Nicole narrated the psychological thriller titled,

Last Breath. The further north she traveled, the moderate traffic grew faster and busier. As cars sped past her, the right lane was perfect for losing oneself in a spell-binding, page-turning novel. Before she realized it, her exit was upon her, and in fifteen minutes, she'd be sharing a glass of wine with her mother, Judy.

Pulling into her mother's driveway, relaxing on the front porch with a glass of wine, Judy waved. As she exited her car, a motherly hug greeted Beth. After a loving embrace, they walked arm-in-arm to the porch. A full bottle of Ecco Domani Italian Pinot Grigio and an empty glass awaited her. While Beth sat in a welcoming lounge chair, Judy handed her a glass of wine. Holding up the wine glass, Judy followed her lead. Glasses met gently for a toast, and smiles of love beamed at each other. It had been several months since Beth last visited her mother. They each took turns catching up with each other. The tone of the conversation described the pain of living far apart; phone calls weren't the same as hugs and kisses. After a sip of wine, their eyes met, and a smile came across Judy's face.

"What, mom?"

"Uh, nothing. I miss you, honey."

"Ah, mom, I miss you, too. How was your week?"

"A normal week, just like all the rest. How about you, my forensic psychologist and profiler?" In a sarcastic tone, she asked, "Solve any big cases this week?" A tear or two rolled down Beth's cheek turning her smile into a troubled frown. "What's wrong, honey?"

Wiping away the tears, a long sip of wine filled her mouth. Swishing it around, Beth savored its fruitiness. Smiling at her mother, she answered. "It's been a long week. Can we just relax and enjoy the evening and the view?" Her mother nodded. "Thanks, mom. I love you."

"Love you, too. You know, I never get tired of this view. The skyline of downtown Cincinnati is breathtaking at night. What do you say we make a day of it tomorrow? Shopping and dinner in Cincinnati will be a lot of fun. We haven't done that for a while."

"Yeah, mom, sounds great."

As the evening waned on, they moved inside the house. The effect of too much Pinot Grigio warmed Beth's body and soul. Mother-daughter time always relieved the stresses of reality, even if only for a short time. After Beth fell asleep in the La-Z-Boy in the living room, Judy placed a blanket over her and turned off the lights. Kissing her daughter on the forehead, she whispered, "Sweet dreams, honey. So glad you are home." Beth nodded as her mother and the queen the house, a fluffy white feline, retired to the master bedroom. A long week, the effect of the wine had done its job, and quiet darkness surrounded Beth's mom.

Only the glow of a streetlight lit the living room. Otherwise, darkness crept in and settled around Beth. The La-Z-Boy, and probably the effect of the wine, sent Beth into a world of peacefulness and tranquility. At two o'clock in the morning, a flash of lightning lit the room up, and a few seconds later, a crack of thunder startled Beth. As lightning illuminated the room intermittently, shadows of the night faded in and out on the walls and ceiling. Something moved in the muted darkness. She whispered, "Who's there?" Nothing but silence in the eerie night answered her. Suddenly, she felt something on her lap, causing her to flinch. Two yellowish-green eyes glowed from lightning illuminating the room. "Oh, it's just you. Have you been there long, Aliyah?" After a soft meow, Aliyah purred while laying her head down on Beth's lap. She picked-up her and climbed the stairs to the guest bedroom. Putting her down on the bed, she visited the bathroom and returned to the bedroom in her favorite nightgown—her ex-boyfriend's long-sleeved shirt. While crawling into the bed, her mom appeared in the doorway.

"Beth, is everything okay?"

"Yeah, mom. The lightning and thunder woke me up. Aliyah was sleeping on my lap, so I brought her to bed with me. Go back to sleep. I'll see you in the morning."

After her mother returned to her bedroom, Aliyah snuggled close to Beth with purring sounds of love. Still a little woozy from the wine, a deep, peaceful sleep surrounded them. An hour later, a familiar voice interrupted her sleep. "Zoe, please help me. You must keep that promise you made after I went missing. I'm waiting for you."

Subconsciously, Beth murmured, "Penny, please let me sleep, and quit doing this to me. Also, if you are going to interrupt my sleep, please show yourself."

A bolt of lightning, then a crack of thunder; Beth's mom stared at the darkness blanketing the bedroom. Another bolt of lightning flashed on the walls, while voices emanated from Beth's bedroom. Still groggy from the wine, Judy rubbed her eyes as more sounds filled the hallway. Slipping out of bed, she followed the voices. Outside Beth's bedroom, her daughter's rambling continued. What promise was she talking about, and whom was she talking to, Beth's mom wondered.

Standing in the doorway, she asked Beth who she was talking to. Nothing but silence flowed from the bedroom.

She repeated the question, and still no response. Entering the room, Judy approached the bed where Aliyah snuggled close to Beth as she breathed heavily and continued mumbling in her sleep. A gentle tap on the shoulder startled Beth. Aliyah was in cat heaven and oblivious to everything.

"Mom, why are you in here?"

"I couldn't get to sleep, and I heard voices coming from your room, so I came to see if you were okay. You mentioned Penny's name. What's going on?"

"Mom, I'm worn out. We'll talk in the morning, now get some rest. We have a big day tomorrow."

"Okay, night, honey. I love you."

"Love you, too, mom."

Sunlight chased away the pale shade of darkness. Aliyah stood on Beth's chest purring loudly. As Beth opened her eyes, she rubbed them, blocking the annoying sunlight. While Aliyah sat on her chest, she pawed Beth's chin, wanting affection. Eyes open again, Aliyah meowed loudly, breaking Beth's stare at the ceiling. The smell of freshly brewed coffee emanated from the kitchen downstairs. "Okay, Aliyah, I get it, you want me to get up." Meowing again, she jumped down, sauntering out of the bedroom. Dragging herself out of bed, Beth walked into the bathroom, turning on the light. In the mirror, bloodshot eyes from too much wine and a broken night's sleep glared back. Her reflection stared back as she whispered, "Penny, I'm going to find you so that I can get a full night's sleep."

Not realizing that her mom was standing in the doorway, she continued talking, hoping for an answer. A clearing of the throat from the doorway startled Beth, and she turned to face her mom holding a cup of coffee.

"Good morning, sweetheart. Coffee is ready."

"Morning, mom. I'll be down in a minute."

Dressed in a white lounging suit, Beth joined her mom on the back deck. As Beth took a sip, the steaming coffee warmed her hands. Adjusting to the morning brightness, Beth squinted. The deck boards appeared damp to her; she saw puddles of water randomly scattered on the deck.

"Mom, did it storm last night?"

"You don't remember?" Shaking her head back-and-forth, a sip of coffee soothed her aching head. "Beth, I can't believe you don't remember the lightning and thunder. You were talking in your sleep, and I heard you mention Penny. I hadn't thought about her much since we moved away. What brought that on?"

Very hesitant about answering that last question, Beth refreshed her cup of coffee. The danish looked enticing, and she tore a piece off, savoring it, buying some time before she responded to her mom. Beth's mom had this stare that she hated because it meant her mom wanted an answer and wanted it now. As a child, Beth endured it every day, and her mom always won. Another sip of coffee, another bite of the danish…Beth knew she couldn't win. After giving in, she reluctantly responded, "Mom, you know I started my new job this week as the forensic psychologist and profiler with the Oakmont Police Department. Specifically, they hired me to work on cold cases…"

"Shit, I don't like where this is going, Beth."

"Well, sorry, mom. Whether you like it or not, Penny Miracle's disappearance is my first case. How ironic is that?"

CHAPTER 7

Silence smothered them. Judy Pendergast looked toward the heavens, praying that her daughter would fail miserably, hoping that this case would remain unsolved, that the secrets of the past would remain just that, secrets of the past. Staring at her mom, Beth could see she was somewhere off in a distant world. She had never acted like this before, or at least in Beth's presence. Her mom's catatonic stare bored holes through Beth's soul. Touching a sensitive nerve, what Beth hoped would be a fun, relaxing weekend had left a sour taste in her mouth thus far.

Several cigarette butts grossly rested in the crystal glass ashtray while an almost empty pack of Camels and a non-descript butane lighter was near. After trying for years to get her mother to stop, Beth's attempts were to no avail. Silence blocked out the peaceful sounds of the chilly morning, at least by June standards.

Wispy clouds slowly moved eastward as a freshly lit Camel smelled awful as it permeated toward Beth. While waving her hand back-and-forth, the smoke floated around Beth until a slight morning breeze drifted across the table, swallowing up the nasty stench. After breathing deeply, Beth sighed, meeting her mom's stoic gaze.

"Mom, please put that out. You're making me sick."

While not responding, her mother took a long draw on the Camel, turned her head, sending the carcinogens away from her daughter. Beth whispered *thank you*. As a subtle smile appeared between puffs, an unbearable silence tested Beth's patience.

"Mom, what's going on? It's just a job. Our chances of solving this case aren't good. Fifteen years have passed, and what little evidence we have is of no use to us. Unfortunately, my memory is the best evidence we have right now, and I don't remember that much. I'm sure those memories are tucked away in somewhere in my subconscious. Maybe you can help me fill in the blank spaces of my childhood, will you?"

Extinguishing her cigarette, her mom got up and left without responding. The storm door to the kitchen slowly closed behind her. As muted sounds from the counter-sized television faded away, bad news in the world matched their mood. The storm door creaked as it was opened. Judy, with a new pack of Camels and a clean ashtray in tow, sat across from Beth. After setting the ashtray down, a brisk breeze carried the scent and smoke away. Unforgettable eyes met each other, searching for some sense of direction.

"Mom, why are you so upset about this?" Another puff. As the smoke dissipated in the breeze, her mother's mouth quivered slightly. "Mom, I see it on your face. I hear it in your voice. Please talk to me."

As quickly as her mother's mood changed from distant to near, it turned to directness. "Tell me about your dream last night. You know, you said Penny's name. I swear I heard you talking to her. What's going on with that?" Beth knew her mom was rather adept at changing the subject. It was her way of answering questions she didn't want to answer. Beth could never win that game with her mom, and there was no use in trying. It was time to confess her dark secret, hoping her mom would eventually open up to her about Penny's disappearance and its effect on her.

"Okay, mom. I made a promise to myself the day Penny disappeared that I would one day find out what happened to her. I never told anyone about it until the other day. Detective Carla McBride was the first to know that deep dark secret. I'm sorry, mom. It may have been a knee-jerk reaction back then. My heart ripped apart, a part of me died that day. You remember, don't you?"

"Yeah, you cried every night. You had nightmares. We even tried counseling to ease your pain."

"I know it sounds crazy, but I hear Penny's voice almost every night. Maybe I'm going crazy. The voice reminds me of the promise. I don't know if it's my subconscious using her voice to speak to me. As far-fetched as it is, I'm beginning to think her spirit is visiting me from the other side. I feel like I'm a hostage, and the only way I can escape and keep my sanity is to solve her disappearance."

"I see. What happened to you and Scott?" Beth rolled her eyes. Her mom had a knack for controlling and redirecting the conversation. Beth knew she could not win even if she tried to. A few deep breaths, and a big sigh, and she poured another cup of coffee, buying some time. "Well, honey?"

"Mom, there you go again, changing the subject. He

wasn't ready to settle down. Scott broke it off. It's that simple. Now, let's quit playing games. You act as though you are hiding something you don't want me to know, either about Penny or my childhood. What is it?"

"Let's just say some things are better left alone. You know, leave well enough and live the life you have. You will be happier, trust your mother. That's all I have to say."

"That's kind of funny, that's the same thing Mrs. Anderson told us as we left the house I grew up in."

"You visited the house where we used to live. Why? Why would you do that?"

"I don't know, mom. Detective McBride and I took a ride and ended up there. As I looked at our old home, it was as though something was pulling me inside…maybe some magnetic force or maybe Penny's spirit. I don't know what it was. However, I had to do it. I visited my old bedroom, traced my fingers on the wall where I wrote something the day before she disappeared. Mrs. Anderson was very nice and accommodating. I felt this strange feeling when I shook her hand. Never felt something that bizarre before."

As another cigarette rested on the ashtray, a fresh cup of coffee tried to mask the nasty smell smothering Beth. Tears dotted Beth's cheeks as the silence continued between them. Glancing at her mom, Beth quickly wiped the tears away.

"Anything else, honey?"

After several deep breaths and a sip of lukewarm coffee, she let out a big sigh while gazing at the wispy clouds. Beth knew she was not good at playing her mother's game. Eyes battling each other, her mother's lips winced.

"Well, is there anything else?"

"We visited Penny's old house for the same reason. An uncontrollable force pulled me in there. I had a flashback while looking at the backyard. I remember a man in a black sedan with tinted windows waving at Penny and me the day she disappeared. Penny said he was her friend."

An eerie silence surrounded them. Her mom stared at the sky, puffing away on her cigarette. Eyes moving back-and-forth, up-and-down, the Camel hung between her quivering lips. Waving arms finally captured her mother's glassy eyes. Sighing deeply, the half-smoked Camel rested on the ashtray.

"What do you want from me?"

"Would you tell me about my childhood while we lived in Oakmont? Even though I remember bits and pieces, there are too many blank spaces in my head. By learning more about my childhood, it might help us find out what happened to Penny."

"I'll have to think about it. Besides, it's time to get ready to go shopping. Let's just enjoy the day, okay?"

"Yeah, of course, mom."

After getting up from the table, Beth planted a kiss on her mother's forehead and hugged her. As Beth began walking away, her mother grabbed her left arm. Turning around to face her, Judy mouthed, "I love you, honey."

Smiling, Beth replied, "Love you, too, mom."

An hour later, as they crossed the Ohio River heading for downtown Cincinnati, normalcy had returned. A long-awaited mother-daughter reunion was born. Laughter and unimportant conversation drowned out the radio. Returning home after a long day of shopping, lunch, and dinner, Beth and her mom settled on the front porch, a glass of vino nearby. Crickets serenaded them while fire-flies sparkled against mother nature's beautiful dark canvas. A crisp Italian Pinot Grigio soothed their tired souls as they relaxed, enjoying the quietness of the neighborhood. Candles flickered as though keeping a beat with the crickets' featured song of the evening.

Aliyah softly purring, slept beside Beth in the lounge chair. While admiring her daughter, Judy rested comfortably across from Beth with her legs stretched out on the outdoor glass table. Aliyah snuggled closer to Beth, dreaming of her nighttime snack and enjoying the caresses of love on her soft, furry coat.

Proud of herself, Judy Pendergast raised Beth as a single mom, and now her daughter was a forensic psychologist working for the hometown police department. Beaming with pride, Beth was everything she wanted to be, but when her husband passed away from pancreatic cancer, her dreams and aspirations were put on hold. While thinking of what she had accomplished, her emotions unleashed her heartstrings. Taking a deep breath, she fought back the tears of joy.

Flickering light illuminated Judy's glistening cheeks and watery eyes. Beth met her gaze. "Mom, are you okay?" She nodded. "Then what are the tears for?"

"Just watching you over there, I was thinking how proud I am of you. Honey, you turned out to be an exceptional young woman, and have your master's degree in psychology, and now a great job. You're beautiful and confident. Everything I wanted to be. That's why those tears of joy sneaked out of my heart, sorry."

Welling up inside, Beth picked up Aliyah and carried her over, sitting beside her mom. As Aliyah purred from her lap, Beth's head rested on her mother's shoulder.

Emotions took over. "Ah, mom, I couldn't have done it without your love, support, and sacrifice. You sacrificed a lot for me. I love you for that." While appreciating her mother's love, her mother's heart cried silently. "Mom, what about what we talked about this morning, you know, helping me fill in the blank spaces. Will you do that?"

Judy Pendergast, enjoying the wine and the intimacy with her daughter, didn't want it to end. However, she wasn't ready to open up the past just yet. Yawning and a big sigh provided the answer Beth didn't want to hear. Judy's last ounce of wine went down harshly as she got up and glanced at Beth.

"Honey, I'm tired. Let me sleep on it, okay? I hope you sleep better tonight." Beth nodded as her mom entered the house and quietly settled in her bedroom hoping for a good night's rest.

CHAPTER 8

Remaining on the porch, Beth enjoyed the coolness of the evening solitude. After replenishing her wine glass, Ecco Domani's crisp fruitiness eased the emotions still lingering in her soul as Aliyah purred softly on her lap. Under the glow of the moon, fireflies finished their impressive performance of the evening as crickets paused before their encore serenade in the crisp summer air. A few sips of vino remained. Her palate savored hints of green apple and melon.

Picking up Aliyah, she entered the house, going to her bedroom. Placing Aliyah on the bed, the soft fluorescent glow in the bathroom reflected off her tear-streaked cheeks. Gently splashing cold water on her face, she washed them away. While smiling at the reflection in the mirror, her eyes had recovered from the emotional day. The glow on her face gave way to muted shades of darkness. With Aliyah fast asleep in her favorite spot, the bed never felt so good. A white summer blanket provided the peacefulness she was craving. Snuggling closer, Aliyah purred softly. Beth listened to her soothing bedtime lullaby as she closed her eyes. Thoughts of a peaceful night morphed into a tranquil serenity.

The sun's welcoming rays sneaked through the plantation shutters landing on Beth's face. Aliyah stretched and crawled upon Beth's chest, gently pawing her chin, interrupting her final minutes of peaceful sleep. After Beth shielded her eyes from the bright sunlight, she tickled Aliyah's favorite spot under her chin. "Aliyah, you know you're just like my alarm clock, annoying as hell, but effective." Meowing, she jumped down, scampering down the steps heading for the kitchen.

The aroma of freshly brewed coffee replaced the smell of the morning air filtering through the plantation shutters. While staring at the ceiling, Beth thanked her subconscious for keeping the voice of guilt and redemption at bay during the night. Yawning and stretching, her tension-free body and soul smiled. After answering nature's call, Beth splashed cold water on her face once more.

The aroma of the coffee beckoned her to the kitchen. Maneuvering the stairs gracefully, her mom, seated at the table sipping on her second cup of coffee, welcomed her. Coffee was first and foremost on her mind; however, an open scrapbook covered what appeared to be a thick photo album, and seized her attention. Giving it a curious glance, she wondered if the answers to her questions were inside. An empty cup waited for her on the table as did a full carafe of coffee. Sitting down opposite her mom, she poured herself a cup, watching the steam dissipate upward and disappearing. Looking at her mom inquisitively, she quickly closed the scrapbook.

"How did you sleep last night, sweetheart?"

Smiling at her mom, Beth replied, "The best night in a long time, mom. No visits from Penny if that's what you mean." Her mom nodded. "Whose old scrapbook you have there?"

"Mine. I guess yours now. I knew one day I would give it to you, but wasn't sure when it would be the right time. I thought about it last night. Guess this as good a time as any. You can take it back with you, but keep it in a safe place. I may want it back someday."

Anxiety was running through her veins, she asked, "May I look through it now?"

"Let's have breakfast first. Then we will go through it together, okay?"

"Yeah, mom, that'll be fine. Thank you."

The aroma of eggs, bacon, sausage, hash browns, gravy, and biscuits filled the house. Although Judy knew how to make Beth's soul happy, her favorite breakfast could ease the anxiety created by the scrapbook and photo album. A lot of blank spaces about her childhood needed answered. Were they in the scrapbook and the photo album her mom carried to the living room? She was hoping to find out.

Appetite satisfied, she cleared the table for her mom. Refilling her coffee cup, she headed to the living room where her mom had settled on the sofa with the scrapbooks. While sitting beside her mom, she waited to see them. While pages of the album were yellowed in places, other pages were taped together. The scrapbooks chronicled Beth's life to date and showed how proud her mom was of her. From elementary school through college, it was all there. Elementary school projects, newspaper clippings of her high school athletic accolades, and college graduation exercises told the story of her life.

Leafing through the pages, the first thing that caught her eye was two pictures, one of her and Penny when they were in the fourth grade. The other was with their mothers; their science project had won first place. Studying a slightly faded picture of them in front of their science project, she noticed how eerily similar they were; the same color of hair, golden blonde to be exact, and the same height. She traced her hand around Penny's face and smiled. "Mom, I can't believe how much we looked alike back then. We almost looked like we were family, you know, cousins, or maybe even sisters, but I know that's impossible."

"Sweetheart, many people thought that same thing, neighbors, your teachers, even our pastor, but you're right, that wasn't possible. None of us knew each other until we moved to Oakmont when you both were two-years-old. We moved from Altmont. I believe the Miracles moved from a small town in Boyd County, Kentucky. Both towns were in the same county; however, we never knew each other. She watched you while I worked after your father died. That's when we became good friends, like sisters."

Fixated on the other picture, she said, "Gosh mom, the four of us, umm, you and Sandy could pass for sisters or cousins as well. Creepy, isn't it?"

"Yeah, sort of, but we were just close friends."

"I remember these photos as well. Near the end of school. Look how mature Penny was in a two-piece." Tearing up, she wiped her emotions away. "Yeah, then several weeks later, Penny was gone. I couldn't believe it." More tears trickled down her cheeks. Judy rubbed her eyes as well, trying to erase the tears before Beth saw them.

"Mom, tell me about that day when she went missing."

"The day started like any other day. You spent it with Penny like always. Sandy watched you while I worked. She was a lifesaver back then. I couldn't have raised you as I did without her. We became close, very close friends, kind of like sisters, like you and Penny. However, the weird thing about that was at times I'd swear you and Penny could read each other's minds. And even more strange, Sandy and I could often finish each other's sentences as well."

"Wow, didn't know that. Please tell me more, okay?"

"It was a normal day until a police officer knocked on our door. I remember it just like it was yesterday. I remember Officer McBride, pretty for a police officer. Anyway, she told me what happened. It was like a part of me died that day. She asked to speak with you, and I agreed. You cried a lot, even though I don't think you understood the gravity of it all. I remember she made a promise to you that she would find Penny. The next day, a dark-skinned police detective came to interview both of us. I don't remember his name."

"Bernie Kowalski, the lead detective on the case back then."

"Umm, I knew the name sounded foreign. His questions were much the same." Beth nodded, wanting more. "I decided that we should seek counseling. You were having nightmares about Penny. I felt like I'd lost a family member. Without your dad here, depression grabbed my soul. I smoked and started drinking. The counseling helped us both. In time, your nightmares ended, and I went on with life as best I could. I had to take time off from my job until I could find someone else to watch you."

"I remember that was Mason's mother, right?"

"Yeah, I was a little hesitant, given he was two years older than you, but it worked out."

"Mom, we were just kids, like brother and sister, he watched out for me. Can't believe you thought something would happen."

"After Penny went missing, I was overprotective. What mother wouldn't be, right? Sandy and I grew apart after that. I think it was too painful for her to be around you and me. Then they moved away. I tried to stay in touch with her, but I guess she wanted to forget the painful and heartbreaking past, and that included me."

"Hmm, I'm sorry you endured such pain back then. Not having family around must have been tough. Thank you for sharing this with me."

"Yeah, it wasn't easy without your dad, but we got through it just fine. You know, he loved you so very much and would be extremely proud of you."

"I don't remember much about him since I was very young when he died. Would you tell me more about him? I'm old enough now to understand what he was really like."

"Your father was the love of my life, thoughtful and kind, funny, and carefree. I worshiped him and depended on him. I knew the first time I laid eyes on him, that I would marry him one day. You know, we were high school sweethearts. He adored you. I can still remember the day we brought you home from the hospital. I'm sure there is a picture of that in the scrapbook."

"Really, where?"

"It's in there somewhere. You know, nothing is in order. Just keep turning the pages, and I'm sure you'll come to it."

While leafing through the pages and stopping at some to ask questions, a page titled, *Coming Home*, grabbed Beth's emotional being. After touching several pictures of when she was brought home for the first time sent chills throughout her body. Wrapped in a blanket; a knitted cap covered her head as her dad held her in his arms; a happy father beamed with pride and joy. In another picture, Judy was holding Beth in her arms, smiling at her. While touching it with her fingers, emotions welled-up inside her soul. Beth swallowed hard, chasing them away.

A deep breath, then she touched a picture of the three of them. Fixated on it, she glanced at her mom briefly. After returning her gaze to the photo, her fingers moved across it. Her mind wandered; children should look like their parents, she thought. Thoughts crept into her mind about that. Eyes were different and noses were different. Her hair was blonde; her parents in the picture had dark hair. Thoughts and emotions ran wild. Judy Pendergast sat motionless, watching her daughter explore her past, oblivious to the expression on her daughter's face.

"Mom, I know I've asked you this before, but I don't remember, what is the name of the hospital where I was born?" Silence, aloofness, signs that her mom didn't want to answer the question. She asked again, "Mom, did you hear me. What was the name of the hospital where I was born?"

A puzzled look painted her mom's face as though she didn't hear the question. "Sorry, I was daydreaming about your dad. The only hospital in Altmont. I don't remember the name. That's a strange question. Why did you ask that?"

"Well, I look nothing like you and dad in that picture, and I look nothing like you now. Makes me wonder whether I was adopted."

With a look of concern on her face, Judy laughed and paused. After a big sigh, she finally replied, "For heaven's sake honey, without a doubt, you're my flesh and blood all the way. Must be the recessive genes that came out or maybe the milkman as they say. I remember the time we conceived you. You want to hear about that, all the spicy details of that night? Besides, a copy of your birth certificate is in here somewhere."

"Hmm, no, mom, uh, that's more than I wanted to hear. I guess I should get ready to head back to Oakmont and get ready for what tomorrow will bring. Thanks for letting me take the scrapbook and photo album back with me."

Traffic was light for a Sunday afternoon. *Last Breath* consumed her mind. Listening to Ali Sandy narrate all the twists and turns, the end was disappointing. She wondered why she ended the novel the way she did. Beth liked the plot and the characters well enough to read more of her books.

After arriving at her apartment, sleep came early because of her exhausting weekend with her mom that had drained her body and soul. She wanted so much to look through the scrapbook and photo album she brought back, but sleep was more important. She knew her mom would always be there to answer all the questions she would have. Thoughts of Scott entered her mind. Her head crashed softly on her pillow. Peaceful darkness moved in, and dreams of him flowed in and out of her subconscious, especially the last time they made magic love. A smile crossed her face as a deep cleansing sleep blocked Penny's voice from invading her subconscious space.

CHAPTER 9

CHASING...TRUE LOVE'S TEMPTATION 59

Six AM flashed its ugly head at Beth. Heart pounding, she gasped for air and hit the snooze button. Drenched in sweat, the remnants of an erotic dream the damn clock interrupted lingered in her mind. Hoping to return to her dream, she closed her eyes, drifting back to sleep. In the dream, Scott found every inch of her sensuality pushing her to new heights of pleasure, waiting to experience the outer limits of her sexual fantasy…buzz-buzz cooled her burning embers once more.

She hit the snooze button again. After eight minutes more of sleep, she would have to shower and get ready for the day. As she breathed heavily, her damp nightgown clung to her aroused curves. While hoping to return to the subconscious sexual fantasy lingering her mind, her eyes closed, willing the final episode to begin. However, her phone screen lit up and dinged. *Damn*, she whispered and wondered who was texting her this early. An annoying ding, but the message made her smile. *Have a great day*, it read, *love mom*.

A quick shower cooled the embers burning inside her soul. After toweling off, she felt refreshed and ready for the day. In Scott's long-sleeved shirt, she saw her four-cup coffee maker was all ready to go. The brew button turned blue. Seconds later, the carafe began to fill. Retreating to her living room with her coffee, she hit the remote and the local news blared. The big story of the morning had just finished; however, an update from last week's top story, the disappearance of Abbie Gardner, was of more interest to her. Although the details were sketchy and limited, there was enough to keep her interested in the report. The information was eerie similar to the disappearance of Penny. Abbie was a pretty blonde with blue eyes and physically mature for a twelve-year-old girl—just like Penny. Clues were scarce, and it seemed that Abbie vanished from the face of the earth just like Penny.

An interview with the girl's parents was heartbreaking to watch as they pleaded for her safe return. Their daughter had been missing for a week now. The lead investigator, Craig Bjornson, was seeking information from the public as they didn't have any substantial leads at this time. A reward of ten thousand dollars, from the Gardner family, had been offered for information leading to the safe return of their daughter. Making a note of the lead detective's name, she knew the reward would probably be in vain given the circumstances; but then again, an award of that significance at least gave them a sliver of hope.

Midway through her second cup of coffee, the morning local news moved on to a more pleasant segment with the weather. The long-term forecast was going to be more like spring than summer, which suited her just fine. She hated the heat and humidity because, to her, it stifled her creativity. Enough local news, she flipped the channel to the national news where the White House was facing another crisis. She shook her head back-and-forth because the White House and the federal government always seemed in crisis mode. *Who cares*, she thought, and the screen went blank. The last few sips of her coffee were cold, so down the drain it went. Her clothes, already selected for the day, consisted of a black pantsuit with a pale pink blouse which dressed her up nicely. Casual, but striking. Comfortable black pumps complemented her business attire perfectly. A pair of casual black sneakers with lightweight socks were in the car, like always, for street work. A fresh cup of coffee in her to-go cup. She locked her apartment, leaving the subconscious remnants of Scott behind.

Monday mornings at the police station were usually slow, especially for those that arrived early, and today was no different. The big clock on the wall was just shy of twenty minutes to eight as Beth entered the station, checking her in-house mailbox; zip, and that suited her just fine. The second week on the job, she didn't expect mail anyway. Checking in with the receptionist, she had no messages as well. Although being early, she was not alone in the common area. When reaching her desk, the file labeled Penny Miracle—June 1997 rested on her desk calendar. Flipping it open, two tattered and torn photos of Penny stared back at her. Chills traveled up her arms; her delicate hairs stood at attention.

Picking up the photo she had carried around for years, the message on the backside took her back to June 1997. More pieces of that horrible time in her childhood surfaced the more she reviewed the file.

Continuing to haunt her was the black sedan in the alley the day Penny went missing. As a young child, her mom taught her to beware of strangers. Did Penny's mom teach her the same thing; she often wondered. Even though she knew Penny well back then; there was something different about her. Penny seemed a little more trusting when it came to meeting strangers. Guilt welled up in Beth as she often wondered had she told Penny's mom about that particular incident, maybe Penny wouldn't have disappeared. Perhaps that horrible day would only be in someone else's nightmare or a horror movie.

Even though she knew from reading the file that the man in the black sedan with tinted windows that waved at them didn't abduct Penny. Although he was a known pedophile and registered sex offender, he had an airtight alibi. The man, Tommy Akers, had been at a group counseling session that afternoon mandated by the court system, a requirement of his parole. Breaking it would have sent him back to prison for a long time. Engrossed in reviewing the file, Beth hadn't noticed Carla had arrived. Reviewing Bernie's notes garnered all of her attention; her intuition was telling her Bernie missed something long ago. Consumed by his notes, she was unaware of Carla standing in front of her. A slight cough broke her fixation on a particular interview on a person of interest.

"How was your weekend, newbie?"

In a very reserved and non-descript tone, Beth replied, "Fine, what about you?"

"Mine was fantastic, but I take it from that tone of voice, yours, well, may have not been so good, am I right?" Beth nodded and remained silent. Carla, in her rather cheery attitude, continued, "I'm sorry, what's on your mind. Why are you so down?"

Deflecting eye contact, she responded, "Weekend was fine. My mom and I had a great time together. Up and back, I listened to an audiobook by Ali Sandy, you know, who writes under the pen name of Annie Nicole. Remember her?" Carla nodded. "Good book titled *Last Breath*. I'll loan it to you some time."

Another nod, and a puzzled expression covered Carla's face as she responded, "Then why the sour attitude?"

"Well, uh, I've been reviewing Penny's file, and when I came across Bernie's notes about the black sedan with tinted windows in the alley behind Penny's house, it brought back unpleasant memories of that day. I realize the individual that waved at us that morning was not involved. However, knowing how trusting Penny was with strangers and other people, I feel somewhat responsible because I never mentioned that to her mom or even my mom."

Carla, trying to lift her spirits, replied, "Hey, you can't beat yourself up over that. You were twelve years old and scared as hell. Also, who wants to rat on their best friend? I wouldn't have."

A wrinkled smile crossed Beth's face as she replied, "Yeah, I know, but that's not all. I had one of those dreams of Scott and me together. The last time he shared my bed before he decided that it was time to move on. I'm sure you've had those types of dreams. I woke up sweating and gasping for air if you know what I mean." Carla offered no response and just nodded. Beth continued, "So, there you have it. I'll get over it. By the way, where's Bernie?"

"Taking a few days off, not sure why. Bernie just said that he and Lydia were taking a trip together, somewhere they hadn't been before. I recommended The Greenbrier Resort in West Virginia. He just said he needed to get away. Besides, he has plenty of days off banked."

"Good for him. You know, he seems like a great guy, but I believe after he realized who I was and that we'd be working together on this cold case, he seemed a little down. He told us that he would relive this case all over again. I could tell he was not looking forward to it."

"Yeah, I agree. Maybe it caught him by surprise. Plus he is still on desk duty because of his street readiness. I think getting wounded affected him more than he believed. I'm sure he will be back later this week and ready to help us solve this case."

"You know him better than I do. Hey, have you been following that case in Lexington about Abbie Gardner that went missing over a week ago?"

Giving her a quizzical look, Carla paused and replied, "I know about it, but haven't seen any more on it. Why do you ask?"

"Well, while I was getting ready this morning, the local news had an update about it. Hmm…"

Carla interrupted her and asked, "Yeah, so they had an update. You seriously don't think it's connected to our case, do you?"

"I know this is farfetched. There are so many similar-ities…we shouldn't ignore it as a possibility. Yeah, umm, I know it's a crazy thought, and yeah, I know it's been fifteen years between these disappearances. Regardless of that, I think we might want to check it out. What could it hurt? Maybe we have a serial abductor out there, and no one knows about it."

Laughing under her breath, Carla shot a strange look at Beth and laughed at her hunch. Being scoffed at, Beth let it go. When the time was right, if the information warranted it, she would bring it up again. While Beth returned to Bernie's notes, Carla logged on to the local television station's website. She immediately found a video stream of that morning's update on the disappearance of Abbie Gardner. She plugged in her earphones to her iPad and hit the play button. Watching and listening intently to the video, thoughts crept into her mind. Although, no matter how farfetched it was, the disappearance of Abbie Gardner was eerie similar and may be worth checking out. Abbie Gardner and Penny Miracle were a mirror image of each other. Physically mature, and pretty. They were both thirteen-going-on-twenty and would catch any male's lustful eyes.

The investigating detective's name and contact information flashed at the end of the video. Before she realized it, Beth was approaching her desk, glaring at her. She quickly closed out the website and removed her earphones. A smile met Beth as she passed by her, heading for the in-house mailbox to check again for any mail or messages. Feeling relieved, Carla pulled out her copy of the Penny Miracle file and reviewed Bernie's notes for the millionth time, hoping something different stood out.

CHAPTER 10

Bernie had left a message with Carla on Tuesday afternoon that he would be returning to work on Wednesday morning. The big clock on the wall approached twenty minutes after eight. In ten minutes, Beth, Carla, and Bernie would meet on the Penny Miracle case. While Bernie had been out of their hair, Beth and Carla had uninterrupted time to review all evidence, interviews, and notes from the case, especially Bernie's. Five minutes had passed, and Bernie was still a no-show. That was uncharacteristic for him. However, since he had taken fire, his demeanor was different. Being on medical leave had given him time to assess his future.

The second hand on the big clock rested squarely in the middle of the number six; meeting time had arrived, and Bernie was missing in action. Fixated on the main entrance of the police station, Carla did not like waiting; Bernie was going to be on her shit list. The door opened, air swooshed out, and Officer Wiesmann entered. The minute-hand approached the big eight, and Bernie was ten minutes late. Patience was not one of Carla's strong suits. Bernie had just moved to the top of her shit list. Dialing Bernie's cell number, she uttered a four-letter expletive. Beth watched as the door opened several times, with no Bernie. Throwing her hands up in the air, Carla redialed his number, and got no answer. Another group of expletives flew from her lips.

As Beth closed her file on the case, a pair of pissed-off eyes followed by a slight frown met her stare. "Carla, where is he? We need to get started."

While shaking her head back-and-forth, the minute-hand was fast approaching the big twelve. Beth, who had her nose in the file and writing notes, had lost track of time and Carla's fidgetiness. Carla like what she was seeing in Beth and had a good feeling about her; on the other hand, her main concern was the whereabouts of her partner. Although being forced as partners, they somehow made it work. Since becoming partners, they discussed the protocol of being open and honest, and given their personalities, that should have been a piece of cake. The most critical thing they adamantly agreed on was keeping each other informed about each other's life affecting their job.

Another glance at the behemoth clock on the wall, Bernie was an hour late, and Carla began to worry. She asked around the station if anyone had heard from him. He was missing in action, AWOL. Making a B-line to Chief Evans' office, she found the door was closed. Voices, especially a familiar one, emanated from inside the office, so she knocked. Voices stopped, the door partially opened, and Chief Evans said, "What do you want, Carla?"

In a nervous-like tone, she replied, "Have you heard

from Bernie? It's not like him to be late and not notify me."

Motioning her in, he closed the door. Seated against the wall, Bernie faced her and patted the seat beside him. Experiencing a queasy feeling inside her gut, Carla sat down. She looked Bernie straight in the eyes, but he deflected her pissed-off glare. She knew something was going on, and it wasn't good. Looking at Chief Evans, she saw his face was expressionless. She noticed a file on the desk in front of Bernie. Seeing his name on it, she knew it was his personnel file. Thoughts swam in her mind, but remaining silent, her feelings subsided. Her patience had run out. She lashed out at him. "Bernie, what the fu…?"

Chief Evans was trying to keep fireworks from exploding and motioned for her to stay quiet. "Carla, just calm down. Bernie has something to tell you. Go ahead, tell her."

"Tell me what, Bernie."

Glassy-eyed, and finally having the courage, Bernie made eye contact with her. He rubbed his eyes to prevent the tears from gushing out. Composed and ready to open up to his partner, he replied, "Uh, there is no easy way to, umm, tell you this." He paused, taking a deep breath, and looked away from her once more. "I'm, uh, well, you know, retiring." Surprised, Carla sat stoically, totally speechless. He returned his gaze at her and said, "I was going to tell you when I finished telling him, but I guess you beat me to the punch. I can see you are really pissed at me. Say something." With blood draining from her face, she sat stoically, remaining silent to collect her thoughts. Bernie knew she was probably likely to explode any moment now, and she had that right. He had not abided by the principles they agreed to. "Please, say something."

While she wiped a few tears of joy and sadness away, the color was returning to her face. "Why? Did I do anything wrong?" Bernie shook his head back-and-forth, and she continued, "Then what?"

Fighting back the tears, Bernie responded, "You know, I've enjoyed our partnership. At first I didn't think it would work, but in the end, I was wrong. We made a good team." He knew her well. She was going to interrupt him as she always did and stuck his hand in front of her. "Don't, Let me finish, okay?" She nodded, biting her tongue. "When I was in the hospital after being shot, they discovered that, uh, that I had prostate cancer. Because they caught it early enough, with proper treatment, I should have a good life. Finding this out and being shot, I reassessed my life and what remains of it. There are many things I'd like to do…that Lydia and I want to do." His lips quivered, and he wiped away tears that surfaced. He continued, "We all have life-altering moments. After being shot and finding out I have prostate cancer, well, they were mine. I need to smell the roses, as they say, and live life like I'm dying. You understand, don't you?"

Speechless, Carla wasn't sure how to respond. Although they hadn't been partners very long, they grew close very fast, and she would miss him, and that hurt. Breaking her silence, she said, "I'm happy for you. I noticed a change in you after you returned from medical leave, and when we had lunch last week with Beth and found out we were reopening the Penny Miracle case, I knew something was up. So, yeah, I'm happy for you and Lydia. I wish you the best. We can still be friends, can't we? I sure could use the kielbasa and kraut sometime, okay?"

Bernie nodded, got up, and left, leaving Carla alone with Chief Evans. He informed her that Bernie had about three months of sick time banked and would take it immediately. He also told her that there was a possibility Bernie could return after that but not to get her hopes up. Carla knew that would never happen. She saw it in his face before he walked out of the office.

Carla returned to her desk, hoping that Bernie was there collecting his belongings, but he wasn't. She noticed the picture on his desk was gone, and maybe that was the only personal thing he had. The atmosphere in the common area hadn't change one bit. Perhaps the news hadn't hit them yet, or maybe no one cared. He wasn't the easiest person to work with, and everyone knew that.

Beth was oblivious to what just happened. Carla approached her and said, "Let's take a drive."

Beth inquisitively replied, "Okay, what's going on? Where did Bernie go?"

In an angry-like tone, she repeated herself, "I said... let's take a ride now."

"Okay... geez, Carla, what's got your panties all in a wad?"

CHAPTER 11

After returning from lunch at McGruder's, Carla and Beth had been meeting for well over two hours discussing and comparing notes on the Penny Miracle cold case without Bernie. Although there was an abundance of material to review, one item seemed to stick out in Beth's mind more than any other. In Bernie's notes, he mentioned receiving an anonymous tip about a youth minister and teacher from St. Anthony's Catholic Church. His notes stated that he checked it out; however, she couldn't find any other reference to this individual anywhere in the file. Beth wondered if Carla ever picked up on this during the numerous times she reviewed Bernie's notes over the past fifteen years, and that's where their discussion began.

Carla, still in a sour mood, replied, "Yeah, from what I recall, uh, he said he checked this individual out, and he was squeaky clean, no criminal record, and that was it. I don't recall his name or anything about him. I was very green and took his word for it."

"Okay. Hmm, I can understand that, but there is no

mention of a name anywhere in the file. A little strange, don't you think?"

"Maybe, but Bernie must have had his reason to leave out that information. I don't know. Over the years, I asked him about it, and he always gave me the same answer, you know, uh, said pursuing him was a waste of time. So, I let it be. You can ask him if you like, but not sure you will get anywhere with it."

"Maybe not, but it's worth a try, given what we have to work with."

"Hmm, well, good luck with that."

Chief Evans tapped on the window of the interrogation room, interrupting their discussion. He pointed toward the door. Carla walked over and opened it. Chief Evans said something to her and stood outside the room, waiting for her. She told Beth to continue reviewing the file, and if she had the courage, she could call Bernie while she met with the chief. Carla followed him to his office. Pushing the partially closed door open, Carla felt acid seeping up from her stomach. Chief Evans motioned her to take a seat beside two well-dressed gentlemen. One she recognized, FBI Agent Donnie Slack; however, she didn't know the other agent. After sitting down, she took several deep relaxing breaths to calm the anger boiling inside her soul.

Chief Evans said, "Carla, before you say a damn word, just listen. First, you remember Agent Slack, don't you?" Carla nodded. "His new partner is Agent Scott Carlson." Silent and fuming inside, she just acknowledged them and remained calm since she knew of no reason they would be here since John Dickerson was in prison. Chief Evans continued, "They are here to update us about an incident regarding John Dickerson. So, please let them talk and do not interrupt them, if you know what I mean. You can ask questions later, okay?"

Carla nodded, and Agent Slack began. "Out of professional courtesy and your experience with John Dickerson, we have some unsettling news regarding him." All this time, even though Carla was holding her tongue, she remained calm and showed her respect for them. Chief Evans was glaring at her with a stern expression on his face. She had experienced that look many times before and knew it was best to keep her mouth shut for the time being. "You remember the circumstances with his placement into the witness protection program and that he would have to testify against Edwardo Cavalla once he was taken into custody." Both Carla and Chief Evans acknowledged them, and he continued, "Well, that time has finally arrived."

Carla, in a very respectful tone, said, "Really, and he will return to Kentucky to serve his life sentence, right?"

"Yes. However, there is a major problem you should know about."

Although Carla had remained calm and collected, hearing the phrase, "major problem," pushed her panic button. "A major problem? Aren't you federal boys supposed to be perfect?"

Angry eyes met Carla's sour disposition as Chief Evans quickly moved his hand across his mouth, hushing her. "Sorry for the interruption, boys. Please continue."

"When the US Marshals were transporting him to the airport, they were run off the road. The van crashed into a cluster of trees down an embankment. With the US Marshals incapacitated, he somehow escaped. A county-wide search began as soon as we knew of the incident;

however, that was not for a few hours, so he had a head start on us."

Carla took a deep breath and swallowed the stale saliva in her mouth, forcing the acid back to her stomach. A ghostly shade of paleness painted her face, and she could no longer keep her emotions in check. However, Carla knew if she lost control it would not go over well with Chief Evans. Silence bounced from person to person as she took several deep calming breaths. Finally, she could no longer bite her tongue. "Let me get this straight, John Dickerson is on the loose, and you have no clue where he is, right?"

Agent Slack did all the talking since Agent Carlson was a newbie and not privy to everything about John Dickerson. Agent Slack responded, "Unfortunately, it appears he planned his escape somehow. The US Marshals transporting him had small puncture wounds on their neck, likely injected with a potent muscle relaxer, putting them out for hours. Law enforcement found his prison jumpsuit, handcuffs, and leg chains at the scene."

Carla, still wearing a frown, remained silent while taking several calming breaths. Her posture showed disgust in the agents and especially for the US Marshals transporting him. Agent Slack glanced at her seeing one pissed-off detective. He continued, "That's all we have. If there are any further developments, we will notify you. Until then, be on the lookout for him. We know he is a dangerous psychotic individual and probably still seeking revenge. Are there any questions?"

Carla glanced at Chief Evans and just shook her head back-and-forth in disgust. There was nothing she could say, and what she wanted to say would get her in hot water. Keeping calm, she responded, "We will. I have no more questions. Thank you for notifying us. We appreciate your cooperation." Glancing at Chief Evans, who was smiling, she continued, "Chief, may I go? I've got a fifteen-year-old case to solve." He acknowledged her, and she left to return to the interrogation room.

Back in the room with Beth, anger grabbed Carla's face. Trying to solve the Penny Miracle case was tough enough. Adding John Dickerson and his psychotic games to the mix would make everything more complicated and unpredictable. Anger and disgust bared down on the walls of the room.

"Carla, what's going on with you, and don't hold out on me. I can see how pissed you are."

With anger emanating from her eyes, she replied, "You remember me telling you about my last case, well the last two cases, involving John Dickerson?" Silence glared back at Carla as the two men appeared in the window catching Beth's gaze. While stunned, Beth's eyes never left the window. "Beth, are you listening to me? You look like you've seen a ghost."

"Carla, tell me that wasn't Agent Scott Carlson."

"You know him?"

"Duh. You remember my ex, don't you?"

"So that was him? What a crappy day." While shrugging her shoulders, a quizzical look painted Beth's face. "Well, let's see, Bernie retires, John Dickerson escapes, and your ex-lover shows up here. Now, couldn't get any better than that, could it?"

Acknowledging her, a knock on the door sent Beth's pulse racing. Opening the door, emotions of love, hate, lust, and disgust filled her soul and glared from her face. "Scott, I didn't expect to see you here. I sort of thought our paths might cross someday, but not this soon; how are you?"

"Doing well. So, this is your new job?"

"Yeah, it is. I'd introduce you to Detective McBride, but you already met her."

"Yeah, well, gotta run. Agent Slack is waiting on me. Just wanted to say hi, it's good to see you again."

Beth acknowledged and slammed the door, laughing aloud. At the table, she flipped through the Penny Miracle file as if nothing happened. Carla, who had watched this awkward moment play out, looked at Beth, who tried to hide her emotions. "See? I told you it's been one hell of a shitty day."

"Ugh, yeah, I guess so, but I'll get through it. After seeing Scott, you know, I guess I'm not really over him just yet."

"Well, it just takes some time, Beth, and it will pass."

"Yeah, I know. Hey, I know it's early, but, you know, I could use a drink after seeing Scott. I've already had way too much fun today."

"Yeah, me too. I could use a Jameson about now… McGruder's okay?"

"Perfect. Maybe I'll have a Jameson today as a glass of wine will not help erase his image."

"Atta girl, because with psycho John Dickerson on the loose, and this crazy case, the fun is just getting started, trust me."

CHAPTER 12

After Carla and Beth drowned their sorrows at McGruder's, they both dragged themselves into the police station a little later than usual the next morning. Although Carla could handle several shots of Jameson, Beth still felt the effects of its power and potency. She was slow to get her body and brain working. Since Bernie retired, Carla suggested that Beth take over his desk across from her.

Seeing her ex-lover yesterday interrupted her train of thought, then after their afternoon soiree with Jameson, Beth forgot to inform Carla after her meeting with the feds about her discussion with Bernie. Any talk about work at McGruder's was a no-no; it was just girl talk. Jameson did his job yesterday in turning their somewhat shitty day into a straight-out girly-fun kind of day, with no worries.

Addressing Beth, Carla broke the alcohol-induced silence stifling their thought process and space. Although Beth's face looked normal, a masquerade disguised her red and tired eyes. Carla didn't look much better;

however, she managed the power of Jameson much better than Beth. Carla stared at her computer screen as though red lasers were zooming in on their target while Beth looked like she was stuck in some kind of time warp struggling to break free. Recognizing the funk Beth was in, tough love was in order. "Get a grip on it, Beth. Did you get a hold of Bernie about the youth minister?"

"Hmm, yeah, let me, uh, grab my notes." Pulling out a small notepad, she tried to focus on her rough scribbling. "He gave me a name, Jackson Walker. Does that ring a bell?" A short head-bob right-to-left met her gaze. "He told me he was squeaky clean, no criminal file, no traffic tickets, nothing. Even though he didn't have a credible alibi, Bernie was adamant that Jackson was not involved."

"Well, maybe that's why there is never a mention in the file anywhere. Maybe Jackson Walker was squeaky clean. Your face tells me there is something else."

"Yeah, with Bernie knowing Jackson personally from church, he was rather hesitant about answering any of my questions. I have to wonder about Jackson. Also, Bernie was evasive about everything I asked him about the case. I know he didn't like that I questioned his investigation notes, but something isn't right. It's a big red flag for me. What do you think?"

"Hey, Bernie is Bernie, and he can be a real dick sometimes if you know what I mean. So, you think we should check out this Jackson Walker dude?" Beth nodded and glanced at her notes one more time. "Beth, is there something else?"

"Nah, that's it, but you know, we definitely should check him out."

"Yeah, I guess it couldn't hurt, let's get to work."

Although they knew the information found would likely be the same, they searched separately for Jackson Walker. About fourteen years had passed since any substantial investigation into the Penny Miracle case had taken place, and they were both finding that the information about Jackson Walker was mostly non-existent. They searched available criminal databases; his name never surfaced. Widening her search to include the states bordering Kentucky, nothing surfaced. He seemed to be a model citizen, no matter where he lived.

Striking out on every occasion, Carla finally gave up and searched for the status of John Dickerson. Unfortunately, the news was not good; he was still on the loose. The area-wide search turned up nothing. As the FBI agents told her, he likely had accomplices and probably was not anywhere Kentucky. However, she knew with him on the loose; he would eventually surface.

Carla had played John for a fool in the Black Rose case. He believed he was meeting his wife and son; however, she arrested him for conspiracy to the abduction of Laura Watson. She remembered his last words to her as though it was yesterday. *"Detective McBride, this game will never be over until I'm back with Gina and Landon, and you are dead. Then it will be 'Game Over' for you...bitch!"* She took his words very seriously and would be very diligent in keeping track of him.

Beth continued to focus on Jackson Walker, finding as much information about him that would eliminate him as a person of interest. From everything she read, he appeared to be a model citizen, youth minister, and a teacher at Catholic elementary schools. The most recent information had him leaving the church and school a couple of years after Penny disappeared. She found that interesting but didn't prove he had anything to do with Penny's disappearance. It was his first teaching job, and he had been there for about five years. She found it strange that there was a gap in the information on him.

The next time his name surfaced was a year or two later in Dayton, Ohio. While there, he was a youth minister and teacher. He then left six years later and conveniently disappeared again for a year until turning up back in Kentucky in Lexington. He had been at his most recent position, as a youth minister and teacher, for about six years. Beth found it quite interesting that Jackson Walker left a year after Penny disappeared. With the recent disappearance of Abbie Gardner in Lexington, she wondered whether it was a mere coincidence or was she on to something.

Beth glanced over at Carla, who had just closed her laptop. She looked as though she had overdosed on internet information; rubbing her eyes, she met Beth's gaze and smiled. Giving Carla a quizzical look, Beth asked, "Okay, you first, what did you find?"

"Jackson Walker, by all indications, is a model citizen. There isn't diddly squat on him. I searched every criminal database I could get into, and nothing. What about you?"

"Well, pretty much the same. However, given the armchair quarterback in me, there's something very concerning." Fixated on Beth, Carla nodded. "There are gaps in his information and his work history, all a red flag to me."

"Really, Beth, and that's a reason this case involves him."

"Hey, that's not all. He left a year or two after Penny disappeared, and he has been in Lexington for almost six years, and now another young girl disappeared. Don't you find that a little strange?" Carla laughed and rolled her eyes. "What is it, Carla? What's so funny about that?"

"Nothing. You're a newbie, and I should take that into consideration, sorry."

"Hey, no problem. I'll still check it out. You never know where it might lead us.

"Have at it, newbie. I think it's a waste of time if you know what I mean?"

Ignoring Carla's nonchalant response, she continued searching for any reports of missing children in the Dayton, Ohio, area from 1998 through 2005. Expecting nothing to surface, it surprised her to discover that there were six such reports. It listed three as runaways and found, family members abducted two, one was a twelve-year-old girl named Melody Morris whose body has never been found. Comparing the dates, it was interesting that Jackson Walker left Dayton about a year after she disappeared. Carla, fixated on her laptop screen, didn't see Beth waving frantically at her. Beth cleared her throat, finally getting her attention.

"What?"

"Hey, listen to this. I find it very interesting." Carla acknowledged her, and Beth continued, "I searched missing children in Dayton while he worked there, and one incident is very interesting. A twelve-year-old girl went missing, her body was never found, and he left a year later. Interesting, huh?"

"Yeah, but it still doesn't prove anything, does it?"

"Well, no, but we can't discount the possibility of his involvement, can we? It may be a break in the case.

Maybe Penny was his first victim. You see where I'm going with this?"

"Yeah, I do, and the more I think about it, you may be on to something. We have to check out Jackson Walker, and quickly. What's going on about the missing girl in Lexington?" Waiting for a reply, Carla did a quick search, and the news was not good. "Hey, Beth, I got tired of waiting on you and searched it. Nothing is going on. The girl is still missing. You know, if this is not a coincidence, he could be our man with a big if, then time might be running out before he bolts again. You know, that's been his MO."

"I'll build a profile on Jackson Walker. It's going to take some time, and if we have enough, we can contact Detective Craig Bjornson of the Lexington Police Department."

"Beth, I'm going to call Father Tim O'Brien at the Catholic church to see what I can find out. You try the Catholic church in Dayton, and then we can discuss our findings."

"Deal. I feel good about this even if you don't."

Feeling right about Beth's theory, hope surfaced that they possibly discovered a suspect after all these years. Smiles and high-fives got them pumped. Googling catholic churches in Dayton, Ohio, Beth stared at her screen and didn't see Chief Evans standing at Carla's desk talking to her. Beth read her lips as she responded to Chief Evans, their smiles and high-fives gave way to disappointment.

CHAPTER 13

Although the discovery of skeletal remains at a construction site was alarming, their investigation of Jackson Walker would continue as planned. The possibility that the skeletal remains found at an Oakmont Centre construction site belonged to Penny Miracle was real. A frayed pink tank top on the torso of the skeleton was similar to what she wore that day she disappeared. Until all evidence was collected, the site preparation for Home Depot was suspended. A well-respected forensic anthropologist was called in to assist in determining the identification and cause of death.

Father Tim O'Brien at St. Anthony's Catholic Church yielded very little information about Jackson Walker. Father Tim had only been there for about five years and just knew of him in name only. They reviewed his personnel file, which yielded very little. For obvious reasons, privacy issues limited what information Father Tim could and would share. The personnel file of Jackson Walker was tiny and contained his annual evaluations and resume. According to his resume, Jackson grew up in Fort Gay, West Virginia, a small, depressed town across from Louisa, Kentucky. He attended the local university in Oakmont and graduated with a degree in elementary education. From all indications, his evaluations were exemplary.

Although Father Tim had only been at St. Anthony's for about five years, the principal of the school, Arlene Flanagan, had been there during Jackson's full employment. Ms. Flanagan had since retired, but still lived in Oakmont, and Carla obtained her contact information. A call to her yielded a different perspective on Jackson Walker. Ms. Flanagan agreed with the contents of the personnel file; however, she remembered several incidents as she called them. The notes of trite incidents or complaints were not part of his personnel file, but rather a separate file that she kept in case more allegations surfaced. He left St. Anthony's in 1999, two years after Penny disappeared. According to Ms. Flanagan, the reason was personal. She heard nothing about him until she received a call from St. Anne's Catholic Church and school in Dayton, Ohio. He was being considered for a similar position there and had listed her as a reference. Given his exemplary work record at St. Anthony's, she found no reason not to give him a good reference.

Jackson started working at St. Anne's in the fall of 2000. Beth spoke with Father Conrad Farrell of St. Anne's, and he referred her to principal Ralph McAndrews who recommended hiring Jackson Walker. Jackson worked there through the 2005 school year and left for personal reasons. His record, according to Principal McAndrews, was exemplary as well. Unlike St. Anthony's, there weren't any incidents or complaints. He was, for all intents and purposes, squeaky clean. After he left

St. Anne's, he disappeared for another year and resurfaced in Lexington, Kentucky, in 2007 at St. Peter and Paul's Catholic School. He had just finished his fifth year, and now, Abbie Gardner was missing.

Carla closed her laptop and glanced at Beth, still fixated on her screen. Carla rose and put her hands on her desk to stretch and to get her attention. Beth couldn't help noticing some movement in her peripheral vision and glanced in Carla's direction and asked, "We've been at it for several hours, how about a break?"

"Great, what do you have in mind?"

"Parsons' Coffee Emporium downtown. I'm sure we can find a quiet table to discuss our findings. Have you been there before?"

"It will be my first time."

"Can't believe you haven't been there. The owner is a hoot. Wait till you meet her. You will love her. You know she was a basketball star at Western Kentucky University. A photo of her hangs in the hallway at the back of the building. Check it out while we're there."

Since it was mid-morning, the coffee shop was not super busy. A quiet table in the back was perfect for them, private and cozy at the same time. In many ways, it was Carla's favorite table. She had interviewed Joanne Alison there and then her sister, Kathy Wilcox. Familiar with the shop, she liked sitting in the back since she could see everyone coming and going. Plus, she was friends with the owner, Alicia Parsons, which made every visit a pleasure. While they waited for their coffee, they discussed their findings. After receiving their coffee, they sipped on it to clear their minds before beginning what would probably be a lively discussion. About five minutes has passed, Beth met Carla's gaze. "You go first since that's where Jackson Walker's history begins, okay?

Before Carla could begin, Alicia Parsons stopped by to greet her. "Detective McBride, I didn't see you come in. How are things going?"

"Hey, Mrs. P, couldn't be better."

"Well, great. Coffee good like always?"

"Oh, yeah, perfect. I'd like you to meet Beth Pendergast, our forensic psychologist. She is working with us on a fifteen-year-old cold case."

Alicia extended her hand toward Beth, taking Beth's hand in hers, she gently squeezed it, sending a strange feeling throughout her body. "Nice to meet you, Mrs. Parsons. My first time here, what a friendly and cozy place you have, and coffee's great."

"Thank you, nice to meet you as well. Hey, I've got to get back to running my business. Come back sometime. The next coffee is on me, okay? Also, I'm all about first names, so please call me Ally."

Beth acknowledged her and watched her walk away. Carla, noticing Beth's gaze, said, "See, I told you that you would love her, and before we leave, check out the picture in the hallway. Now, where were we?"

"Hmm, your interview with Ms. Flanagan?"

"Right, in speaking with her, who was principal when he was there, he was an exemplary teacher. She indicated a few incidents, kind of silly things, and wasn't sure she believed the students. Fourth and fifth-grade students make up stuff, you know. She spoke with him, and there were no further incidents."

"What kind of incidents?"

"Touching on the shoulders and arms, that kind of thing. One incident was a girl that thought he was looking up her skirt. You know they wore pleated skirts back then, and you know young girls don't always sit ladylike and all. He left for personal reasons and ended up a year later in Dayton. Other than that, this guy was a model teacher. What did you find out?

"Honestly, not much more. It pretty much mirrors your findings. Model teacher, no problems, and left for personal reasons."

"Then maybe Bernie was right. Jackson Walker is squeaky clean."

"I still believe something's not right. He has gaps in his work history, two girls the same age disappear, bodies never found, and then he leaves. He surfaced in Lexington five years ago, and now another young girl is missing. I don't think that's a coincidence, do you?"

"Hmm, I see your point, but that doesn't make him a child molester or killer. We need more to go on, and we don't want to take this flimsy theory to the Lexington Police. We need something more credible, or we look foolish. Do you remember him when you were in elementary school at St. Anthony's?"

"I didn't go to St. Anthony's. My mom couldn't afford the tuition, so it was a public school for me."

"Then, that means that Penny didn't go there either, right?" Beth acknowledged her. "Then that shoots big holes in this theory, that it involved him, unless he held other jobs during the summer months, maybe a lifeguard or something else. Maybe after school activities, uh, like gymnastics or something similar. We need to check that angle out. I'll call Ms. Flanagan and inquire; you do the same with the person you spoke with."

"Sounds good. Anything else on your mind?"

"Yeah, we've never talked about Penny. I only saw

pictures of her. Tell me about her and why someone might have abducted her for whatever reason."

"What do you mean, physical appearance?"

"Yeah, that would be a good place to start since these types of abductions usually involve sexual predators."

"Seriously, she was just a sixth-grader and innocent."

"Beth, we live in a whacky and sick world. Whether it's a sexual predator or a recruiter for sex trafficking, young and mature innocent girls are targets. Tell me more about her."

"Okay, she was pretty, and she developed way earlier than me. Sometimes I felt she was older than me even though we were in the same grade. That summer, she filled out quite a bit. I remember that because she boasted about it all the time. Me, on the other hand, I was a late bloomer, and if you look at me now, I still don't have much, but then, you, well, you get the picture."

"Honey, big boobs can be a curse sometimes, if you know what I mean?" A quirky grin moved from her lips. "Anything else?"

"You know at the pool, she wore a two-piece. I wouldn't call it a bikini, but she wore it well. She attracted the young boys, I guess boys period, and loved it, flirting with them all the time. Regardless, why would a twenty-three-old man be interested in a budding sixth-grader for pleasure?"

"I don't know. It's a sick world. If it's him, he'd be around thirty-eight now, why would he be interested in Abbie Gardner—same reason."

"Ugh, let's talk about something more pleasant, okay?"

"Sure, let's get out of here and head to the Apollo Café for lunch, and once we get back to the station, we can follow-up on Jackson Walker, the exemplary teacher."

Before leaving, Carla showed Beth the picture of Alicia Parsons when she played for Western Kentucky University. Beth studied the photo, and weird thoughts danced in her head as they left the coffee shop. After a quick lunch, they were back at the station, following up on getting further information on Jackson Walker and any extracurricular activities of his. A call to Ms. Flanagan indicated she remembered him working at a gymnastics center and as a lifeguard in the summer.

Beth found out that he was also a lifeguard in Dayton and coaching a girls' softball team as well. They ended the day going over the similarities of his after-school and summer activities. Being a lifeguard was a common occurrence and another thing to check out. They would have to track down Melody Morris's parents and ask them questions about her daughter's after-school and summer activities. Although it would be painful for them, it was essential to know that information to build a case.

CHAPTER 14

With the weekend upon Beth and Carla, each was looking forward to time away from the job. However, Beth would have to make it through today before she could enjoy the weekend. She had to contact the parents of Melody Morris, the young girl that disappeared in Dayton, Ohio, where Jackson Walker lived and worked. A quick search on the internet for a phone number yielded nothing. Evidently, Melody's parents were ordinary everyday people. A call to Ralph McAndrews to inquire if Melody attended a Catholic school in Dayton would hopefully yield something. Mr. McAndrews knew the name because of the media coverage regarding her disappearance. However, he informed Beth that she didn't attend school at St. Anne's, but the Morris family were members of the church.

After explaining her reasons for contacting Melody's parents, he provided her with their contact information. Ed and Dot Morris were just ordinary people in the community and involved at the church. Dot was a lay minister while Ed was in the Knights of Columbus. According to Father Farrell, they turned to the church when their daughter disappeared, which helped them cope with the loss. Dot worked at a local retail store in the home goods department while Ed was a paramedic. Their faith in God got them through the difficult years. With counseling, they could have a happy life as best as possible.

Even though it had been five years or more since Melody's disappearance, she knew that the call wouldn't be easy for her or them because this was about the time their daughter disappeared. Even though Beth knew time heals even the deepest wounds, losing your only child was probably something a parent would never get over. In her mind, if she were to have children, losing one would devastate her.

Approaching the call, she knew to treat it with kid gloves. A caring, sympathetic attitude and tone of voice while showing respect for Melody would be vital in getting them to open up about their daughter. With no landline, she had to choose which one to call, Ed or Dot. Not knowing the family dynamics, it was like flipping a coin. Carla voted for the mother first. Talking to either of them would be painful, however, it was necessary. For privacy, Beth retreated to a vacant interrogation room. She dialed Dot's mobile number; it rang and rang, eventually going to her voicemail. Leaving a message bringing up her daughter's disappearance would be disrespectful so she ended the call. That left Ed. Dialing his number, it rang twice, and then it was answered. Beth placed the call on speaker. A solemn and soft voice filled the room.

"Mr. Morris?"

"Yes."

After taking a deep breath to calm her nerves tugging on her heartstrings, Beth said, "Mr. Morris, my name is Beth Pendergast with the police department in Oakmont, Kentucky. Do you have a few moments to speak with me?"

"Oakmont Police Department, Kentucky. What's this about?"

"Mr. Morris, I don't want to pry or mean to upset you, I just want to ask you several questions about Melody's disappearance." Silence exuded from the other end. She felt she heard him taking a deep breath. She interjected, "I'm so sorry for your loss, and I don't mean to upset you, and if this is not a good time, please let me know."

"Did you find Melody?" Not expecting that question, she had to take a deep breath herself and collected her thoughts before she answered. It was apparent he had not given up hope in finding his daughter. "Are you there, Ms. Pendergast?"

Calm and collected, she replied, "Yes, I'm calling to ask a few questions because my best friend from my childhood disappeared just as your daughter did. However, my friend disappeared fifteen years ago. Her body was never found just like your daughter. I'm a forensic psychologist re-opening that case and have discovered some leads we are chasing. I don't know what you experienced back then, but the pain I experienced in losing my best friend was excruciating. Your daughter's disappearance may or may not be relevant to the case I'm investigating. I'm thinking outside the box at any lead we discover. Your answers may help us substantiate our present direction in the investigation."

Again, Mr. Morris was silent on the other end. She heard what she thought was a sniffle or two and assumed emotions were erupting in his soul. She quietly asked, "Mr. Morris, is everything okay?" The silence continued, and she knew this conversation was causing painful memories. Thinking that maybe she should end the call, she asked, "Mr. Morris, would there be a better time for you?"

"Uh, Ms. Pendergast, what do you want to know?"

Taking a deep breath, she collected her thoughts before asking what would result in painful memories. "Why not start and tell me about your lovely daughter. What was she like, what did she liked to do, you know, those kinds of things? May we start with that, and I will just listen, okay?"

"Yeah, that will be easier for me, and thank you for being so respectful to Melody and me."

"Mr. Morris, thank you for wanting to help. I'm ready when you are, and if you need a break, just let me know, okay?"

Over the next thirty minutes, she listened to a loving father describe his precious little girl. Melody was very friendly, never met a stranger. She was a pretty child and looked older than her real age. Melody was just a few weeks shy of her thirteenth birthday when she went missing. With long blonde hair and blue eyes, she had just started modeling and entering beauty pageants at her mother's insistence. She was mature beyond her years, thirteen-going-on-twenty her mother described her. She loved swimming and playing softball; he described her as an all-American girl. Beth listened to him ramble on about her, realizing how much he still loved her.

He finally said, "Ms. Pendergast, is there anything else you want to ask?"

Showing sympathy in her voice, she responded, "Mr. Morris, thank you so much. I only have one more question to ask. Do you remember who might have coached your daughter in softball?"

"I don't remember his name, but he was an excellent coach and taught her a lot about playing and getting better. She loved him. I believe he was a teacher at St. Anne's Catholic School. Anything else?"

"Yeah, did Melody attend school there?"

"No, she attended public schools. Why do you ask?"

"Just wondered. Thank you so much. You've been a big help. Once again, I'm sorry for your loss."

She was just about to end the call when he asked, "Ms. Pendergast, if something develops, please call me, okay?"

"Yeah, oh one last thing, do you have a picture of her you could text or email me?"

"Yeah, I'll send it right away."

Beth ended the call and waited for the picture to arrive. About five minutes later, her phone alerted her of a text and the photo. Melody Morris, pretty, blonde, and blue eyes, in a dress she wore in a beauty pageant. She was definitely thirteen-going-on-twenty. A familiar theme was surfacing, and one they couldn't ignore.

While Beth had been on the phone with Mr. Morris, Carla checked on updates about John Dickerson's escape. Even though his mugshot had been all over the news, nothing new existed. He had just vanished, probably went underground. With a vast network of business associates that would help him, that was a big problem for Carla and her friends because he was a psychotic and vengeful person on the loose.

Beth had returned from the interrogation room, where she spoke with Mr. Morris. Drained and frazzled, Carla knew how difficult it was. She'd made that call many times. "How did it go?"

"It was difficult, but I used my charm and empathy, and he told me all about Melody and sent me this picture. Take a look."

Carla took Beth's phone, studied the picture, and handed the phone back to her. Carla continued, "Let's get some coffee and go somewhere we can talk in private. How about the interrogation room in five minutes or so?"

With a cup of fresh coffee, the interrogation room was command central seven minutes later. Beth explained what she found out about Melody Morris. They realized coincidence or not, there were many similarities between Penny and Melody, and there was the Jackson Walker connection. On the surface, he was a model citizen no matter where he lived; however, their brief investigation was a different story. Jackson Walker was now a person of interest.

As Beth was leaving the room, her phone rang, startling her. The caller ID sent chills up and down her spine. Answering, tears surfaced. "Yes, this is she." The silence was deafening as she listened, wiping away more tears. "Thank you." The call ended. Stunned, she sat down before she collapsed.

Sitting beside her, Carla consoled Beth the best she could. All Carla knew was something tragic had occurred. As the sobbing continued, a blank expression slowly covered Beth's ghostly face. Carla reached for

Beth's hand to comfort her. "Beth, what's going on? Talk to me."

Beth's eyes met Carla's compassionate concern. "Umm, my, my mom's been in, uh, a serious, umm, serious accident. She's in a Cincinnati hospital. She's, umm, in an intensive care unit, on a ventilator. I have to go now. The outlook isn't promising."

As those words came out, Carla wrapped her arms around Beth, comforting her as best she could. Carla had felt this pain before and knew the heartbreak that comes after receiving a call like this. "Beth, you're in no shape to drive. I will take you if that's all right." Beth just nodded. Carla continued to hold her and comfort her and whispered, "Honey, everything's going to be fine. Stay here and compose yourself the best you can. I'm going to let Chief Evans know what is going on. When I get back, we'll leave, okay?"

Again, she just nodded. Carla left, and in that time, Beth had composed herself. Returning with Chief Evans, he expressed his concern making her feel a little better. He went to the common area to inform those working that Beth's mother had been in a severe accident. Beth and Carla exited through a side door to avoid the common area and employee reaction.

Even though it was only a two-hour drive to downtown Cincinnati, it would seem like an eternity to them. Carla had experienced this same living hell when her parents died, rushing to the hospital, hoping to hug them one more time, expressing your love, or saying goodbye.

CHAPTER 15

Arriving at the hospital by mid-afternoon, the glorious and sunny June morning morphed into a gloomy, misty afternoon of despair. After entering through the main doors, patient information services was a few steps away. The downtown hospital was old and looked its age. It wasn't particularly inviting, but Beth's mom had emergency surgery to remove her gallbladder there while Beth was in high school. She knew her mom was receiving the best care as she did many years ago. The receptionist on duty directed them to the intensive care unit on the fourth floor.

Stepping off the elevator, ICU was to the right. A set of double doors separated Beth from her mom. Anticipation was churning inside her stomach, creating an uneasy feeling. Entering through the double doors, the nurses' station was straight ahead. There was a scurry of activity with nurses moving in and out of the command center. Doctors in white coats stood in front and behind the counter, reviewing charts. Ready to inquire about her mom, she identified herself. The charge nurse instructed her to sit in the waiting area until the doctor treating her mother was available to speak with her.

The private waiting area was just to the left of the nurses' station. Opening the door, they sat across from a television attached on the wall. CNN was quietly barking out today's top story. Several chairs to the left, a man and a woman, presumably husband and wife, waited patiently for some good news. With his arm around the woman, her head rested on his shoulder, tired and worried eyes silently described their demeanor. The clock on the wall was imposing. It appeared to stand still even though the second hand was moving at its normal speed.

———

3:47 PM.

As the door swung open, a doctor entered. Beth's heart pounded furiously. However, the doctor went straight to the other couple and sat down beside them. She over-heard the doctor telling the couple that they could see their loved one now. Smiles painted their face as they quickly followed the doctor out of the room. Beth and Carla were all alone in the waiting room with the big clock of uncertainty.

———

3:55 PM.

The minute hand moved slowly on its predestined circular path. Outside the door, nurses and doctors scur-ried about, oblivious to their pain. Even though the television created muted noise, Beth could not hear or comprehend the conversation. Thoughts and questions about her mom consumed her mind. While trying to focus on the good things in her life, uncertainty ravaged her soul. Her mom was the only relative she had left as far as she knew. Her dad died when she was five years old; she barely knew him. Her mom became her best friend, confidant, and protector. She was her life, and Beth could never fathom life without her. A tap of reassurance on the arm startled Beth; Carla squeezed her hand once more. Looking at Carla for a moment, Beth's gaze returned to the clock on the wall.

4:10 PM.

Beth closed her eyes tightly, embedding a mostly black image in her brain. After opening her eyes, the image slowly faded as the door swung open. She turned toward the door; the news she was waiting on stood in front of her. The doctor identified himself as Doctor Lex Charles. He pulled up a chair and began explaining her mom's condition and prognosis. Tears trickled down Beth's tired face. Carla held her hand while the doctor continued his explanation. Beth's mom was in a comatose state, and her chances of recovering weren't good. The doctor explained to her that tough decisions were ahead of her should her mom deteriorate further. The next twenty-four hours would be crucial to any chances of survival, but what kind of survival she wondered.

Even though Carla was not family, she was permitted to go with Beth to see her mom for a brief moment.

Beth's heart was exploding inside her body as she followed the doctor to the intensive care unit. The vision of her mom was too much for her to bear, and her emotions erupted in her soul. While hooked up to machines monitoring everything vital—the sight of the ventilator shook her to her core. Walking over to her mom, she grabbed her hand, expecting a response. It was cold and lifeless, and tears surfaced on her face and she wiped them away. After leaning down, she whispered her love in her mom's ear. Hearing the doctor tell her that this was all the time he could permit, she gently squeezed her mom's hand and planted a kiss on her forehead.

As they entered the waiting room, it was empty and cold, just like death. Beth glanced at the clock, 4:35 PM glared back at her. Dr. Charles, who accompanied them back to the waiting room, reassured Beth that her mom was getting the best care possible. The rest was up to her mom to fight for her life. He suggested they get coffee because it was going to be a long night. After asking Beth if she had any further questions, he left to check on her mom again. It was up to Carla to ease the pain that Beth was experiencing and thought coffee would be a good idea as well. "Why don't we go to the canteen in the downstairs lobby, and we can just talk if you want to?"

"Thank you for coming with me, it means a lot, and I couldn't have handled this by myself. Coffee in the canteen would be nice."

Before leaving the floor, Beth stopped by the nurses' station, leaving her phone number should they need to get a hold of her while they were in the canteen. Back on the elevator, they exited on the ground floor, found the canteen quickly, and placed an order for two large coffees. After receiving their coffee, they found a table for two on the far wall. Sitting across from each other, Beth was silent and reserved. "Beth, why don't you tell me about your mom?"

With her hands around her cup of coffee trying to warm her spirits, Beth took a sip of the steaming java. After meeting Carla's comforting smile, she replied, "Awe, my mom, best mom ever, was my rock growing up, always there for me. I remember the first time my first real boyfriend broke my heart, my mom talked me through it and cried with every tear I shed. My mom gave me tough love when I needed it. I would not be the person today without her love and devotion."

Beth paused for a moment to take another sip of the coffee, which allowed Carla to respond and comfort her as well. "Umm, I understand, my dad was that way although he never cried with me much. He always used to tell me, suck it up, honey, that kind of tough love, and you know, it made me stronger. Tell me more about your mom?"

Beth appreciated Carla opening up and doing her best to ease the painful thoughts bouncing around in her mind. "Well, she never remarried after my dad died, said she didn't need a man, her focus was on raising me the best she could. You know, my mom told me after she had me, she couldn't have any more children, you know, complications in giving birth."

Noticing her emotions were beginning to erupt, Carla gave her some consoling words. "Hey, I'm sorry about that, but it wasn't your fault. There are always underlying conditions, so don't beat yourself up over that, okay?"

Beth nodded and continued opening up to her, "You know, only a few people know this, but my mom never knew her birth mother." One of those looks of disbelief painted Carla's face as her eyes flew wide open. "Yeah, adopted. My mom never said much about it because, well, she was just a baby when it happened. She told me she never had the desire to find her real biological mother."

"Wow, that's something else. Being adopted, I would want to know my biological mother for medical reasons, what about you?"

"Well, that's a strange question since neither of us is adopted, but I would have to agree. I would do everything I could to find my biological mother. You know my mom and Penny's mom were so much alike, I asked her if they were related. She laughed it off and always changed the subject every time I brought it up."

"Umm, you know, I remember when I met Penny's mother and then your mom that same day, it hit me how much they resembled each other. Also, there's you and Penny, well I guess this conversation is going in a weird direction, wouldn't you say?"

Beth was showing some signs of happiness. She smiled and laughed. Suddenly the screen on her phone lit-up; she stared at it for a moment, taking a deep breath before answering it. Hitting the accept button, she listened, then ended the call. "Carla, we have to go to ICU now."

"What's going on?"

"I don't know. They said I needed to come right away."

Stepping off the elevator, they quickly walked through the double doors that held the fate of Beth's mother. Walking to the nurses' station, she inquired about her mother. A nurse told them to go to the waiting area, and the doctor would be in shortly. Another wait was not what she wanted, and the strong coffee she drank began its upward trek into her esophagus. She swallowed hard, pushing it back down. Her stomach already churned from the uncertainty of the situation.

5:14 PM.

Waiting was excruciating. Thoughts seeped into Beth's mind of what was going on. The doctor said the next twenty-four hours would be crucial, and it was up to her mother to survive.

5:16 PM.

It seemed like fifteen minutes had passed. What was taking Dr. Charles so long, she asked herself? She glanced at the door, seeing him approaching the waiting room; however, he quickly made a sharp left turn, false alarm, she thought.

Tension and stress painted Beth's face; her eyes were glassy and red from tears of fright and uncertainty. Carla took Beth's hand in hers and gave it a gentle squeeze. Reacting to the caring gesture, Beth glanced at her and smiled a thank you at her. The silence sucked the air out of the room. Waiting was hell.

5:35 PM.

Suffocating air swooshed out of the room as the door opened. Pulling up a chair in front of Beth and Carla, the silence in the room was surreal. Dr. Charles swallowed hard before grabbing Beth's hand. A loud deafening atmosphere hung from the ceiling. His mouth appeared to move in slow motion trying to console her, while forcing comforting words out. As he released her hand, a brief smile of hope and prayer met Beth's red and swollen eyes. As Dr. Charles left, more sorrow and helplessness captivated the waiting room. Sitting in the chair in front of Beth, Carla grabbed her hands as emotions erupted as Carla became a consoling surrogate mother.

Judy Pendergast's untimely death shattered Beth's soul. Her mother, best friend, and the only living relative she had died of a massive pulmonary embolism. Mad at the world, at God, for taking her mother away so soon, the heartbreak left her soul empty. Her mother deserved much better, a chance to grow old and be a grandmother. However, the finality of death stole that from her. Beth's family, as she knew it, except for Aliyah, vanished as the horrific force of crunching metal and shattered glass exploded on a concrete highway. Just the other day, Beth and her mom laughed together, cried together, sharing their love. As Beth grieved, she questioned why life was so cruel.

Chief Evans granted Beth as much bereavement leave as necessary to grieve and settle her mother's estate. Fortunately for Beth, her mom's will would make the process much more manageable. Also, in Beth's favor, the house her mother owned had been titled in both of their names when her mom suffered a medical scare several years back. With no other known family members, settling her estate would be a relatively painless and quick process. Stated in her mother's will, Judy Pendergast would undergo cremation. Beth was not happy with her wishes even though she agreed to it several years ago.

CHAPTER 16

With Beth on bereavement leave, the investigation into Jackson Walker's past would fall on Carla. On the surface, his past appeared normal except for the missing years in his work history and was a red flag in Beth's mind. Initially, Carla discounted Jackson Walker's involvement in the Penny Miracle case. However, several red flags changed her mind, and nothing else credible has surfaced. If they were going to solve this case, this might be their best shot since that fateful day, their best shot in getting redemption, and closure. Jackson Walker's life was about to be picked apart, piece by piece, and would start in his hometown of Fort Gay, West Virginia.

Before disturbing that tiny West Virginia coal town, a quick review of his activity in college was necessary. Although Jackson graduated over twenty years ago, records would not be that difficult to get through the Freedom of Information Act. After receiving Jackson's school records two days later, the packet she received only contained a copy of his transcripts, filling her with disappointment. Filing another request, disappointment again, nothing but his transcripts existed. She wondered whether Bernie was right in the initial investigation that Jackson Walker was squeaky clean.

The transcripts revealed Jackson was one smart individual. His cumulative grade point average was a three-point-eight out of perfect four-point-zero. A more detailed analysis showed that he only attended the university campus in Oakmont for two years. His transcripts revealed his first two years of post-secondary education was at a community college in Prestonsburg, Kentucky. His GPA there indicated he was a smart individual; staying at home and commuting to Prestonsburg saved him a ton of money, allowing him to maintain a job in his hometown.

Fort Gay, approximately 145 miles from Oakmont, was a two-hour drive. The trip would take her east on Interstate 64 till she reached Exit 191. From there, she would take US 23 South along the Big Sandy River dividing West Virginia and Kentucky. Once reaching Louisa, Kentucky, a trip across the bridge led her to the downtown area. Being a small town should make it easier to find out information about Jackson Walker; local restaurants or barbershops were her best bet. Driving through town, she made mental notes of those types of establishments; barbershops would be the last resort for a female detective.

A local restaurant near the high school was an excellent place to start. Parking on the street just down from it, Carla walked toward the restaurant taking in the town's cityscape—an old city still thriving in the grand scheme of things. For years, it depended on the coal industry, just like its counterparts in Kentucky. At this time of the day, Grace's Diner wasn't too busy, which suited her just fine.

Entering the diner was like going back in time; a checkerboard tile floor flowed throughout the restaurant. The nostalgia of yesteryear hung on the faded white walls. Wooden tables and chairs flanked each wall. Straight ahead, a long bar with a stainless-steel countertop set the tone of the vintage feel. The cash register was on one end, while on the other end was a sign that read place order here. Old vintage backless stools with red vinyl seat cushions fronted the bar giving the diner its classic yesteryear style.

With her pick of stools, the center one suited her just fine. As her elbows rested on the counter, flashbacks of her childhood rushed in. In the kitchen, a woman glanced in her direction. Carla smiled at the lady. A set of western-style swinging doors separated the kitchen from the counter area. The badge on the woman's blouse read Grace Atkins. While eyeing the menu on the wall, an old-time soda dispenser caught her eye as Grace appeared in front of her.

"Grace, I hope you don't mind me calling you that, but do you have the old-time fountain drinks, you know the real Coca-Cola? I haven't had one in, well, I don't know when."

Abrupt and a little unfriendly, she responded, "Of course, coming right up. May I get you anything else while I'm at it?"

"Tell you what, let's just start with that." Within a minute, an old-time fountain soda fizzed in front of her, with an old-time straw included. Still fizzing, she savored the first sip. Smiling, she hoped to get Grace to open up. "Hmm, many places don't make them like this anymore. This is great. You worked here long?"

A frown and downward eye movement met Carla's strained smile. Grace had been around for a long time and knew most of the locals. She knew Carla didn't quite fit the mold, and Grace's disdaining frown morphed to a crooked grin. While wiping off the counter where Carla's soda left a streak of water when she grabbed it, Grace retorted. "Didn't you see the name on the building? I'm the only owner this place has ever had."

Carla's rosy cheeks felt the heat as they glowed. "Sorry. Guess you know I'm not from around here."

"Wasn't hard to figure that one out. Where are you from?"

"Oakmont, Kentucky."

"Hmm, what brings you to old Fort Gay? Did you get lost?"

"Nah, I'm trying to get information on some guy that I met at the university in Oakmont. I believe he grew up here. Umm, Does Jackson Walker ring a bell?"

"Well now, haven't heard that name in a while. Ole Tommy they used to call him. He was a real charmer back in the day. Had all the ladies after him, even young girls, and I mean the young ones. They wanted his admiration, jealous of each other. I guess they all had a big crush on him."

Making quick eye contact, she responded, "Tommy, what's up with that?"

"Uh, everybody called him Tommy because he hated Jackson. His middle name was Thomas. What do you want with him?"

"Oh, yeah, Tommy. I remember now. You knew him personally?"

"Yeah, he worked here. His mom helped me start this place, and his mom would still be my business partner and working here if it hadn't been for her accident about fifteen years ago."

"Really, what kind of accident?"

"You're awful nosey, you know."

Grace was wiser than Carla thought; it would be a little more challenging to get the information she wanted. "Hey, give me another soda, and how about a chili dog, just mustard and slaw, no onions, please?"

A strange look met Carla's eyes. Grace pushed open the western-style swinging doors, sounds of tongs clattered against a stainless steel pan, a metal spoon scraped against the inside of the chili pot. Observing Grace through the opening, Carla got lost in her nostalgic flashbacks. The swinging doors squeaked, carrying an off-white melamine plate with a chili-dog with slaw on the side brought back more memories of yesteryear. Grace reached behind her and grabbed the bottle of mustard, and placed it in front of Carla. After Grace fixed another old-fashioned soda and placed it on the counter, Carla's nostalgic culinary trip was complete. As she took a bite of the chili dog, Grace threw her another quizzical look.

"What are you really doing here, and what do you want?"

"As I said, he's an old friend from college. Ran across his picture the other day, and since I was on my way to Pikeville for business, thought I'd stop and see if anyone had any contact information on him, that's all."

Getting information out of Grace was difficult, and Carla let it be for the moment. The tasty chili dog with an old-time fountain drink brought back happy memories of her dad taking her to the local pharmacy and treating her to a root beer float. Lost in the moment, she didn't notice Grace placing a napkin in front of her plate. She couldn't understand why she did that; several clean napkins already flanked the plate. An address and phone number in red ink made Carla smile.

"I don't have his contact information, but his mom probably does. She lives in a small frame house up on the hill overlooking the river. The accident left her paralyzed from the waist down, and her house had to be retro-fitted to her situation. I bought out her partnership because she needed the money. It wasn't much, but it helped. She told me she never wanted to live in a nursing home. She still has a mortgage and needs a full-time housekeeper. I understand Tommy helps her as much as he can, but teachers don't make that much. Not sure where he gets all that money, but it's no business of mine. I visit her from time to time. She's doing fine and adjusted well to a life of confinement."

Looking at the napkin and the information, she glanced at Grace and smiled. "Chili dog and soda were awesome. What do I owe you?"

An old-style nostalgic check laid in front of her, a double-take at the amount, Grace nodded. With the nostalgic culinary lunch finished, carrying the soda glass and plate, Grace bumped the swinging doors open and disappeared. Twenty dollars stood tall on the counter; Grace returned from the kitchen and snatched it up. Seconds later, one ten, two ones, and a quarter sat in front of Carla. Nostalgic memories were worth every penny, Carla thought. She smiled at Grace as she rested her elbows on the counter. "You keep it. I haven't had a chili-dog that good in a long time, and the old-fashioned sodas reminded me when my dad would take me to the pharmacy for a root beer float. Those memories are priceless. Thank you for that memorable journey. Have a nice day, you're the best."

Grace smiled back, and Carla left, hoping Jackson Walker's mother would allow a visit from a total stranger. After turning up the hill to her home, the old neighborhood houses showed their age. Parking in front of her home, a lady in a wheelchair sat on the small but adequate porch. Beside her in a rocking chair, another lady, presumably her housekeeper, rocked back-and-forth. An older black and white cat purred softly on the lap of the lady in the wheelchair. Other than frail and feeble, she appeared healthy. Ever since Carla exited the car, the two ladies stared in her direction.

Approaching the porch, Carla said, "Mrs. Walker?"

"Yes, please call me Phyliss." Carla nodded. "You after money? I know I'm late on a few bills. Tommy will give me some soon."

"I'm sorry to alarm you like that. I know how it is, you know, struggling to pay bills." A smile met Carla's stoic expression. "I'm Carla Sizemore from Oakmont, Kentucky. I was on my way to Pikeville for business and stopped in town to see if I could find anyone that had contact information for your son, Tommy. We were friends in college. After that, I lost contact with him. I came across a picture of him the other day and wondered where he was and what he was doing. I took a chance, ate at Grace's place. She gave me your address. I hope I'm not intruding."

A broad smile crossed her wrinkled and weathered lips. "Oh my, please have a seat. I don't recall Tommy ever mentioning you before. He had many girlfriends, you know. Tillie Carter is my housekeeper. She takes excellent care of me."

Carla acknowledged Tillie and replied, "Yeah, he had many girlfriends, but, well, we were just friends, studied at the library together. Besides, I was dating someone else." Tillie rocked faster in her wooden rocker. The black and white cat repositioned itself and snuggled deeper in Phyliss' lap. "What's his name?"

"Gizmo. Just showed up one day, and I took him in."

"Umm, anyway, do you have Tommy's contact information? I'd love to catch up with him."

Phyliss motioned Tillie to fetch her address book. While Tillie was gone, she continued. "Well, you know, he lives close to you." Tillie returned and read off his contact information. Carla jotted it down and stood up to leave to the disdain of Phyliss. She motioned Carla to sit back down. "You like iced tea?" Carla nodded. "Tillie, fetch her a glass. She's going to sit a spell with me."

Several minutes later, Tillie returned with a tall glass of iced tea with lemon. Carla took several sips, savoring its freshness. Real teabags, she thought. "Tea's great. I can't stay long, but thank you." Silence surrounded them as the birds chirped, insects buzzed around. Iced tea half gone, Carla studied Phyliss, eyes closed, must have dozed off, she thought. "Phyliss?"

Suddenly, her eyes opened. She moistened her lips, took a sip of her tea, then licking her lips, said, "I'm sorry, what were you going to ask?"

"Does Tommy come home often?"

"Now that he is back in Lexington, he comes home about every two weeks or so. You know, he helps me with the expenses and mortgage, always brings cash. I asked him about the extra money. He says he works other jobs from time to time. You know, he's such a nice son and will make some lucky lady a wonderful husband one of these days. Are you married?"

"Nah, but I've found my soulmate. He just hasn't popped the question yet."

"Oh, I see. What do you do for a living?"

"Uh, I'm a pharmaceutical rep. Umm, that reminds me, I better leave for my meeting. Do you have a Styrofoam cup for my tea? I'd love to take it with me."

"Sure. I'll have Tillie go get one."

As the full-length storm door closed, Carla stood up and walked toward the door, peering inside. Newer furniture and what appeared as a new hardwood floor made for a comfortable living space. As far as she could see into the kitchen, it seemed renovated recently as well. In the shadows of the house, Tillie reappeared, carrying a large Styrofoam cup and lid. Carla walked back over to Phyliss, who was petting Gizmo. Tillie had poured Carla a fresh glass of tea and handed it to her.

Carla smiled and said, "Thank you for seeing me. I can't wait to talk to Tommy. By the way, what does he do now?"

"Oh, he's a teacher and a good one. He tells me so. He even coaches girls' softball in the summer."

"Well, that's great. I must leave now, or I'll be late for my meeting. Have a nice day."

"You too. You come back and see me, you hear? Friends of Tommy are always welcome here."

Carla nodded and patted Phyliss on her arm, and left the porch. Her car backed out of the driveway, she snaked down the hill to the main road, and turned left. The trip back to Oakmont was quiet and peaceful as the hills of Eastern Kentucky passed by. It was once a booming area as long as coal moved on the railroad tracks or the Big Sandy River. The big question bouncing around in her mind was, how was Jackson "Tommy" Walker helping his mother on a teacher's salary.

CHAPTER 17

Although her mother's death lingered on in her soul, with each day's passing, memories replaced the pain and emptiness Beth felt. She knew life must go on and carried out her mother's wishes of cremation. Meeting with her mom's lawyer revealed nothing she didn't already know. Several years ago, after a short illness, her mom gave her a copy of her will. With the house already in her name, the only thing she had to deal with was the financial provisions contained in the will. Although her mom wasn't rich by any means, what she had in a retirement account through her employer would be resolved outside the legal process of the will.

Beth had a house now, a mortgage, insurance, and taxes that eventually she had to manage. She also had a fluffy white cat named Aliyah that depended on her. Parking in the driveway of her mom's house, the realization that the house was hers now hit her hard as her heartstrings exploded. Two weeks ago, her mom greeted her with a glass of Pinot Grigio on the porch. Today, the porch was lonely and cold. As she sat in her car, she remembered the day her mom purchased this fixer-upper and made it her own. Beth remembered how proud her mom was the day she entered the home after its modern renovation was completed. Her mom's smile still etched in her subconscious world, brought a smile across her face.

Exiting her car, she walked onto the porch carrying a beautiful and elegant multi-colored urn. She picked one out that best allowed her mom to live on in her mind. Her ashes rested peacefully inside. The mailbox was over-flowing. Opening the storm door, she inserted the key and turned it. Opening the door, a rush of memories greeted her. Swallowing hard, she squashed the emotions churning inside her soul. Wiping away the tears trickling down her cheeks, she flipped on the light switch illuminating the cold, dark, and somber room.

Pictures flanked each end of the fireplace mantel. Beth smiled from one photo, Judy and Brian Pendergast smiled from the other. The eternal urn filled the emptiness in between as she placed it on the mantel. Beth smiled and said aloud, "Mom, you're home now." Stepping back out on the porch, she retrieved the mail, tossing it on the table just inside the door, just as her mom always did. Although the living room was just as she left it two weeks ago, it seemed different; emptiness replaced laughter and hugs from her last visit.

Suddenly, a noise from the kitchen startled her. Wondering what could have caused it, she walked to the kitchen seeing Aliyah sitting in the doorway. She picked her up and held her in her arms. Aliyah purred loudly, meowing and grieving even though a neighbor checked in on her a few times. When spotting her feeding bowl, the automatic feeder dispensed no more, the automatic water dispenser hissed and spurted. Although Aliyah had been several days without food before, it didn't concern her; in fact, she always told her mom that Aliyah could stand to lose a little weight. Her mom always said a fat kitty loved you more. After replenishing the automatic water dispenser and feeder, the automatic feeder filled the bowl with her favorite food. Aliyah ate and purred simultaneously; she wondered how cats did that and not choke themselves. As Aliyah filled her tummy, happiness replaced her grieving.

A half-empty bottle of Ecco Domani Pinot Grigio stared back at her from the refrigerator. It called her name. Taking a wine glass off the holder under the upper kitchen cabinet, she poured herself a drink. As she watched the wine swirl to the bottom of the glass, her last memory of sharing a glass of wine with her mom flooded her mind. Taking a sip, she could tell it wasn't very fresh, but that didn't matter; memories of her mom washed away its blandness. Tears speckled her cheeks as she picked up the glass and retreated to the living room. Her tears left a trail on the floor as she placed the wine on a table beside the sofa. The loneliness of death's aftermath welled-up inside her; a deep breath pushed them away. Another sip of wine, it tasted better, but not great. Her mother's spirit was on the bottle; her scent, although invisible, still lingered in her mind easing her tension and pain as she prayed for peacefulness.

Aliyah purred softly at her feet. With her belly full and satisfied, she sauntered up to the master bedroom. Beth grabbed her mother's urn and followed her upstairs. Aliyah jumped up on the bed. Continuing to purr and meow, Beth sat on the side of the bed holding the urn as she found Aliyah's soft spot she loved so much. With her sleeping soundly, Beth got up, placed the urn on the bedside table and slid open the closet revealing an array of her mom's clothing. It wasn't particularly Beth's style, but they were her size. Ruffling through them, a few looked like something she might want to keep. In the closet, a safe set upon a shelf, she tried to move it, but it wouldn't budge. Her mom had it bolted from the inside. The digital combination was easy to remember; it was a combination of the day they both were born. She keyed in 1,8,2,3, and the door popped open.

A mysterious gray metal box sent her thoughts wandering. Taking it out, Beth tried to open it, but it didn't budge. Where was the key, she asked herself? Several number-ten envelopes laid on one of the lower shelves. Leafing through them, one of them had something written on it. Open and read me first it stated. Her mother's cursive writing was beautiful—a six-by-nine manila package laid on the upper shelf. The metal box must have been sitting on it. After taking the envelope out, tape sealed it. Her mom was always a stickler about following directions. Beth didn't want to disobey her instructions because her mom was watching from Heaven and would be pissed if she didn't follow them. Scattered on the bed, her mother's most private thoughts and affairs grabbed her soul.

The white envelope that stated "read me first" stared up at her. Picking it up, she felt it and knew that there couldn't be much in it, maybe a letter. Taped shut, she took it down to the kitchen to find something that could open the envelope. A paring knife would do, she thought. Opening the mystery envelope, she peeked inside and took out what appeared to be a letter, and unfolded it.

Her eyes flew open. Her lower lip quivered; tears

flowed as she stared at her mom's perfectly placed cursive writing. Dated, her mom wrote the letter just after her last visit two weeks ago—the last time she saw her mom alive. Tears dropped randomly off her cheeks, her pulse steadily thumped louder as she opened the back door to the deck, gasping for strength to understand her mother's last message of love.

CHAPTER 18

After some fresh air, she returned to the bedroom, placing the letter on the bedside table. Aliyah repositioning herself on one of the bed pillows brought a brief smile to her face. She continued to purr and sleep peacefully, oblivious to Beth's defining moment. Her mom's hand-written letter weighed heavily on her soul. Her mom's cursive was exquisite, just like her. Picking up the letter, she sat in a lounge chair in the corner staring at the date written on the letter, June 10, 2012.

After a long sip of wine, she stared at her mother's urn feeling her presence. After a big sigh, she whispered, "Here we go, mom." She knew her mom was watching her somehow, someway. Gazing at the ceiling for a moment, she swallowed hard and began to read the letter aloud.

Dearest Zoe,

I know you go by Beth now, but you will always be my Zoe. If you are reading this letter, I must be dead. I hope I'm in Heaven because I deserved to be there. I did everything to raise you to be a responsible woman and look at you now. I accomplished what I set out to do. Hopefully, God rewarded me for that. Now that I'm dead, I'm probably with your father in Heaven. What a wonderful man he was, too bad we didn't have more time with him. However, as it turned out, I get to spend eternity with him now. Not bad, I'd say.

I hope you are laughing and smiling instead of balling your eyes out, making you look older than you are, you know. We had a good life together, right? You have our memories to celebrate and enjoy for as long as you live. At least we had that time together. You know, God brought us together, a strange statement, isn't it? As you read on, you'll understand why.

Pausing for a moment while collecting her thoughts and composing herself, she sighed. While looking at the urn again, she whispered, "Mom, you always had a way of cheering me up." She returned her gaze to the letter, wondering what she would understand in time. After a big sigh, the rest of the letter loomed large on her soul.

I always did my best to tell you the truth, but I must confess, now that I'm dead, I've kept something from you for a very long time. When you were home last time, we laughed and cried together, looking at the old scrapbook and photos. That's when I realized I had not been honest and fair with you and decided it was time to write this letter.

Once again, she felt her mom's presence as she stared at the urn. "Mom, what are you talking about?" She grabbed a Kleenex and gently patted her tears away. Returning to the letter, she continued reading it.

Now that I'm gone, you deserve to know the truth. I'm sure you will probably be mad at me, scream and yell at me, but that's okay; you have that right. Yes, I'll probably be able to see you getting upset; however, I won't be able to hear you cuss me out, which I know you will. Brace yourself for what will change your life forever. I'm sure your emotions are boiling over, and your pulse is racing; take several deep breaths and calm down before reading what will change your life forever.

After that revelation, Beth needed a break as she wondered what her mom had been hiding from her all these years. With the floodgates open, wiping away tears of sadness was useless. A drink of wine and a deep breath, she returned to the letter waiting for the other shoe to drop.

You knew I was adopted, and my adoption was closed; however, your private adoption was not. See, I told you to brace yourself. Let me decipher that—you were adopted. You are not my flesh and blood, but I was your mother, and there is a big difference in that. I loved you like you were my flesh and blood, didn't I?

Breathless, she searched for calmness and clarity. Shock-and-awe painted her face as she addressed her mother's presence, "Yeah, mom, you did. I love you for that, and I miss you terribly." Emotions erupted once more, tears of sadness and hatefulness streaked down her cheeks. Needing a break and another drink to ease all the different feelings in her soul, Pinot Grigio wasn't strong enough to get her through this life-altering revelation.

In the kitchen cabinet, several ounces of Woodford Reserve gleamed at her, seeing a suitable glass, a double-shot colored the bottom of the glass. Opening the refrigerator, she dropped a few cubes of ice in the bourbon, chilling its amber color. As the ice floated gracefully, Woodford coated her mouth and tongue. Woodford's soothing power took her breath away. Swallowing hard, she closed her eyes, wincing as the burn faded away. Taking a deep breath, she returned to the bedroom, wanting to find out what her mom had been hiding from her. Page two teased her inquisitiveness, her sanity. Another loving look at her mother's urn; Woodford's smooth silkiness went down easier the second time around, sighing, she continued reading her mom's last words.

Now that you know you're adopted let me explain how that came to be. When Brian and I got married, we weren't ready to start a family immediately. However, just before our first anniversary, I discovered I was pregnant. As the baby grew inside me, I fell in love with it even more and knew the time was right to have a real family. Not to drag this out, I lost the baby. It was a boy; we named him Nicholas Alexander. Some complications with delivery would never allow me to give birth again. It devastated us; the heartache never left us. Adoption was the only way we could ever have a family.

After a long wait and passing all the prerequisites, we finally had our opportunity to adopt a little boy, but it was not to be. Devastated again and depressed, we sought counseling with our pastor. Earlier in this letter, I told you God brought us together, and he did. With all hope fading away, our pastor, Terry Clark, came to us with an opportunity to adopt. In the congregation, a young teenager, pregnant with twin girls, was being raised by a single father. The girl's father could barely make ends meet, and raising his seventeen-year-old daughter was all he could handle.

Given that situation, they made the agonizing decision to put them up for adoption and instructed the pastor to find a good home for them both. Pastor Clark approached us about adopting both girls; however, we couldn't afford two babies at one time back then, especially with your father taking a new job in Oakmont. Somehow things worked out for us, and through the church and their attorneys, Pastor Clark delivered you to us. We didn't get the chance to pick which one we wanted, but I know we got the best of the litter. Yeah, this is where you could probably use a drink, but I suspect you have one already, right?

Glancing at her mother's urn, Woodford blessed her once more. Rising out of the chair, she approached her mother's urn and tapped it gently with her glass, saluting her. Returning to the chair, she was ready for the next revelation.

Anyway, your biological mother named you Elizabeth Annie Williams; we didn't care for Annie as a middle name. The legal name we gave you was Zoe Elizabeth Pendergast. Assuming your twin sister is alive, she's out there somewhere waiting for you. As for your

biological mother, Alicia Williams, soon after she gave
birth, I believe they moved to Bowling Green,
Kentucky, and that's all the information I have on her. I
never met her personally, just knew of her. She seemed
like a sweet young girl. As for your biological father,
no one knows. Alicia wouldn't divulge the identity of
the father, who never came forward to claim you or
your twin sister, and probably for a good reason.
Everything regarding your adoption is in the grayish
metal box; the key is in my jewelry box on the dresser.
What you do with the information is your business
now; however, I advise you, sometimes things are best
left alone if you know what I mean?

I love you and miss you, Mom

Woodford called her name one final time. Filling her glass in the kitchen, she walked back up to the master bedroom with an almost empty bottle of the bourbon. While staring at her mother's urn, feeling her presence, she saluted her mom's spirit once more. With a weird emptiness in her soul, she prayed to God for guidance and courage. While returning to the lounge chair, tears replaced her prayers.

CHAPTER 19

After all the ice had melted in her glass; she tasted the last remnants of Woodford in her mouth. Initial numbing had worn off or maybe were drained by an unexplained force from the urn that invaded her body, cleansing her soul. Adopted, a biological mother and a twin sister were surreal, taking her breath away, stunning her soul. With her glass in hand, Woodford found new life. Two cubes of ice nestled in the amber-colored liquid unlocked new and exciting flavors.

What next, she thought, opening the metal box was heavy on her mind. However, her emotions weren't ready for what the metal box may reveal. Needing to decompress and absorb the fact that a metaphorical earthquake had just hit her world, she carried Woodford downstairs to the deck. Twilight had given away to twinkling stars and constellations. After lighting a candle, the flames danced in a cooling breeze, the memory of the candle bouncing off her mom's face flashed in her mind. A brief smile crossed her mouth as she held Woodford up, toasting her mom looking down on her.

A scratching noise interrupted her ceremonial toast. A pair of yellowish-green eyes wanting comfort and love cried out from the kitchen. Outstretched paws moved in tandem, and the only friend she had that could comfort her at this moment meowed loudly. Opening the door, Aliyah pawed at her leg gently meowing. Picking her up, purring against Beth's shoulder made her smile. Beth sat in a lounge chair, placing Aliyah on her lap. She purred and reverently snuggled closer to Beth's body. As she gently stroked Aliyah, a grieving meow raised the hair on Beth's arms. Comforting her, Beth whispered, "It's just us now, I know you miss her too. Don't worry. I'll take good care of you." A double-wink of glassy eyes met Beth's somber soul. After snuggling even closer, the purring warmth felt good against Beth's chilling soul.

Out of her peripheral vision, a shooting star streaked across the sky. Many evenings, she and her mom watched the heavens, hoping to catch a glimpse of one; every time one occurred, they would argue who saw it first. Never agreeing; they would end up laughing at each other, waiting for the next one to bring joy into their lives. Her soul was feeling the numbing effects of Woodford. While focusing on the brightest star in the sky, she thought about the metal box and its contents, until her phone rang. The name and picture on the screen sent mixed emotions throughout her body. While resisting the temptation to answer, the ringing soon stopped.

She thought she had erased that person from her life. A missed call and voicemail message appeared on the lime-green icon. Woodford eased the anxiety building inside her. Only a few months since they broke up, she still loved Scott but didn't quite know how he felt. He loved her once, but not enough to commit to a deeper, more meaningful relationship for the long haul, which Beth really wanted. Another sip, she listened to his message, five seconds of silence buzzed in her ear.

With the bourbon diminishing before her eyes, she picked Aliyah up and carried her along with Woodford back into the house. Jumping down, she scurried to her bowl, savoring the fresh morsels. As Beth traversed a few steps toward her mom's bedroom, chimes interrupted her private thoughts. She wondered who it might be because many of her current friends didn't know where her mom lived.

Chimes rang out once more. Walking to the door, she looked through the peephole, took a deep breath, and opened the door. Emotions exploded as she wrapped her arms around Scott. In her mind, she wasn't sure whether that was the right thing to do. Vulnerable and under the effects of Woodford, she might lose control of her emotions.

Beth had just lost her mom, crushing her. Learning about her adoption and having a twin sister would be easy for her to forget her grief and sadness while wrapped in his arms. She remembered the last time he held her tight; she felt secure. Holding on to him, she didn't want to let go. Emotions were erupting fast and furious as he continued to hold her against his warm and sensual body. He whispered words of comfort and sympathy in her ear, words she so desperately longed to hear. A voice of reason in her head cooled her vulnerable hormones. She pulled away from his loving and tempting embrace. The silence created an awkward moment just as their last encounter at the police station a few days ago. "Scott, why didn't you leave a message?"

"I didn't feel it was appropriate. I felt I needed to tell

you in person how sorry I am for your loss. I always liked your mom. How are you doing?"

"All things considered, umm, I'm doing okay. I'd offer you a drink, but I drank all the good stuff."

"Hmm, I'm fine, but are you really okay?"

"Yeah, umm, what are you doing here?"

"Honestly, when I found out what happened, I didn't know what to do, given all we had been through, expressing my condolences in person just seemed right. You know, I miss you, when I saw you at the police station, well, let's say, uh, I realized just how much I missed you and wanted to be here for you, I realized I still love you and want you."

Words she wanted to hear, she needed to hear. Scott didn't know half of what was going on in her life, and she wasn't sure how much she would tell him, but then again, he was her best friend while they were together, and she could use a good friend right now. In her mind, emotions battled her vulnerable hormones, wanting satisfied. Eyes upon eyes, lips yearning for hers, two fingers touched his lips, stopping him, he backed off and apologized.

"It's okay," she said. "I want you, but I can't let that happen with what I'm feeling right now."

"I understand, sorry."

As her mother's spirit watched over them, they talked for hours about the good times they had. It was so easy for her to melt into his arms, make love to him, experience the magic they made many times before. He made her feel at peace, and she was grateful for his friendship, but she wasn't ready to open up her bed to him. With Scott in the guestroom, she put on her favorite nightgown —his long-sleeved white shirt. Buttoning it up over her sensual and aroused curves, she crawled in bed with Aliyah. Scents of his love kissed her body as Aliyah snuggled close to her bosom.

While rays of sun filtered through the blinds, fresh coffee permeated the house. Beth awoke alone in her bed as Aliyah had already made it to the kitchen for breakfast. Stretching and breathing in the aroma of bacon and eggs, she headed to the bathroom for a shower. Although tempted to wear his shirt in front of him, she didn't dare even though he knew every inch of her body. They weren't a couple anymore, and until she was sure he wanted to commit to her entirely, every inch of her body was off-limits to him.

In a comfortable baggy jogging suit, she made her way to the kitchen. Dressed in his casual khakis and a short-sleeved polo shirt, Scott was cooking away. An empty coffee cup on the counter awaited her. It was her mom's favorite, but he wouldn't have known that, but that was okay. Fixing herself a cup of coffee just how she liked it, she took a seat at the table.

"Your specialty, huh?"

"Yeah, be ready in a few minutes. How did you sleep last night?"

"All things considered, pretty good."

"Great. I hope you don't mind me fixing breakfast. Everything was in the fridge, so I figured you could use a good breakfast."

"Nah, I don't mind, thank you. Smells and looks great."

"We're about ready. Would you mind getting the toast while I plate everything?"

By the time she had buttered the toast, the breakfast was on the table. She sat down and put two pieces of toast on each plate. After replenishing each cup of coffee, Scott suggested a short blessing before digging in. A peaceful serenity surrounded the table. She smiled at him counting her blessings; having him here was the difference between hope and despair.

"What's going on with you? Umm, you look preoccupied and all, you know, I'm here for you, anything you want to talk about stays here, you can trust me, you know that, don't you?"

"Yeah, I know."

Not sure she wanted to tell him everything, she remembered her mom always telling her it was better to get it off her chest, then she would feel better. Catching his gaze, she opened up. "I'm adopted."

With eggs in his mouth and a piece of toast in his hand, awe-and-shock grabbed his face. "Scott, didn't you hear me? I'm adopted." His stare continued past her. "I also have a twin sister." His stare never met her angry eyes. "Dammit, Scott, please say something."

His eyes finally met hers. Tears glistened in her eyes. Compassion touched her hand, pulling her hand away; she wiped away the tears. "I'm speechless at the moment. How did you find out?"

"Let's finish breakfast, then I'll tell you the whole story, okay?"

After he acknowledged her, silence destroyed what appetites remained. While they cleared off the table, she asked him to take the coffee out to the deck, and she would join him in a few minutes. At the table enjoying his coffee, she came out carrying several sheets of paper. Across from him, she handed her mother's letter to him.

"What's this?"

"Just read it, okay?"

He slowly read her mom's life-changing confession. His expression never changed throughout; never once did his eyes leave the letter. Handing it back to her, he said, "I don't know what to say. Your mom dying and then finding out all of this…life's just not fair."

"Yeah, I guess. She had to die for me to find all this out. That sucks, but I understand why she never told me. I think she was afraid of losing me, so I get it. We had a great relationship, but difficult at times, and I always felt something was different between us."

"What are you going to do?"

"Well, umm, I'm going to find my biological mother and my twin sister. I have to. I have no choice if I want to be happy again. There's a reason my mom wrote this letter. I don't have any family that I'm aware of except my twin sister wherever she may be. Since my mom's adoption documents were sealed, my mom didn't know if she had any family. I may have grandparents out there, an aunt or uncle. So, yeah, finding my sister is the key to maybe uncovering my past, maybe even finding out what happened to Penny. Heavy stuff, huh?"

"Maybe I can help if you let me."

She acknowledged him, with coffee finished, they retreated to the living room. As their eyes met, she put her arms around him, hugging him tightly. Before releasing her arms, she planted a kiss on his cheek. He remembered their last real kiss and missed tasting her sweetness, her sexiness, but after last night, he knew the time was not right to make a move.

He left later that morning, hoping there was a chance to mend their relationship, that he could taste her sweetness and make magical love to her again. As she watched him drive away, emptiness deep in her soul cried out for his love and affection. With her mother's urn back on the mantel, she wrapped her hands around it. Leaning her forehead against the mantel, she searched for guidance, and a message from her mom that things would all work out.

CHAPTER 20

R eturning to work after a week of mourning, Beth, for the most part, seemed to be healing. Entering the police station, colleagues expressed their sincere condolences brought a few tears. She appreciated the expressions of sympathy. It was something she would have to get used to for some time. Not working at the police department that long, seeing the caring attitude was refreshing and lifted her spirits. If that was the typical behavior in the law enforcement brotherhood, she was fortunate and thrilled to be part of it.

Approaching her desk, she noticed that it was just as she left it, clean and orderly. However, she was only off for a week, even though it felt much longer. Being a psychologist, she knew to lose a loved one; time didn't fly quickly for anyone, especially not her. Carla's laptop was open, her nose to the grind. Hearing familiar foot-steps on the tile floor, in her peripheral vision, Beth was back. A smile came across her face as she reached her desk and placed a large file on it, then sat down. While staring at Carla, a quizzical expression covered Carla's face. "Beth, please don't tell me you took Penny's file back with you. I know everyone has to have a relief mechanism when dealing with the loss of a loved one, but work-related, especially, in this case, I don't get it."

"Interrogation room, now." Beth's abruptness crushed Carla's welcoming smile.

Once inside the room, taking a seat across from each other, she handed Carla her mom's confession. Glancing briefly at the handwritten letter, she said, "This is not from Penny's file, so, what is it?"

"Just read it, my mom wrote this knowing someday I would find it; unfortunately, she didn't know it would be this soon."

Carla, seeing tears changing a face of happiness into one of sorrow, replied, "I'm so sorry for what you've been through."

Tears wiped away; a quirky smile crossed her lips. A quick sigh of composure, Beth responded, "Thanks for being there for me, I owe you."

Carla acknowledged her and read Beth's mother's final message to her daughter. While reading, Carla's expression on her face was, well, expressionless, except for an occasional raising of her brow or a slight quiver of her lower lip. Carla had lost her mother long ago and knew the pain Beth was experiencing. Finished with the letter, she slid it across the table. Emotions raging in her soul from such a personal confession hit home. Reverent serenity bloomed in the room as they stared at each other in silence. Reaching for Beth's hand, Carla said, "What are you going to do?"

Trying to lighten it up a little, she replied, "Well, you know, how did I answer this situation the other day?"

"You know, you're getting just like me, uh, answering a question with a question. You said you try to find your biological mother, are you?"

"That's what I said. I have a twin sister out there, and a biological mother, so yeah. Today, I begin my search for the secrets of my past."

"Whew, girl, umm, you're something else. You lose your mom, then find out you're adopted, and you have a twin sister as well. Umm, not sure I could handle that if you know what I mean?"

"Yeah, and you know, I'm not sure I can either, but I'm going to find out. Now, where are we on Jackson Walker?"

"We'll get to that in a minute. Anything else, because I get a sense you're not telling me everything."

"Okay, you're right. My mom kept all the adoption papers in a metal box, you know one of those little money safes. Well, I haven't opened it yet. I fear that it will be just like opening Pandora's Box. I get this feeling there is more than just adoption papers inside. So, I need support when I open it. I want you there when I do. Now let's get to Jackson Walker and solve this case."

Carla filled Beth in about her visit to Fort Gay, the town where he was born and grew up, and visiting his mom. Beth was pleased that Carla had embraced her hunch that Jackson Walker was a person of interest and requested he and his mother's financial records. They both agreed it was a long shot, but anything was better than what they had now.

"So, there you have it, we have to wait on at least Jackson Walker's financial records. I have heard nothing on the second request for his mother's information, so we'll see what happens. I still sense you are holding something from me."

"You're good, well the other night, Scott visited me." Carla flashed a big smile at her, and Beth returned it with a smirk on her face. "Don't get any ideas, nothing happened, and he didn't try anything, given my vulnerability. He was caring and respectful. It was nice seeing him. I asked him about John Dickerson, and he didn't have much to say, but I'm sure you already know they have no leads."

"Yeah, he's probably underground, but eventually he'll surface, and I will put him away this time for good even if it costs me my job."

"You don't like this guy, do you?"

"Hell no. He kidnaps my best friend and keeps her captive in an abandoned cottage to die unless I can find his wife, who is in a witness protection program. That made it personal, so, yes, if I get the chance, I will not hesitate to kill him if it comes to that."

"Seriously, and risk your career, come on, I doubt it." Carla flipped her the bird, and a quirky grinned, painted Beth's face. "Okay, I believe you, now, when should we hear about the court order?"

"I would suspect any day now."

Returning to their respective desk, Beth opened her laptop and typed in Alicia Williams in Bowling Green, Kentucky. According to her mom's letter, she thought that's where they moved to, which was over twenty-seven years ago. She didn't think she stood a chance in finding any information at all. It took many search pages to read through, but finally a story popped up about two women named Alicia Williams, about the same age. Alicia Williams number one was the valedictorian at the local high school and received an academic scholarship to attend Western Kentucky University. The second listing was about another Alicia Williams that attended the university in Oakmont on a basketball scholarship. Taking a deep breath, she made a note of both and reviewed other search pages.

She knew she had to pick one and start there. The intriguing one was the second one. Alicia Williams attended college on an athletic scholarship in basketball, as she did, and that was the best place as any to start. Alicia Williams, the real smart one, would have to wait for another day. Not that she couldn't be her biological mother, but she knew athletic ability, in most cases, could be inherited, and that was where she would start. Typing in a new search for Alicia Williams and the university in Oakmont, it took a while for the search pages to load. Feeling frustrated, she said to herself, "Come on, please, come on."

Carla studied Beth, who was glued to her laptop screen, breaking her focus, she asked, "What did you say?"

"Oh, you know the damn internet can be so slow when you want information quickly. Ah, here we go."

At that moment, Chief Evans approached their desk. He said, "The two of you in my office now."

Carla immediately got up. Beth closed her laptop and let out a big sigh. With disgust painting her face, Beth followed Carla to his office. Once inside, he informed them the court order for Jackson Walker's financial records came through; however, the one for his mom was denied. After reviewing and analyzing Jackson Walker's information, if it turned out to be what they suspected, then they could file for a court order on his mother at that time. Beth, feeling anxiety and disappointment simultaneously, knew that solving Penny Miracle's case was priority one, and getting the court order brightened her spirits. Alicia Williams number two would have to wait for now. She knew she had the rest of her life to discover the secrets of her past.

CHAPTER 21

Jackson Walker's financial records were vast but not complicated. Bank statements from Chase which included checking, savings, and retirement. His financial footprint was under one entity, making their job easier. Since he didn't own a home, no mortgage existed, and auto loans were paid in full. Credit card debt was minimal, with only one account. From all indications, his financial record was spotless with a credit score in the excellent range.

His checking account maintained an average balance of one-thousand dollars for most of his financial life. His rent, utilities, and phone comprised most of the line items in the monthly statements. On average, that totaled around fifteen hundred dollars per month. There were several transactions for groceries and auto fuel on the credit card statements. He appeared to eat out a lot, but he wasn't extravagant or outlandish by any means. Based on his credit card charges, O'Charlie's and Applebee's were favorite hangouts of his. Monthly credit card purchases totaled about two-hundred dollars, and he always paid it off in full each month.

Jackson's savings account was modest, with about ten-thousand dollars in total. His deposits were erratic; however, ironically, there were several large deposits about five years apart. A red flag, they thought. Venturing on to his retirement account, a Roth IRA, it had a current value of fifty-thousand dollars; maybe not unusual for someone employed for over fifteen years. Monthly contributions of two hundred dollars each were automatically transferred to his IRA, with the rest deposited each summer. Again, they noticed more substantial amounts every five years or so. The market had seen its share of difficulties, and amassing this amount of money wasn't out of the realm of possibility. Furthermore, they were more interested in the fine details and whether everything added up or raised even more red flags.

His tax returns revealed gross income beginning at twenty-thousand starting in 1993 and increasing to around thirty-thousand for the 2011 taxable year. His tax returns were simple, always using the standard deductions in determining taxable income. Having all his financial information, they would have their forensic financial expert build a balance sheet similar to a profit-and-loss statement. They thought by analyzing the data, red flags would glare back at them. Forensics indicated they should have the spreadsheet ready first thing in the morning. In a waiting game, Alicia Williams, number two, that attended the local university, was on Beth's mind, while John Dickerson's escape demanded Carla's attention.

Beth reopened her laptop, and within a few seconds her last search page loaded. She read in detail the story of each Alicia Williams. Photos accompanied each story, but the fact that they were at least fifteen years old, either of them could be a possibility that one of them was her biological mother or maybe not. As she read each story, she wondered if she was doing the right thing or opening Pandora's Box. Googling Alicia Williams and the university brought up pages from her years of playing basketball. She was a star at the university, making all-conference honors beginning her sophomore year. From the team picture during her playing years, she appeared to be about the same height as Beth. Pulling up her bio information, she was five feet, ten inches tall with a slender build. She studied Alicia's face close-up; she thought it was a distinct possibility that Alicia Williams number two could be her biological mother. Still, she dispelled it because finding her wouldn't have been this easy. Continuing to more search pages, the information got sparser and sparser. She graduated in four years and took a job in education and coaching. A year later, she was married to her college sweetheart.

The most recent information had her teaching high school in Knoxville, Tennessee. Her most recent bio information stated she had twin teenage boys, a red flag in her mind. If it was her biological mother, was it possible to have twins later in life? Googling this question resulted in a high possibility of this occurring. A recent picture of Alicia resembled Beth, but not striking enough for her to have a definitive opinion. Closing her laptop, she glanced at the big clock on the wall, then turned her gaze to Carla, who had her nose glued to her computer. Beth said, "What did you find out on John Dickerson from Agent Slack?"

"He wasn't available, so I spoke with your ex. Nice guy, anyway, it's pretty much what you told me. They have nothing and no reported sightings or tips. His picture is up in post offices and federal buildings in the region, but like me, it's a waiting game until he makes a move. What about you?"

"Well, Alicia Williams number two is a possibility. Same physical characteristics and she did earn a basketball scholarship to the university, the same as me. She was a star there, like me. She's married with twin teenage boys, teaches high school, and coaches girls' basketball. As I said, characteristics fit. However, I'm not getting my hopes up because finding her this early would be way too easy. Besides, my biological mother may not be any of these women, or she could even be dead."

"That's not being positive, you know. Wow, look at the time. What do you say we get a drink at McGruder's and continue our conversation there?"

Ten minutes later, McGruder's was unusually busy when they arrived. Tables were at a premium; a table in the back of the pub on the left-hand side would have to do. After taking a seat, Sam approached them, "Hi, ladies, what can I get you?"

Beth chimed in and replied, "Jameson on the rocks for both us."

Sam responded with the thumbs-up gesture and said, "I see Carla's already corrupted you."

"Umm, let's just say it's been a trying day."

Jameson waited to taste their lips, and a ceremonial toast pleased Carla's liquid lover. The table in the back allowed Carla to see everyone coming and going. Although crowded, especially the bar, an individual caught her eye. As long as John Dickerson was on the loose, looking over her shoulder, she expected the unexpected. She gave up on the thought that he would be so stupid to show up here; she dispelled that idea. Beth noticed that Carla was staring at the bar area, "What are you looking at?"

"Ah, nothing. Tell me more about Alicia Williams number two?"

"Nothing else to tell you, depending on what we get into tomorrow, I'll check out Alicia Williams number one next."

"I thought you would be gung-ho about this and spend all your time searching."

"My job is more important, and I'm not getting my hopes up because I may never find my biological mother, so I've got plenty of time to search."

Nodding, a man in a baseball cap at the bar fascinated Carla. Sam had spent a lot of time talking with this guy; maybe she knew his name. Jameson was gone. Carla held her glass toward Sam, motioned for two more. Arriving with Jameson, Carla asked, "Sam, that dude in the baseball cap, who is he?"

"Oh, said his name is Corey Hawthorne. Said he was here on business and heard about McGruder's. He thought he would give us a try. It's the second time he's been in here. Is there a problem?"

"Umm, just wondering. He looked familiar to me, thanks."

Sam gave Carla the thumbs-up gesture and left. Paranoia was getting the best of Carla. Unexpectedly, she got up. Beth said, "Where are you going?"

"Nowhere. I'll be right back." Carla noticed a vacant seat beside the individual and approached him and asked, "Hi John, is this stool taken?"

The man gave her a strange look. However, noticing how hot she looked, he thought that maybe this was his lucky night and replied, "Excuse me, not sure who John is, but may I buy you a drink, honey?"

Looking the man square in the eyes, she replied, "Oh, I'm sorry, I thought you were someone else. Forgive me for intruding. Have a nice evening."

Feeling used and disappointed, Corey scowled as she walked away. Returning to her booth, another man at the front of the bar did a double-take and quickly left the building through the front door.

When Carla returned to the booth, Beth asked, "What the hell was that all about?"

"Nothing. I thought I knew him, but when I got a closer look, I realized I didn't. I apologized and left before I made a fool of myself. Sorry I left you stranded."

"Hey, no problem. Did you notice the man that just left through the front door? He stared at you long and hard, then quickly left." Without hesitation, Carla got up and dashed outside, looking in every direction. Whoever he was, he had disappeared. She returned out of breath and sat back down. Beth asked, "What was that all about, what's going on with you?"

"John Dickerson. What did that guy look like?"

"Baseball cap on, dark wraparound shades, dark complexion, at least six-foot, very slender. Now, don't you think you are a little paranoid?"

Carla never liked being questioned about what she was feeling, and she certainly didn't want to be accused of paranoia. "Listen, newbie. John Dickerson is a psychopath who will stop at nothing to find his wife and son. He ended up killing all of his brothers from the Alpha Tango Special Forces unit, so if I want to be para- noid about him to save your ass, I will. He is out there, and he will eventually come after us or our loved ones. Don't ever forget it."

Beth, feeling like a child that had just been spanked by their mother, didn't say another word. She downed the remainder of the Jameson. Sam made a pass by to check on them again, and Carla asked, "Sam, are the security cameras still rolling?"

"Of course. What do you need?"

"The last fifteen minutes, showing Corey at the bar and the man with the dark complexion that just left through the front door."

"Is there a problem?"

"Umm, maybe. Please make me a copy and bring our check, okay?"

Within a few minutes, Sam returned with a copy of the video segment and the check. As they got up to leave, the man at the bar that called himself Corey Hawthorne followed their every move. Carla locked eyes with him and made a mental image of him in her mind.

CHAPTER 22

A simple spreadsheet detailed Jackson Walker's financial footprint. Of course, all Carla was interested in was there enough to move forward and contact Craig Bjornson of the Lexington Police Department. She also hoped the final analysis was enough to get a court order for his mother's financial affairs. Head of the forensic department, Sherry Caudill, planned to meet with Carla, Beth, and Chief Evans to explain her results and expert opinion on what action they should take. The mood inside the interrogation room was like waiting for Santa to arrive. Sherry was never in a hurry, which always pissed off Carla. She always believed Sherry did it on purpose to irritate her because Carla always wanted it done yesterday. Patience was not a strong suit of Carla's; Sherry knew that and exploited it.

Finally, the door opened to the interrogation room, and Sherry entered carrying several file folders. She took a seat at the head of the table, sending a message to Carla that she was now in charge. Promptly, she passed out file folders to each of them. "Okay, folks, what you have in the folder is a detailed spreadsheet of Jackson Walker's financial history. As you can see in the first column, his earned income is solely from his teaching positions. The second column is money that he deposited in his bank or IRA account. Next, we have all his expenses from multiple sources, you know, rent, auto loans, groceries, you get the picture. We've highlighted anomalies to his normal activity, and..."

A clearing of the throat disrupted Sherry's train of thought, giving Carla the opening she needed. Sherry threw Carla her best bitchy look; it wasn't the first time Carla had seen that from her, but she didn't care. Carla said, "Sherry, I know you get your rocks off explaining all this information in detail and all that shit, but just give us your expert opinion. You are an expert, aren't you?" Another bitchy look hit Carla square in the face but didn't faze her. "Just tell us, are we barking up the wrong tree, or do we have a concrete reason to meet with the Lexington Police Department about bringing in this dude?"

Fuming and ready to explode, Sherry glared at Chief Evans, who wasn't paying much attention to the exchange between them. "Carla, you're a bitch, you know. I don't tell you how to conduct investigations, so don't rush me when I'm just doing my job, okay?" Ready to lash out at Miss CSI as Carla sometimes called her, Chief Evans intervened, shutting Carla down.

While a disgusting glance met Sherry's quirky smile, she ignored Carla's arrows of hate zipping by her. Continuing with her detailed analysis, Carla somehow kept her mouth shut, and finally, Sherry finished sitting like a queen on her throne. Looking around the table, she waited for questions. Chief Evans looked at Beth and

Carla for direction. Impatience was eating at Sherry. After a long sigh, she responded with sarcasm. "Well, folks, cat got your tongue?"

Beth glanced at Carla, who was close to exploding; they had a love-hate relationship, always wanting to show each other up. Beth responded, "Now that you have explained everything so precisely, in your expert opinion, do we have reason to discuss our findings with Craig Bjornson and hopefully convince them to question Jackson?"

"His income doesn't support his total financial footprint. The large irregular deposits are very suspect and red flags. It's possible, a lucrative summer job would explain it. However, I feel it would be prudent to interview him, but I would tread lightly. Just because red flags exist with his financial footprint doesn't mean he committed any crimes. Are there any other questions?"

Beth looked at Carla, who just shook her head back-and-forth, then at Chief Evans, who did the same. "Well, I guess not, Sherry. Thank you so much for putting all of this together. You've been a big help."

Sherry nodded and smiled as she left the room, declaring victory. As soon as she left, Carla said, "Hey, newbie, you know you don't have to be so nice to her. She is a bitch sometimes."

"I say kill her with kindness, and you'll get what you want. Try it sometimes."

Carla laughed and rolled her eyes at such a lamebrain comment. After a short discussion, a meeting with Craig Bjornson of the Lexington Police Department, the lead detective on the disappearance of Abbie Gardner, would move forward. A call to him resulted in a meeting that afternoon at 2:00 PM in Lexington. At first, Detective Bjornson was a little skeptical about Jackson Walker as a person of interest in their case, but after inflicting her Irish charm on him, Carla convinced him to at least hear them out.

Arriving at the police station about fifteen minutes early, the receptionist escorted Beth and Carla to a cozy little conference room and informed them Detective Bjornson would join them shortly. A well-appointed table surrounded by six leather winged-back chairs was impressive. A Keurig with a full complement of coffee offerings set next to a small dorm-sized refrigerator. The sign on it read, *bottled water, please help yourself*. Carla often thought about inquiring when the Lexington Police Department had openings; however, she liked the close-knit community of Oakmont and its people.

1:55 PM, A well-dressed gentleman entered and introduced himself as Detective Craig Bjornson. Medium height, red hair with a sandy-like tint throughout it, would be a good catch for any woman, but not them. Hair cut short, not quite a buzz cut, more like a short flattop of the sixties, gave him a militaristic persona. He took a seat across from them. After a few moments of chit-chat, the door remained wide open.

Carla asked, "Craig, will someone else be joining us?"

"Oh, I'm sorry. Yes, Nicole Hernandez will be joining us. Her position is similar to Beth's. We have different terminology for her title."

Another minute passed, then an attractive young woman entered and took a seat beside Craig and introduced herself. Ironically, she was about the same height as Beth. Hair was darker and shorter, but otherwise, she had many of the same physical characteristics and facial features as Beth. At first glance, one could think they could be related. After another moment of casual talk, Craig said, "Shall we get started?"

With confirmation around the table, Carla began, "Thank you for meeting with us. We've re-opened a cold case that has been dormant for fifteen years. Beth, recently hired, provided a fresh set of eyes, and after reviewing the file, noticed that a Jackson Walker, who was a person of interest back then, was not pursued as aggressively as he should have been. Our case involved the disappearance of a twelve-year-old girl, Penny Miracle; to this day, her body has never surfaced. Does that sound familiar?"

Craig and Nicole acknowledged her, and she continued, "Well, Beth started tracing his movements after leaving Oakmont, which by the way, was a year or so after Penny disappeared. Her research indicated that he showed up again in Dayton, Ohio. After being there for about four or five years, another twelve-year-old girl goes missing. Her name was Melody Morris, and like our case, her body never surfaced. He left Dayton and ends up here in Lexington, and now you have a twelve-year-old girl missing. We've been following the case, and her body has not been found as well. Follow me so far?"

Both Craig and Nicole had been glued to Carla's explanation and frequently nodded, showing their interest. Carla continued, "We then got a court order to investigate his financial footprint, and without going into a full-blown analysis, we discovered that many red flags might suggest some illegal activity. Also, I visited his hometown and discovered his mother's house was renovated to accommodate her disabilities. She told me her son brings large sums of cash home every two or three weeks. His mother also has a permanent caregiver. All of this adds up to maybe something illegal, past or present."

Craig asked, "So, based on all of that, you think that he may be involved in all three disappearances?"

Beth had remained silent since Carla is heading the investigation but felt this was her opportunity to get her feet wet. "I've been building a profile on him, and I believe that Penny may have been his first victim. His mother, disabled, had to sell her stake in a business in Fort Gay, West Virginia. Her house had been renovated over the years to accommodate her disabilities, and then eventually she required a housekeeper or caregiver. The good son that he is, he gets involved in something illegal to help his mother because a teacher's salary in a Catholic school would not be enough."

Craig replied, "Okay, I can see where you are going with this, but what kind of illegal activity are you thinking?"

Beth continued, "Keep an open mind, but sex trafficking is a real possibility. All the cities where these abductions occurred have Interstate 75 in common, easy abduction, easy disappearance. He has had various summer jobs, especially a girls' softball coach and a lifeguard. In his younger days, he was a real charmer with young girls. It would be easy for him to gain a girl's trust and when the time was right, abduct them, and then arrange the delivery to sex-traffickers. That's why their bodies have never been found. Tell us about the victim in your case. I believe her name is Abbie Gardner, right?"

"Nicole, why don't you bring them up to speed on our case?"

"Of course. Her name is Abbie Gardner, and she was a beautiful child. Even though the media reports stated she was twelve-years-old, she was just a few weeks shy of her thirteenth birthday. According to a recent picture her parents gave us, she was quite mature for her age. Here's the picture." After viewing the photo, Beth and Carla acknowledged her. "As you can see, she was quite mature and pretty. Her parents reported her missing after softball practice. The field is only a few blocks from her house, and she walked home after practice most of the time; however, that evening, she didn't come home. After canvassing the area, nothing turned up. She had never been in any trouble, never ran away or anything like that before. We used the standard protocol, including an Amber Alert, and thus far, nothing has surfaced. Interviews with friends turned up nothing useful as well. We interviewed her softball coach, a woman, soon after she went missing, and we got nothing. It appears she just vanished without a trace."

Beth added, "That's very similar to our case and the one in Dayton, Ohio. Little evidence and leads that went nowhere. I don't believe it's a mere coincidence that these disappearances are very similar. Jackson Walker could be involved, and who knows, there could be other victims we don't know about in other cities. Maybe we need to dig deeper and analyze his financial footprint again. Maybe we're missing something. I admit we were looking at the big picture, but maybe it's the fine print we should be dissecting. Is there anything else you can tell us?"

"That's it. Craig, do you have anything else to add?"

"You've covered everything, Nicole. Where do we go from here, detectives? Your scenario is very intriguing."

Carla responded, "If you want our help, and I hope you do, then let's get back together tomorrow afternoon after we dissect the fine details of his financial footprint. There is no need for you to request the same information. Why don't you come to our turf, and we can go from there?"

Craig said, "Sounds good. What time would you like us there?"

Carla replied, "Let's make it around four o'clock in the afternoon; that should give us enough time to review the information again and research our findings. Oh, and one thing you should probably know. In our case involving the disappearance of Penny Miracle, Beth was Penny's best friend growing up and was one of the last people to be with her before vanishing."

Mouths flew wide open, as Nicole and Craig's eyes met each other. A 'wow' expression painted their faces. Craig replied, "Interesting, we'll see you at four o'clock tomorrow afternoon."

Exchanging pleasantries with each other, the four of them left the plush conference room with many questions and no answers. Non-work chit-chat accompanied them to the common area. Carla and Beth exited and walked toward Carla's car, while Nicole and Craig watched them from just outside the main doors. Before Beth opened the passenger door, she turned around, meeting Nicole's glancing stare; strange energy was flowing between them. Interrupting their fixation on each other, he said, "What do you make of all this?"

Nicole remained silent, oblivious to Craig's question. Tapping her on the shoulder, he repeated the question breaking her stare. "I don't know, we'll see. You know, Beth looked familiar, like I should know her somehow or I met her somewhere. It's a weird feeling that I can't explain. I think it's time I get to work researching

Jackson Walker on our own and be ready for the meeting tomorrow."

"Sounds good. If you need me, let me know, okay?"

Nicole nodded, returning to her desk, and opened up her laptop immediately. Staring at the screen for a moment, Nicole pondered where to start. As she placed her fingers on the keyboard, her subconscious made her enter Beth Pendergast; Jackson Walker was not currently a priority. After hitting the enter key, Beth Pendergast's life loaded. Fixated on the information, Nicole was oblivious to Craig standing beside her. Feeling a presence, she quickly closed the search page, and keyed in Jackson Walker, the page loaded, and Craig left.

As Carla took the ramp for Interstate 75 South to Oakmont, Beth seemed distant. "What's going on with you?" Carla asked. "Talk to me?"

"Nicole, I have a weird feeling, strange vibes about her, can't explain it."

"How so?"

"As I said, I can't explain it. It's like I'm drawn to her. Let's talk about Jackson Walker, okay?"

Carla nodded and focused on the heavy traffic of leaving the big city. Once they arrived at the police station, the interrogation room would be command central for digging into the fine print of Sherry's presentation earlier that day. She hoped that Sherry was still there to assist them. After the forty-minute drive, they pulled into the police station parking lot. Carla smiled as she pulled in beside the space that occupied Sherry's six-year-old Nissan Altima. Before getting out of the car, she turned to Beth. "Okay, work your charm with Miss CSI."

"Trust me, no problem, just kill her with kindness, we'll get her cooperation, watch and learn."

Carla rolled her eyes at Beth, shooting her an indiscreet bird. Inside, Beth headed for forensics, while Carla opened up command central. Within a few minutes, Beth, followed by Sherry, entered the interrogation room and closed the door behind them. It would be a long evening for the three of them. Tomorrow at 4:00 PM would be a defining moment in their cold case.

CHAPTER 23

The giant wall clock imposed its will at Beth. 3:00 PM glared back at her. Sixty-minutes stood between being considered a genius or a fool. The past twenty-four hours had been excruciating for Beth and Carla; their integrity and credibility were at risk. Command central was home to them throughout the previous evening as Sherry went into great detail about the fine print in Jackson Walker's financial footprint. Carla had to admit that Beth was right, kill Sherry with kindness, make her feel important, and she will help anyone.

One half-hour to go before they either looked like geniuses or fools. Jackson Walker was just a hunch, maybe his past was legitimate, or perhaps something sick and sinister was part of his financial footprint. As the hour of reckoning approached, Beth's pre-game butter-flies fluttered randomly, while Carla impatiently doodled on her legal pad. Although prepared and confident as best they could be, Sherry was their safety net.

Father time ticked slowly for Carla. Her doodling

increased. Although she had no artistic ability, she doodled a likeness of John Dickerson. A glance at the big clock indicated Craig and Nicole should arrive soon. Beth's desk had a direct line of sight to the entrance of the police station. As 4:00 PM glared at her, a reflection of two individuals on the doors caught her attention. Craig opened the door for Nicole, and they approached the receptionist, asking for them. Beth rose from her desk and approached them. After exchanging pleasantries, she led them back to the conference room where Carla and Sherry were waiting. Carla introduced them to Sherry, who would explain her analysis. Not enthused about hearing her detailed report for the third time in two days, Carla would endure it all the same to make her feel important and gain brownie points with her for future use.

Over the next hour, Sherry felt important as Craig and Nicole seemed very interested in her research and presentation. After finishing, she inquired if there were any questions. Beth and Carla heard this for the third time and shook their heads back-and-forth in unison.

Craig glanced at Nicole meeting her negative wave of the hand. "Okay then, Sherry, thank you for taking the time to explain in detail your findings. Now that we have seen it, we concur that Jackson Walker is a person of interest in our case, right, Nicole?"

After nods of affirmation, smiles of excitement flowed around the table. While Sherry excused herself, Carla took control of the meeting. She followed-up Sherry's presentation with a few opening comments of her own. After a brief exchange of assumptions, Beth expanded on a specific detail in Jackson Walker's financial footprint from the summer of 1999, where he worked as a lifeguard in Richmond, Indiana. On a gut feeling, Beth searched any abductions that summer in the Richmond area. One person stood out, Natalie Arthur, a twelve-year-old girl. She went missing after softball practice, and to this day, her body has never surfaced. She explained that Natalie's parents emailed them a picture of their daughter. Based on the photo passed around the table, it was easy to see that Natalie was quite mature for a twelve-year-old. She was very striking with long blond hair and blue eyes. She was definitely twelve-going-on-twenty, and desirable.

After a short break and a few questions by Nicole, Beth continued her findings. She spoke with Detective Paul Patterson of the Richmond, Indiana police department. He initially investigated the abduction as a patrol officer, but when he made detective, he took a personal interest in the case. Little evidence and no witnesses fit the profile of that case. She explained that the disappearance of Natalie still haunted him to this day.

Beth finished her comments and solicited questions. Since there were none, she continued, "It is my opinion that Jackson Walker is our man, and Penny Miracle was his first victim. I remember Penny was quite mature, and even the older boys in the neighborhood couldn't keep their eyes off her. Natalie was his second victim, and Melanie Morris was his third. Abbie Gardner was his fourth, as far as we know, and if we don't act soon, there will be others. Their bodies have never surfaced. Abduction for the lucrative business of sex and human trafficking is the only possible reason for that."

Nicole responded, "That's a pretty bold statement, but in some ways I guess given the whacky world we live in, it's not that farfetched either. Sorry for the interruption. What else do you have?"

"Keep an open mind as I continue. Jackson Walker's mother becomes disabled from an accident. He can't bear it and wants to help. Somehow, he gets introduced and involved with a sex trafficking ring and succeeds with the first abduction, Penny Miracle. He moved on and felt confident enough to strike again. He took summer jobs and abducted Natalie. Three years later, he strikes again with Melanie and eventually leaves Dayton and turns up in Lexington, where Abbie disappears. All the missing girls are very similar, as you've seen. All of these cities have an interstate highway passing through them, making an easy delivery possible. This guy flies under the radar because he has no past association with the victims other than through a summer job, which goes unnoticed."

While intenseness moved around the table, each person took notes as Beth continued, "According to the lady Carla spoke to in his hometown, he's a charmer where females of all ages are attracted to him. Jackson picks his victims based on physical appearance, maturity, and gullibility. He gains enough trust to easily pull off these abductions. He delivers the girls, gets paid in cash. Even though his mom still needs money, he gets hooked on how easy it was to make money and allowed him to take a year off from teaching. I know this is far out there, but these girls may still be alive, and that's the real reason their bodies have never surfaced. That's it. Are there any further comments or questions?"

Nicole responded, "I can see how the dots are connecting with me. Craig, do you have any comments, you've been silent throughout all of this?"

"Okay, let's say you are right, Beth. How do we proceed and not spook this guy?"

Carla, who also had been very quiet up to now, jumped in, "I don't know, the information we have indicates he works at a local country club, maybe Abbie's parents are members and their daughter went to that pool. Let's check that out. Also, is it possible there is a connection between Jackson and the softball coach? Craig, is it possible to contact Abbie's parents now and find out?"

"Yeah, I have their numbers. Why don't you all take a break while I try to reach them? Give me about ten minutes, okay?"

Beth, Carla, and Nicole acknowledged him and left the conference room. A pleasant afternoon, they walked outside for some fresh air. Ten minutes later, Craig summoned them back to the conference room, explaining what he found out from Abbie's mother. Jackson is an employee at the country club where they are members. Abbie's softball coach, Sally Fredrickson, and Jackson are a couple, and he helps her when he's not working. Smiles and excitement replace somberness and tension around the table.

"So, ladies, there you have it. We may have just gotten a break. We need to bring him in and ask him a few questions, hopefully not to spook him enough that he would lawyer-up."

Smiling and beaming with confidence, Beth interrupted Craig, "Yes, yes, I knew it. I just felt he might be our guy."

Carla replied, "Beth, don't count your chickens before they hatch. We have reasonable cause to speak with him, doesn't mean he is our guy."

"Yeah, I know, but I still feel good where we are.

Anyone interested in a drink, and to celebrate? We've been at it a long time."

Craig said, "I'm going to head back and think about how we question him without spooking him. Thank you for all your help. I'll be in touch with you on how we will proceed."

Carla added, "Sorry, Beth, I've got plans already."

"That leaves you, Nicole, what do you say?"

"I'd love to, but my ride home is leaving."

"Hey, no problem. I'll take you home later. Just one drink, okay?"

"Umm, why not celebrate a breakthrough in these cases...yeah, I'm in."

An empty booth nestled in the front corner of McGruder's was the perfect place to celebrate. Pinot Grigio was the drink of the day. An eerie presence surrounded the booth as they explained the history of their lives. In many ways, their paths were very similar. Even their birthdays were one day apart. Nicole, raised in a small town near Altmont, attended the University of Kentucky on a volleyball scholarship, and graduated with a degree in psychology. She was single after a recent breakup from her college sweetheart as well.

Beth kept her promise of one drink. As they were leaving, a man she recognized from the other night entered and took a seat at the bar. Corey Hawthorne was back. Taking Nicole home proved longer than she had imagined, and after an eighty-minute round trip, Beth pulled into her parking spot at her apartment. After opening the door, a loud meow greeted her. Picking Aliyah up, she hugged her until she squirmed to get down. Following her into the kitchen, Aliyah went straight to her feeding bowl, which was empty. Filling it to the brim, Aliyah purred while eating. Laughing, she wondered how cats could do that.

Opening the refrigerator, an unfinished bottle of Pinot Grigio stood tall. Taking it out, she poured herself a generous portion. After a sip or two, she retreated to her bedroom with her wine. A gray metal box sat atop the dresser, imposing its will. After a few more sips, her moment of truth laid inside the metal box. Initially, she wanted Carla with her when she opened it. However, feeling happy about the progress of her first case, she could handle whatever was inside the gray metal box.

CHAPTER 24

The grayish-green metal box loomed large on her massive dresser. Its presence sent chills up and down her spine. Answers to her questions were just inside the keyhole, waiting to expose the secrets kept from her. Her glass was empty. Knowing she couldn't open it without more to drink, she went to the kitchen and grabbed the Pinot Grigio from the refrigerator and headed back to her bedroom. Another generous pour filled her glass, and she put it to her lips, tasting its fruitiness and nuances. After a few more sips and a deep relaxing breath, she put her glass down on her nightstand.

Walking over to her dresser, she took the metal box in her hands and returned to her bed. Opening the nightstand drawer, she grabbed the key, inserting it into the keyhole. She paused for a moment before turning the key to the right, unlocking it. Slowly raising the lid, she stared at the items inside. Immediately grabbing her attention, a white envelope grabbed her soul as her pulse raced. She turned it over; scotch tape secured its content. Sliding her finger under the flap, she opened it pulling out the tri-folded document. Unfolding it, she knew what it was. She had seen it before, her birth certificate. It looked official with the state seal. Zoe Elizabeth Pendergast, July 18, 1985, was born at 11:58 PM at Queen Ann's Medical Center in Altmont, Kentucky. Seven pounds-two ounces, twenty inches long. There it was in black and white. Placing it back in the envelope, she laid it on the bed.

A large manila envelope titled "Adoption Documents" took her breath away. She briefly flipped through it, noticing lots of signatures and seals. Every document looked official, and she breathed a sigh of relief. Ever since finding out her adoption was private, thoughts crept in and out of her mind whether her adoption was legal. After reviewing it much closer, it all appeared legal, and her doubting feelings subsided.

There was one final item in the bottom of the metal box, another white envelope with her name on it looked very familiar. The handwriting was unmistakable. After taking the envelope out of the gray box, its contents appeared to be another letter. Placing it on the bed, she picked up her wine glass and took a very long sip. She studied the envelope more intently, trying to think of what was inside. The first letter was enough to digest, why a second letter she thought, and what could it reveal that wasn't in the first one?

A few more sips finished the wine in her glass. She would need more to get through what was inside the envelope; pouring the wine into her glass, she was ready to discover more secrets of her past. She slipped the letter out and unfolded it. Her mother's beautiful cursive handwriting brought a few tears rolling down her cheeks. Brushing them away, she stared at the letter and turned it over briefly. Just two pages this time, neatly spaced between the notebook paper lines; not a vowel nor a consonant violated the line below it or above it.

Her mom's eloquence was everywhere in the grey metal box; she was a beautiful person inside and out. Her care and patience in writing this letter said a lot about her mom. Tears dried up, another sip of wine, she read the letter dated June 14, 2012.

My beloved Zoe,

It's been just a few days since I wrote the first letter. Because you are reading this, I'm no longer alive. I hope your grief had subsided enough to comprehend the things you have found out, foremost, your adoption, and what you will learn when you finish this letter. It is not as shocking as finding out about your adoption, who your birth mother was, and that you have a sister somewhere in the universe, but you also have a family. Grandparents, for sure.

Beth wiped more tears away and took a deep breath, then a long sip of wine. Looking at the date, she realized her mother wrote this letter the night before she ascended into Heaven. Beth wondered whether her mom felt something, an omen of impending death. Through her education, a premonition of death was possible even if suicide was not in the picture. Life was strange and unpredictable. After another lingering sip of wine, she read on.

Let's start with your twin sister wherever she may be. That brings me to Penny. We've talked about it before, most recently during your last visit. Growing up, the more you and she got to know each other, and the rela-

tionship grew between you two, the more I thought Penny could be your sister. You and Penny were like sisters; it was surprising how alike you and she were. You could almost finish each other's sentences. Sandy and I talked about it a lot. Sandy treated you just like you were her daughter, she was your second mom, but that didn't bother me because she loved you as much as I did.

I asked Sandy if they adopted Penny, she adamantly denied it, but I didn't believe her. I even asked her if she would commit to DNA analysis to determine if you and Penny were indeed sisters. Again, she said that it didn't matter because Penny was her flesh and blood. Even though I'm dead, I still don't believe Sandy. No, I feel that Penny is your sister, and you should not stop investigating until you have an answer, but that is up to you because if I'm wrong, it will hurt you. Now that her case has been re-opened makes that decision even more difficult because the results could be devastating. Be careful, and by the way, you and Penny have the same birthdate.

Refreshing her wine glass, she took a long sip and contemplated her mother's last thoughts. She couldn't dispel that possibility. After all, Penny's voice had visited her many times and knew about her promise. The other thing she wondered about was whether Penny could be alive somewhere. The possibility of that, albeit a small one, must be pursued until evidence proved it differently. Another long sip, she turned the page over and continued reading her mother's final written words.

I hope you will search for your birth mother, Alicia. I think she would be proud of you. I tried to find her, see what she made of herself, and of course, for medical reasons. I didn't get far, as you know, I wasn't that good with the Internet. I know you are much better, so; I urge you to find her, then decide whether you want to pursue a relationship with her. It could be risky.

Now, for me, you know I was adopted, a closed adoption. My real mom, your grandmother, didn't keep me in the dark about my adoption. Through the years, I searched and talked to people where I grew up. I even tried the adoption agency, but with no success. After my mom died, I contacted the agency again; they wouldn't divulge it. Then one day out of the blue, I received an anonymous letter indicating my birth mother was known as Lilly. Maybe you should try to find her, my birth mother, and tell her I don't hate her; I love her. My adoption documents are in the final envelope with a picture of me as a baby and the DNA analysis I had performed recently.

A lump rose in her throat, but she swallowed, pushing it down. Tears glistened in her eyes and began to zig zag down her cheek. Wiping them away, she looked at the wine bottle. One more glass, she thought and poured it in. It might be enough to get her through the night. She looked at her mom's letter; one more paragraph of emotions to go. Pain, sorrow, hate, love, and joy were all erupting in her soul. Whether or not she was ready for the final paragraph, she continued reading as all the emotions inside her exploded.

One day we will be joined in Heaven, and you can tell
me everything you found out. I see a bright future for
you, a loving husband and children. Love and cherish
every day as if it was your last on earth. Chase your
dreams, never give up on anything. Life's too short.
   I love you so much...Mom

The last paragraph sent aftershocks through her body.
A river of tears gushed from her eyes and dropped on her
lap. She put the wine glass to her lips and sipped its final
breath of life. She looked at the empty bottle and
continued to sob, and Aliyah jumped up on the bed and
purred as though she was feeling the same pain and
sorrow. The envelope containing her mother's adoption
records glared at her. She picked it up and caressed it but
placed it back in the cold grayish-green metal box and
closed the lid. Aliyah meowed and nestled even closer on
her lap. As Beth's head fell softly on her pillow, she
closed her eyes and prayed. Within minutes, quiet darkness soothed the emotions burning inside her soul. Aliyah
snuggled next to her chest, purring a soft-like lullaby
easing her pain and grief.

CHAPTER 25

Carla arrived bright and early at the police station the next morning. Yesterday was a breakthrough moment in the Penny Miracle case. They had enough to proceed with Jackson Walker as a person of interest, at the very least, in the abduction of Abbie Gardner. Checking her mailbox, she was elated that it was empty. With her last two cases, her mailbox had been the bearer of bad news frequently. Carla had developed a slight paranoia toward the mailbox. Anytime there was mail in it, she expected something terrible, but today she smiled as she headed for her desk.

After setting her items down, her purse, and coffee from Starbuck's, she immediately noticed her voicemail light was blinking. She hit the button and listened to Beth's message that said she would be in a little late, and she would explain later. She was hoping to have a voicemail from Detective Bjornson; unfortunately, the only one was from Beth. She hung up the phone receiver and fired up her laptop. She inserted the thumb drive that Sam gave her the other night. After selecting the video file, the fifteen-minute segment played. She observed the man with the baseball cap sitting at the bar. According to Sam, Corey Hawthorne was his name, or that's what he told her. He looked like an average guy having a beer. She remembered that Sam said the man was in town on business and had been in the night before. Another man sitting beside him got up and went out of view of the camera. She didn't recognize that man either.

Next, she saw Beth and herself enter through the front door and go to their booth, leaving the view of the security camera. Several minutes passed, and she saw herself come into the picture going to where Corey Hawthorne was seated. After a brief exchange, she saw herself leave and return to her booth. The man that had been sitting beside Corey appeared in front of the main doors and stopped. He was staring at the booth where Beth and Carla were seated. After a moment, it showed him quickly leaving. A minute later, it showed Carla running out the front door. Reviewing it several times, focusing on Corey, she did the same thing with the mystery man with dark glasses, dark complexion, and a baseball cap, and she noticed it appeared he was bald. Beth had given her a great description because she saw the same thing in the video.

Carla was focusing intently when Beth finally entered the station and walked over to Carla's desk. Carla was oblivious to Beth peering over her shoulder.

"What are you looking at?"

"Shit, Beth, don't creep up on me. You scared the hell out of me. I'm viewing the video from McGruder's. I don't recognize either of these men. Maybe just passing through or here on business. Sam said he was there the night before. Is everything okay?"

"Umm, I opened the metal box last night. I'll tell you about it later over a drink, okay?" Carla nodded, and Beth sat at her desk. "Hey, you know the Corey guy, well, he was there last night. As Nicole and I were leaving, he entered and took a seat at the bar. He gave me a strange look, just thought you ought to know."

"Umm, was Sam working?"

"Didn't see her. Have we heard anything from Detective Bjornson?"

"Not yet. How did your bonding go with Nicole?"

"We hit it off and have a lot in common. She played volleyball for the University of Kentucky and lived in the same area where my mom grew up. Weird, huh?"

"Hmm, I guess so."

"Even weirder is that our birthday is one day apart, and we are the same age."

"Don't tell me, you think she is your twin sister?"

Beth laughed and rolled her eyes. She was beginning to respond when Carla's phone rang. Carla looked at the caller ID and said, "Maybe this is Detective Bjornson." She answered and listened. Beth was trying to eavesdrop; however, the call was short, and she heard Carla say we'll be there and hung up the receiver.

"Well, you going to keep me in suspense, what's going on?"

"They asked Sally Fredrickson to come back in and answer a few more questions. Craig told her, if she had anyone help her coach, to bring them in as well. Sally told them the only person that helped her was her boyfriend, Jackson Walker. They set up a meeting for around four o'clock today after Jackson got off work. They want us there by three-thirty. We'll be able to observe the interview on a monitor in another room. We'll see how it goes."

"Great, what else is going on?"

"Nothing, let's go to Parsons for some coffee, and you can tell me about last night and the metal box."

"That's not the drink I was referring to, but coffee's fine, and we might run into Ally again."

Parsons' Coffee Emporium was not busy, but because they wanted absolute privacy, they ordered coffee and took it upstairs to the quiet, and empty loft area. Ally was not there as she had to take care of some family business back in her hometown. The upstairs room, deserted and comfortable, is what they wanted as she told Carla everything. Beth knew it was not healthy to keep things bottled up inside her. Even though she appeared calm, emotions continued to run rampant inside her soul as she finished.

"There you have it, I know it's a lot to take in and think about."

"Do you think Penny is your sister?"

"I don't know. It's a lot to digest."

"Yeah, I get that, but you know how you can find out, DNA analysis. All the evidence, including the DNA analysis from her clothing, is available in the evidence locker at the station."

"I know, but I don't want these issues to cloud my judgment on our current case. Let's get this case solved, and depending on what we find out, I'll decide whether to pursue it or not. The case is a priority."

"What about your mom?"

"The same answer; let's get this case over with first. I've got the rest of my life to find my sister, birth mother, and grandparents. Let's talk about something else, okay? Any more news on John Dickerson?"

"Nothing. I called your ex; everything is quiet, no leads, no tips, Scott said to tell you hi."

"Did he now? What about Corey Hawthorne and the mystery man, any ideas?"

"No, he's someone I'll keep an eye out for, as far as the mystery man, he appears way too young to be John Dickerson. Besides, I still don't think John would show his face here, too much at risk, but we'll keep an eye out for the mystery man or anyone else that looks out of place. I'm sure John's out there somewhere keeping an eye on us. Maybe not him, but someone else is. Maybe Corey or the mystery man or both. I'm going to see if Sherry can do facial recognition from a still shot of their faces."

Back at the station, each reviewed their notes to prepare for the interview with Sally Fredrickson and Jackson Walker that afternoon. They won't be in the room, but they'll be able to see and hear everything. Before making their way up to Lexington, Carla took the video segment to Sherry and killed her with kindness. Sherry informed her that she would get right on it, but Carla told her it was not a priority and tomorrow would be just fine.

CHAPTER 26

Carla and Beth arrived at the Lexington police station a little early, and the receptionist escorted them to the conference room they occupied just a few days ago. Carla enjoyed the amenities of the room. The more times she visited this building, the more she thought about working here one day. However, she remembered her dad's advice about the grass being greener somewhere else when it is not.

Beth, relaxing in one of the well-appointed wingback chairs, couldn't keep her mind off all the revelations discovered when her mom died and the contents of the metal box. She wondered when she opened it, would it be like opening Pandora's Box creating more problems and stress in her life. Unfortunately, she would have to take that chance and then deal with the consequences no matter the outcome. While waiting, she did a quick search on her iPhone. Typing in Nicole Hernandez, she waited for something to pop up. Just as a page was loading, the door to the conference room opened, and in walked Nicole. Beth quickly closed the page and put her phone away as Nicole sat opposite her. Silence in the room was eerie awakening. After a moment had passed, Craig entered and closed the door behind him, sitting beside Nicole.

After exchanging pleasantries with them, he began his comments. "Here is how we will proceed today. Nicole and I discussed our options for interviewing them and decided I would be the only person in the interview room. The three of you will observe everything on the monitor on the wall. Beth and Nicole will pay particular attention to the body language. Carla, please focus on the answers they give. I will approach this interview as a casual conversation and see where their answers lead me. I don't want to spook anyone. Questions?" After a brief pause, he continued, "Great, well, it will be showtime soon. Wish me luck."

Craig left and closed the door. The television on the wall was already on, showing a vacant and silent interrogation room. A soft buzz filled the conference room as they waited. Just below the television, the remote was on a table. 4:00 PM, they knew any minute now it would be showtime. Within a few minutes, they heard the door opening in the interrogation room. When seated, Sally and Jackson would be in full view of the video camera behind the glass window. Carla walked over and picked up the remote, adjusted the volume, and returned to her seat.

The commotion coming from the video screen alerted them that the interview would begin soon. Sally came into view first, and Jackson followed. He pulled out the first chair and motioned for her to take that chair. After she sat down, Jackson, in full view now, nuzzled the chair forward. He pulled out the other chair and sat down, scooting it a comfortable distance from the table. Craig walked into view carrying a manila folder and took a seat across from them. Placing it on the table just to his right, he hoped its presence would impose itself on them.

Craig didn't immediately begin. He remained silent to observe them before starting the interview. Even though a minute had elapsed, Jackson seemed to be a little fidgety, while Sally exhibited a calm demeanor. After letting them stew a little and allowing the room temperature to rise, he began, "Thank you for coming in on short notice, we appreciate your cooperation."

"Detective Bjornson, Jackson, and I want to help. What else did you want to ask me? Didn't I answer all of your questions the first time around? Also, why did you want me to bring anyone that helped me coach?"

"It's been several weeks since Abbie went missing, and I just wanted to talk with you again since you were one of the individuals that saw her last. Revisit your answers because some new information has come to our attention, and we are checking it out."

"What new information?"

"Hmm, we'll get to that a little later. Sally, tell me again about practice the day Abbie disappeared."

"It was like any other practice, about an hour and a half, all the basics, and I ended it with a pep talk. The girls helped gather up the equipment, and Abbie helped me put it in my car. I asked her if she needed a ride home, and she told me she'd rather walk home today. I left, and that was the last time I saw her."

"Thank you, Sally. Jackson, if I recall from the previous interview with Sally, she said you didn't help that day, correct?"

"Yeah, that's right. I had to take care of some personal business."

"Okay, when did you last help?"

"I usually help every day after I get off work, but I was off that day and needed to take care of some personal business."

"Sally, how long have you two known each other?"

"That's a strange question, but we've known each other for about two years now. I met Jackson when I took the teaching job."

"Are you two romantically involved?"

"That's another strange question, but we've been seeing each other for the past year or so. That's when he started helping me."

"Thanks. Jackson, you mentioned you had personal business to take care of. What kind of personal business?"

"Just stuff, personal errands, doctor's visit."

"Umm, did either of you ever give any of your players a ride home after practice?"

Sally replied, "Yeah, sometimes."

"What about you, Jackson. You ever give any of them a ride home?"

"Hmm, occasionally. What are you implying?"

"I'm not implying anything. Sally, you ever give Abbie a ride home?"

"Yeah, once or twice."

"Jackson, what about you?"

"Same, once or twice. Why do you ask?"

"No reason. We are just having a casual conversation here. You can leave anytime you want, but I hope you want to cooperate so we can find her, isn't that right?"

"Of course we do, right, Jackson?" He was getting a

little nervous but nodded while deflecting Craig's probing eyes. "Detective Bjornson, what other questions do you have for us?"

Craig, noticing Jackson was showing signs of anxiety, pulled out his phone and looked at it as though he had received a text. "I'm sorry, I have to step out for a moment. I'll be right back. May I get either of you some water?"

Sally replied, "No, we're fine, but thank you."

Craig left the room to let them stew a little more, hoping to raise the nervousness between them. He stood just outside the interrogation room. Beth, Carla, and Nicole watched the two of them whispering to each other but couldn't tell what they were saying. However, by the expression on their faces, anxiety was growing inside them, especially Jackson. After several minutes, Craig returned to the room and sat down. He slid the folder over in front of him, picked it up, and opened it. He closed it and laid it back down on the table facing them. Abbie Gardner's file was imposing.

"I believe you are both teachers, do either of you work in the summer?" Although he already knew the answers to both questions, he inquired, all the same, to keep the conversation informal.

"We both work at the country club. I teach tennis, and Jackson manages the pool area."

"Did Abbie play tennis?"

"No, I think she was on the swim team, right, Jackson?"

"Correct. I used to see Abbie finishing up as I began my shift. We'd occasionally talk since we already knew each other from the softball team. She was always very friendly to me. Pretty young girl."

Craig's line of questioning was working as Jackson seemed to get more agitated as time went on. He was fidgeting even more and glancing at the file on the table off and on. He refrained from making eye contact, always looking away from Craig. After Craig acted as though he would open the file, he pulled his hand away and said, "Okay, I think that will do it for now. If we need to talk to you again, we'll get a hold of you, do you have any questions?"

Sally replied, "You said earlier, you mentioned you had new information and would get to it later. What is it?"

"Oh, yeah, I'm sorry." Staring straight at Jackson looking deep into his soul, he continued, "Yeah, we got a tip that someone saw something that day, you know, a witness. They're coming in tomorrow morning."

Sally responded, "Oh, that's good, right?"

"We hope so, but you never know. If either of you don't have any other questions, you're free to leave."

"I don't have any. Jackson, what about you?"

Nervously, he quickly responded, "Uh, me, uh, no questions."

"Okay then, thank you both for coming in and wanting to help. I'll walk you out, okay?"

They nodded, and Craig escorted them out of the building and watched them walk toward a shiny new Mustang. Jackson opened the passenger door for Sally, a real gentleman, Craig thought. She got in, and he closed the door. After he got in, there was a moment that nothing happened. Finally, the Mustang growled, followed by squealing tires as Jackson's car left the parking lot. Craig returned to the police station and the conference room where Beth, Carla, and Nicole watched it unfold.

With all of them seated, Craig began, "Well, what do you think?"

Nicole broke the silence and said, "Nice job. They both got agitated a little, Jackson a little more. When you mentioned new information, I could see Jackson's face light up, and it looked like his respiration increased. It caught his interest, and he seemed to glance at the folder a lot. Like wondering what was inside."

"Beth, what did you see?"

"When you got to the part about giving Abbie a ride home, he reacted nervously, and then again about seeing and talking to her at the country club. I firmly believe he's our man."

"What about you, Carla?"

"Everything they have mentioned, but when you brought up about a witness coming forward, Jackson's face lost all color. I'm with Beth, this guy knows something, or maybe, he is even our guy."

"I agree with each of you, now, where do we go now without spooking him. I don't think it involves Sally at all. She remained fairly calm throughout, and what you didn't see was him squealing the tires leaving the parking lot in his hot new Mustang."

Carla interjected, "We need to bring him back in for further questioning, and the sooner, the better. Maybe go to the country club tomorrow and ask him to come in that your witness said they saw a car like his in the area. You know, not come right out and say he's involved, pressure him a little, but not enough that he would lawyer-up."

Craig responded, "Yeah, just what I was thinking.

Nicole and I will handle it since we are bringing him in based on our case only. I'll call you tomorrow after we are through with him. We'll see how the interview goes and then proceed accordingly. Carla, are you okay with this plan?"

"Umm, Craig, I think we should be here because of our case, and if it wasn't for us..."

"I understand, but until we can connect him to Abbie Gardner, we have nothing. If we can get him on this one, he might be cooperative and tell us about your case and the other two missing girls. I have a gut feeling there are much bigger fish to fry than just him in this deal. If it is sex or human trafficking, he is just a small-time player delivering the goods."

Disappointed, Carla agreed to his plan, and the meeting adjourned. As they were walking out, Nicole suggested they all go for a drink. Craig, not wanting to mix business with pleasure declined, Carla mentioned she needed to get back to Oakmont. Beth told her she wouldn't mind, but that would mean Nicole would have to give her a ride home. Nicole agreed, and in less than twenty minutes, they sat in Harry's Bar and Bistro in the Hamburg Shopping district for a drink and more bonding time. Both were single and not looking for love at the moment. Finding out what happened to Abbie Gardner was all that mattered to them.

CHAPTER 27

Sally informed Craig they would come in again after work. He was confident they would show up because she really seemed like a responsible, honest person and genuinely wanted to help find Abbie. The meeting was the same as yesterday, 4:00 PM. Since Craig had made a small change to the plan, he called Carla and informed her of that change. Once the interview was over, he would contact her with all the details.

As Craig had predicted, Sally and Jackson arrived a few minutes early. He informed them of their right to have legal representation during the meeting. After some ice-breaking casual conversation to put them at ease, he was ready to begin. Just as yesterday, Abbie Gardner's file sat on the table facing them. He also had another folder to the right of him to pique their interest. The name on it read Melody Morris. Picking up Abbie's file, he flipped it open for a moment, glanced at them, and back at the folder. After closing it, and repeating the same process with the other file, it drew their attention, especially Jackson.

Glancing at Sally, he said, "Okay, let's begin. Sally refresh me about the day Abbie went missing. I know you have told me your story several times, but I think it is a good place to begin, if that's okay?"

Sally nodded, being a trusting and honest person as well as a little naïve, told her story for at least the fourth time. It hadn't changed one bit. While she was talking, Craig focused on Jackson, looking for any sign of anxiousness. Nicole, watching from the conference room, studied Jackson's every movement. Sally finished, and Craig responded, "Thank you, Sally. I know you feel this is unnecessary, but sometimes people change their story." He glanced back and forth between Sally and Jackson several times before making eye contact with Sally again. "I appreciate your cooperation."

Sally acknowledged him and put her left hand on the table, searching for Jackson's nervous hand. Finding it, she gave it a soft squeeze of assurance and released it. Jackson smiled at Sally but cringed when he heard Craig speak. "Jackson, tell me about the day Abbie disappeared. You said yesterday that you took care of personal stuff; I recall you mentioned a doctor's appointment. The more open you are, the sooner we can get you all out of here, okay?"

Jackson's face, painted with white anxiety, said in a soft, mumbling tone, "O...okay." Jackson paused for a moment to collect his thoughts. Craig showed signs of impatience, tapping his fingers, and doodling on Abbie's file created more anxiousness on Jackson's face. Craig traced Abbie's name repeatedly; Jackson wiped beads of sweat off his brow. Finally, opening up, Jackson began. "Okay, earlier in the day, I ran personal errands and then lunched with an old friend from college. That afternoon around four o'clock, I had a dentist's appointment. They were running behind, umm, I didn't get out until well after five."

All the while Jackson was talking, Craig focused on Sally, watching her facial expressions. Although the interview was being recorded, he knew that Nicole was observing it as well. Craig thought for a moment, then he responded. "Jackson, look at me. Yesterday, you said a doctor's visit, now you say you went to the dentist. Which is it?"

"Did I say doctor yesterday, uh, guess I forgot, sorry. It was a dentist appointment, yeah, the dentist."

"Can anyone corroborate any of this?"

"Well, yeah, I had lunch with Lou Chilton, you want his number, and you can call my dentist if you like?"

Craig pulled a business card out of his shirt pocket and handed it to him. "Write down your friend's name and number on the back, and your dentist's name and number, okay?"

Jackson took the business card and quickly wrote on the back. He looked at Craig, whose stare was invading his soul. Jackson paused for a moment and said, "I don't have my dentist's number with me; I'll just write his name, okay?" Craig's nodded. Watching Sally's expression on her face, Craig could see the distrust and disbelief in her eyes. Jackson finished and handed the card back to him. He read aloud the information so Nicole could hear it and do a quick check on its legitimacy.

"Thank you, now I mentioned yesterday about a person that had some information they wanted to bring to our attention. They met with me this morning for a short while. I asked him similar questions; it wasn't a long meeting. I wanted to talk to you about that information."

Suddenly, he pulled out his phone and stared at it. "Gosh, I'm sorry, I have to step out for a moment to take care of this, I'll be back shortly."

While outside the interrogation room, he looked up the dentist's name on his phone. The website loaded, and he clicked on the phone number and waited for an answer. After listening to the receptionist's greeting, he said, "Hi, this is Jackson Walker. I was there on June fourth for a cleaning, and I forgot to make a note of my next appointment. Would you look that up for me?" After a short pause, he said, "Oh, I'm sorry, I must be mistaken when I was there last. I'll make a note of my next appointment. Thanks and have a nice day."

All the while he was checking out Jackson's alibi, Nicole was watching Sally and Jackson whisper to each other. Like yesterday, she couldn't make out what they were talking about, but it appeared very personal, and each showed signs of nervousness. Craig re-entered the room and came into view and took a seat at the table. He said, "I apologize for being so long. Where were we?"

Jackson, who was becoming fidgety and nervous, replied, "I was recounting my day."

"Right." Changing the subject quickly, he asked, "How long have you had that new Mustang I saw you leave in yesterday."

"About six months. What does that have to do with all of this?"

"Maybe nothing. The person we interviewed this morning told us that a Mustang matching yours was in the area that Abbie would have used to walk home."

Sally's mouth flew open, and she turned to Jackson. "What's going on, Jackson? Did you have something to do with this? Please tell me no…"

While flushed with anxiety, sweat dotted Jackson's forehead. He quickly wiped it away. His respiration increased as his heart pounded inside him. He took a deep breath and finally responded in a defensive tone, "Of course not, honey. I wouldn't do anything like that. Come on now, you know me better than that. There are several Mustangs like mine in the area."

Craig, making eye contact with Sally, quickly fired back, "Jackson, if you had anything to do with her disappearance, speak up now; you'll make it a lot easier on yourself."

Silence filled the room until there was a knock on the door. The door opened, and before the receptionist could say anything, a well-dressed man with a briefcase barged in and identified himself as Jared Lester. He handed Craig his business card. As he stood behind Sally and Jackson, he stared at Craig.

"I'm here to represent Jackson and Sally in this matter."

"What's this all about, Mr. Lester? Neither of them has asked legal representation."

After placing his firm hand on Jackson's shoulder, he asked, "Jackson, do you want legal representation?" A quick nod met Craig's dumbfounded eyes. "Good, then we are finished here. If you have any further questions, Detective Bjornson, you have my contact information. Let's get out of here."

Sally and Jackson didn't know quite what to think about what just happened. However, on the way out of the room, Craig heard Sally asking Jackson about Jared Lester. He didn't respond. Craig watched them leave the police station and get into his car and drive off. A black Malibu sedan with dark-tinted windows followed them.

In shock about what happened, Craig returned to the conference room where Nicole was sitting dumbfounded. "What was that all about, Nicole? I don't like what is going on. I've got to notify Carla about this." He immediately called her, who had been anxiously waiting to hear from him. After answering, Carla placed the call on speaker. Craig's authoritative, but anxious voice filled the room. "The interview was going very well, and I was getting somewhere. I think I was close to getting some real information. However, unexpectedly, a man entered the room, introducing himself as Jackson's lawyer. Jackson looked as shocked as I did. His business card looked official, and his name is Jared Lester." Silence captured the room as Carla quickly Googled Jared Lester. "Carla, are you there?"

"Yeah, I don't like this. Jared Lester doesn't come up on my search anywhere. Is there a way to send me a still image of his face, and as quick as possible?"

"It'll take a minute or two. What's going on?"

"I've got a bad feeling about this. Do you have Jackson's home address?"

"We'll get it. The still image is on its way."

After a short pause, Carla grimaced. "Got it. I've seen this guy before. This is not good. Get over to Jackson's place immediately and text me the address as soon as you get it. We are on our way. Be careful. I smell trouble."

Craig, not sure what was going on, sent Carla Jackson's address. Craig and Nicole were en route to his apartment with two patrol cars following them. When the convoy arrived, Jackson's Mustang was in front of his apartment door. Craig exited his vehicle approaching the front door. He motioned two of the patrolmen to go around to the rear of the apartment. Two other patrolmen backed him up at the front door. He rang the doorbell, and it chimed inside. A moment passed, no footsteps, all he could hear was the eerie silence inside. He checked the doorknob; it didn't turn at all. A pair of curtains partially covered a window just to the right of the door, through a sliver of an opening, he peeked inside. Not liking what he saw, he motioned one of the patrolmen to break in the door.

After two swift kicks, the door exploded open. With weapons drawn, they entered. Directly in front of them, slumped back on the sofa, Jackson and Sally stared into a very dark and dead space. Execution style, each had a single bullet hole in their forehead. Craig didn't know what to think about what had just transpired, but he was sure that Jackson was involved in Abbie's disappearance and that this situation may be larger than anyone had ever imagined.

Craig returned outside as Carla and Beth arrived. They exited the car and met him just outside the front door. Carla already knew what happened inside, but walked in just the same, viewed the bodies, and walked back outside where Craig, Nicole, and Beth had gathered.

"Okay, Carla, tell me what's going on and how you knew something like this would happen."

"Craig, the still photo you sent me. I recognized the man. I had a run-in with him at McGruder's in Oakmont. That night he went by Corey Hawthorne. Unfortunately, that is an alias, which spells trouble. We are running facial recognition but haven't found anything yet. That means that Jared Lester is an alias and was ordered to shut Jackson up, which means someone big is behind this. Unfortunately, Sally was collateral damage and didn't deserve such a fate."

"Someone big, what do you mean, Carla?

"Umm, someone big is behind this alright. I have an idea although I wouldn't have suspected it or even Jackson's connection to him."

"Hmm, who or what are you referring to, Carla?"

"My nemesis, John Dickerson. Never would have figured it, but wouldn't put it past him. He had his hands in many illegal ventures besides being in bed with a drug lord. When the FBI took him into custody, sex-trafficking was one of the charges mentioned in the newscast."

"Who's John Dickerson?" Carla explained the entire story of John Dickerson to Craig and that he was on the loose, and his whereabouts were unknown. After hearing the whole story, Craig asked, "Where do we go from here?"

"If I'm right that John Dickerson is involved, we need to bring in the FBI. This case just got way bigger than us. I'll make the call and set up a meeting as soon as we can, hopefully as earliest as tomorrow, because what happened today will not be the end of the killing."

With a concerned and worried pale complexion on his face, Craig inquired, "What, you can't be serious?"

"Dead serious; I know him all too well. Seven people are dead at his hands. He will kill until he gets what he wants."

"And what is that?"

"His wife and son back, they're in a witness protection program that he orchestrated when he agreed with the FBI last year for helping take down a drug kingpin named Edwardo Cavalla. John was on his way to testify when he conveniently escaped. I know where his wife and son are, and he knows that. We all need to be on high alert. Any more you want to know?"

During Carla's explanation, Craig's demeanor remained reserved as a pale color framed his masculine face. He had nothing more to say and walked back inside the apartment, where an execution-style double murder demanded his attention. Forensics and the coroner were working the scene combing Jackson's apartment for evidence. However, Corey Hawthorne, a professional hitman, was good at what he did, and finding any evidence would be a waste of time.

CHAPTER 28

Agents Donnie Slack and Scott Carlson had agreed to meet Carla and Beth in Oakmont on the following Monday at 3:00 PM. Carla hoped that nothing else would happen before she and Beth could lay all of their cards on the table and convince them to get involved. She didn't have any real proof of Jackson Walker's involvement. However, given that he had never been in any trouble in his life, she was sure that his murder was not just a coincidence. It was clear that someone wanted to keep him quiet. A single bullet to the forehead silenced him forever.

Carla hoped that facial recognition would turn up something on Corey Hawthorne and the other mystery man seen at McGruder's. She was sure of their involvement with John Dickerson. Although it took longer than Carla would have liked, facial recognition had been successful. Corey Hawthorne, aka Jared Lester, was positively identified as Nathan "Hawk" Moribito, while they identified the mystery man as Paul Francisco. Both were members of a government contractor security firm called

Lifestar, LLC. More in-depth research indicated they assisted military special forces, especially Alpha Tango, and it was precisely the link Carla was hoping to discover. They were connected to John Dickerson as she suspected. At least in her mind, John Dickerson knew something about the disappearance of Penny Miracle fifteen years ago and the other missing girls, most recently, Abbie Gardner. She contacted Craig and informed him about the facial recognition results. Craig put out a BOLO on them, but Carla knew they were likely long gone or even more likely dead. That's how John Dickerson worked. He uses people, then disposes of them.

On a hunch, Carla contacted the Federal Correctional Facility in Boyd County, inquiring whether John Dickerson had any visitors while incarcerated there. That hunch turned up nothing since he was under the highest security, and with an alias, he was not allowed visitors of any kind. She found out that he was a model prisoner and had gained the trust of the employees and guards.

While isolated from the main prison population, technology amenities such as a television and limited use of a laptop with internet were at his disposal. Although she found out that audits of his usage discovered nothing suspicious in nature, she knew he was a smart man. Somehow he must have communicated with Hawk Moribito and Paul Francisco, who were likely the accomplices that helped him escape, and the men who executed Sally and Jackson.

While Carla was preparing everything necessary for the meeting with the FBI team, Beth had moved forward with the DNA analysis to prove her mother's gut feeling that Penny was her twin sister. She knew it was risky. If

Penny was her twin sister, the case could get very personal, and she might have to recuse herself from it. Furthermore, the results of the DNA analysis would answer the burning question inside her mind once and for all. Beth signed out the box labeled "Penny Miracle" and set it on a table outside the evidence locker room. It wasn't a large box since there was very little evidence. After cutting the tape, she removed the lid revealing the box's content.

Inside was a candy wrapper and a picture of the tomato left on the counter. The tomato had decayed weeks after Penny disappeared. A pair of socks, a hairbrush with complete hairs samples, and a pale-yellow tank top were in plastic evidence bags. She remembered the tank top; a vision of Penny wearing it flashed in her mind, causing tears to trickle down her cheeks. Quickly, she wiped them away. A copy of Penny's DNA analysis stared back at her. At this point, all the graphs and numbers meant nothing to her.

The Forensic Department, in the same room as the evidence locker, Sherry stood behind a counter working her magic on something. Sherry glanced her way; Beth motioned her over. Upon reaching her, Sherry asked, "Looks like the Penny Miracle evidence, what's going on?" Beth pulled up a photo on her phone of she and Penny growing up. Handing the phone to Sherry, she studied it enlarging it on the screen and gave it back to her. "You and Penny, wow…guess you do look like each other a lot. How can I help?"

"My mom left me a letter in my adoption documents that she firmly believed that we were sisters. She could never prove it, and Penny's mother always adamantly denied it. In the letter, my mom encouraged me to have a DNA analysis performed. I want to do that."

"Okay, let me get a kit."

"What about Penny? Is the DNA analysis from fifteen years ago going to be a good comparison, or would a new one be better since the whole DNA thing has improved significantly? Is there anything contained in the box we could use?"

"Let's see what we have. The hairs in the plastic bag appear to have a bead or follicle on them, so that might be our best bet."

"Okay, what about the tank top? I remember she wore it the day before she disappeared. It was hot that day, and we were sweating like crazy."

"Sure, I'll cut the section out under the armpits and send it in with the hair samples and see what we get. No promises, you understand?"

"Of course, I'm ready."

"Okay, open wide. I'll send all of this out today and check with the lab once they receive everything. I'm sure you will be anxiously waiting on the results, so I'll persuade them to make it a high priority to shorten the waiting period. We should have them back in about one week. Hope you get the results you are looking for?"

"Yeah, me, too. Thanks for your help."

"There is one thing you should know. The results may not be definitive; there's a better chance if we had the birth mother or birth father's DNA as well. We'll see what the results show and go from there."

"Thanks."

Sherry nodded and walked away. Beth looked at all the evidence again before placing it back in the box. Putting the lid back on it, she returned it to the attendant who taped it back up and labeled it according to police policies. Beth signed the login sheet and returned to her desk. Immediately, she noticed a note taped to her phone. It was from Carla. She had left for the day and would see her on Monday. It also said she assembled the material for the meeting, and they would review it on Monday morning.

Beth pulled out her iPhone and found Nicole's contact information; she hit the call button and waited for her to answer. After a few rings, Nicole's voice greeted her. "Hey, how's everything in Lexington?" She listened to her response and replied, "That's great. Do you have any plans for tonight?" Again, listening to her reply, she responded, "Great. Do you want to do dinner and drinks tonight? My treat. How about McGruder's here in Oakmont, say around seven? Great, see you then."

As usual, McGruder's was busy on Friday evening, but Beth found a high-top table on the outside deck. She left word with Sam to be on the lookout for Nicole. Around ten after seven, Nicole appeared, walked toward her, and sat opposite her. Within minutes, Sam arrived to take their drink orders. Beth ordered a bottle of Pinot Grigio for them to share and two shots of tequila. After about five minutes, Sam arrived with the tequila, a bottle of wine, and two glasses. Sam poured each a generous amount, then put the wine on ice and left. Beth raised the shot of tequila toward Nicole, she followed her lead and raised her shot glass for a toast.

"Nicole, thanks for meeting me here tonight."

"Thank you for inviting me; I was all prepared to spend another Friday night alone in my apartment. I'm not seeing anyone, and the weekend nights get kind of lonely if you know what I mean?"

"Yeah, I just got through a break-up several months ago, so I know about those lonely nights. Maybe we can do this more often?"

"Sounds good to me, next Friday, it's my treat up in Lexington, okay?"

"You're on. What are you going to order?"

"What do you recommend, Beth?"

"Rueben and fries, you can't go wrong. The sandwich is huge, and we could easily split one accompanied by a side salad, is that okay?" Nicole nodded. Sam returned, took their orders, and left. "Nicole, I need to excuse myself and visit the ladies' room; I'll be right back. Then you can tell me more about you, you know, parents or siblings, all that kind of stuff, okay?"

After a visit to the ladies' room, Beth returned and sat across from Nicole, taking a few sips of her wine before continuing bonding with her. "Now where were we, oh, you were going to tell me all about your past."

"Not much to tell. First, I was adopted as my parents tried to conceive, but it was not to be, so they turned to adoption. All I know is that I was only a few days old when I was adopted. I Grew up in Russell, Kentucky. I played volleyball in high school and received a scholarship to the University of Kentucky. I graduated with a degree in psychology and a minor in social sciences. Also, I have a cat named Hobbs. Like I said, not much to tell."

"Adopted, that's interesting, you ever try to find your birth mother?"

"Nah, that doesn't seem that important to me. I know my birth mother gave me away for a good reason, but my adopted parents raised me. I believe in fate, and I want to leave well enough alone. Okay now, I've spilled my most private secrets; what are you hiding that you haven't told me yet."

"Okay, umm, I was adopted as well. However, after my mom died several weeks ago, she left me letters with my birth mother's name, but nothing else. I also have a twin sister out there somewhere, not identical, though. In my mom's letter, she firmly believed that Penny is my twin sister."

Beth pulled up the photo on her phone and showed it to Nicole. She studied it carefully and returned the phone to Beth. "Yeah, you do look like you could be sisters, but is that possible?"

"I'm going to find out; I did a DNA analysis. Also, because my mom was adopted, in her letter, she encouraged me to find my biological mother and possibly her biological mother. I have no other family from my parents' side, so I'm on a mission to find both. Not sure what I'll find, but I think it's worth the risk."

"I understand, and good luck."

Beth nodded as Sam arrived with their order, and the conversation turned to their current case. Usually, business and pleasure don't mix, but with them, it was unavoidable. They agreed that Jackson Walker knew something or was involved, and he died because of it. The execution-style hit sent a message that someone powerful was involved, and other lives connected to the case were in jeopardy.

CHAPTER 29

After a relaxing weekend, a somber attitude ran throughout Carla's soul as she sat at her desk, reviewing the information for the meeting with the FBI that afternoon at three o'clock. Beth arrived a little late and sat opposite of Carla. She fired up her laptop and waited for everything to load. While glancing at Carla, Beth could tell that she was down about something. She smiled at Carla, but she ignored Beth's friendly greeting. Finally, Carla acknowledged her, and Beth smiled again, which got Carla to break the silence between them.

"What are you so happy about? Did you meet up with somebody over the weekend?"

"Hmm, sort of, but not what you are thinking."

"You're a mind reader now?"

"Nah, I know how you think, but yeah, I met up with someone Friday evening. Nicole and I met at McGruder's for dinner and drinks. I think once this is all over, her and I will become good friends, kind of like sisters."

"You and this sister thing, it's getting on my nerves.

You going to ask her to do a DNA analysis if Penny and yours don't pan out?"

"Maybe. She's adopted as well." Changing the subject, she asked, "You have everything ready for the meeting, and do you want me to play the role of being the silent one?"

"Your responsible for where we are, I don't mean that you have blood on your hands, but we wouldn't be here if you hadn't convinced me that Jackson Walker might be a person of interest. So, yeah, I want you involved when the opportunity presents itself; otherwise, I will lead the meeting, got it?"

Beth nodded and returned to her laptop screen and Googled "sibling DNA analysis" to learn as much as she could about what the result might reveal. She wanted to learn as much as she could to understand the DNA analysis better. Sherry mentioned having the biological mother or biological father's DNA would generate more definitive results. However, that wasn't possible.

While Beth studied DNA analysis of siblings, Carla had left to check their mailboxes. As usual, Beth's mailbox was empty; however, she had one piece of mail, and retrieved it. While staring at the number ten envelope and how it was addressed, it sent chills up and down her spine. She had seen this before. What caught her eye, even more, was that it didn't have a postmark on it, meaning someone delivered it in person. She immediately rushed out of the main doors of the station looking around. Seeing nothing out of the ordinary, she cursed under her breath. Re-entering the station, she went to the receptionist's desk to inquire if she saw anything. The receptionist informed her that a young lady dropped it off about thirty minutes ago.

Carla returned to her desk and examined the front of the envelope again. After turning it over, she pulled the flap out and reached in, pulling out what appeared to be a letter. Unfolding the piece of letter-sized paper, she stared at the printer generated text. Carla read the first sentence to herself and stopped. She glanced at the sender's name at the end of the letter; her face quickly turned a snow-whitish tint of fear. Beth, seeing a ghostly expression painting Carla's face, knew the letter had clearly grabbed her soul.

"What's going on, Carla?"

"Follow me to the interrogation room."

"Why, what's going on?"

"I'll tell you once we are there."

After entering the conference room, Carla closed the door, and they sat opposite each other. Carla took a deep breath as some color had returned to her face. Looking at Beth, she said, "This letter is from John Dickerson, and that's not good. Some young lady dropped it off, probably someone he found on the street. Paid them to deliver it. Listen closely; here we go."

Dear Detective McBride,

We meet again, Detective McBride. I hope your day is going well, Carla. I can call you that now, can't I? We seem to know each other quite well, don't we? I didn't think we would meet this soon again, but fate has brought us together once more. I know what you want, and of course, you already know what I want, and where they are.

When you tricked me into believing my wife and son were in the safe house, I told you I would come after you again and that I would be with my wife and son one day, and that day has arrived.

Game back on, wouldn't you say, bitch?

Let's start with Jackson Walker. I liked him, and until your new associate stumbled onto him in the re-opening of the cold case, he was doing fine in one of my little ventures. He got involved fifteen years ago because his mother needed lots of money. He would do anything for his mother as you found out.

I'm referring to the abduction of Penny Miracle, his first score. I'm sure her name caught your attention. Penny is doing quite well and living a good life. Yes, I know where she is, but we will get to that later.

I think Jackson liked the easy money and moved on to other scores; you know Melody, Natalie, and Abbie, to name a few, there are many others. Now that he was crumbling under pressure, he had to be eliminated. Sorry that his girlfriend got involved with him, collateral damage, but you know how that goes, don't you?

As far as Hawk and Paul are concerned, they are long gone. As you probably have discovered by now, they were known associates from my Alpha Tango days. They paid their debt to me just like you will in the end if you know what I mean?

Oh, by the way. I met a lovely lady, Lydia Kowalski, at the grocery store on Saturday. I'd love to see your face about now. Beth and Nicole seemed to enjoy themselves Friday evening at McGruder's. Also, Sam served me a beer that night as well. Finally, I met your boyfriend, Chris, on Saturday as I inquired about a membership at the country club. He seemed like a nice guy and perfect for you. I'm sure you are fuming about now.

That should do it, for now, I'll be in touch, and oh,
you can look at the video from McGruder's if you like,
but when you think you know what I look like, I'm not
that person at all. I've learned how to be invisible
to you.

You want Penny, and I want my wife and son, I'll be
in touch soon.

Game on, may the best person win.
John

Silence captivated the room as blank, stoic expressions of fear faced each other. The letter affected Beth more than Carla because she knew that after Jackson and Sally were executed, something like this was coming, and John was involved.

"He was watching Nicole and me on Friday evening; shit, Carla, what the hell is going on?"

"Beth, I told you he was one sick bastard, and we all need to watch each other's back because he will strike, trust me, it's just a matter of time, no one is safe. I believe Hawk and Paul are dead, and I wouldn't be surprised if their bodies showed up somewhere soon. That's how he does business. He eliminates any ties to him, anyone that would talk, like Jackson Walker. Craig said he was close to getting information from him and look what happened. Also, I wouldn't be surprised the young lady that delivered this letter is dead as well."

"Okay, I get it, what next?"

"This letter explains a lot, and I'll make copies for our meeting this afternoon, and hopefully, this will be enough to get the FBI involved and solve these cases and, more importantly, take care of John Dickerson for good. I don't mean back in prison. Furthermore, we need to visit

Sam at McGruder's and warn her to be very careful. I don't think he will go after her, but she needs to know what is going on. They should open soon; hopefully, she is working today. Let's go, I'm not all that hungry, but we can visit her and check out some video although it may be in vain."

Arriving at McGruder's, they immediately saw Sam behind the bar prepping for the lunch crowd. Approaching the side of the bar where she was, they sat at stools in front of her. Sam glanced at them and said, "What brings you here today. Beth, didn't I wait on you and Nicole Friday evening?"

"Right, can we both get a Diet Coke, and we need to review some video from Friday night between seven and nine. We need it from every camera, and I believe you have three of them, correct?"

"Yeah, what's up?" She quickly poured them a Diet Coke and continued prepping for the lunch crowd.

Carla said, "I don't want to alarm you, but I received a letter from John Dickerson, and in it, he indicated he was here Friday night and saw Beth and Nicole. You need to be careful because I don't know what his next move is. I don't think he will come after you, but you need to be very careful, just the same."

"Got it. I'll be right back with the laptop."

"Great, we'll move to the corner booth and be out of your way."

After Sam dropped off the laptop, Carla selected the first video and hit the play arrow. This segment was from the left side of the bar. As usual for a Friday evening, the pub was very crowded. To view every second of each video segment, Carla put it on fast-forward just looking for someone that didn't fit. After spending several hours reviewing the video with several refills of Diet Coke, Carla closed the laptop and signaled for Sam.

She came over to the booth and asked, "More refills?"

Shaking her head back-and-forth, Carla replied, "I think we saw him, but not knowing what disguise he was using, it could have been any of the guys you served. We have nothing to go on, be careful, but I don't think he will show up here again. If you see anything suspicious, please call me immediately, okay? Sam, be careful."

Sam nodded and left with the laptop. She informed them she would review the video herself and try to remember anything that might help from that night. After they returned to the police station, Carla contacted Bernie about John meeting Lydia at the grocery store. She contacted Chris about John being in the clubhouse over the weekend. She felt in her mind that Chris, unfortunately, was the most likely target that could hurt her the most.

Carla also called the General Lewis Inn in Lewisburg, West Virginia, to inquire about John's wife, Gina, now using the name Alicia Maddox given to her as she entered the witness protection program. Carla feared that since she knew where Gina was, the US Marshals might move her to another city with another new identity.

However, she was relieved that Gina was still in Lewisburg, working at the General Lewis Inn. Luckily for her, Gina was off today because Carla didn't want to alarm or spook her. Carla would need her cooperation later and knew that it would not be easy to convince her to help solve this case. Gina made it clear she wanted nothing to do with her husband, no matter the life or death consequences.

CHAPTER 30

With her phone calls finished, Carla gathered her materials for the meeting and entered the conference room. She had made seven copies of everything as Chief Evans would sit in on the meeting. Her iPhone screen lit up, and her phone chimed. The hour of reckoning was about to begin. While pacing back and forth, her pulse raced as she waited for everyone. After arriving first, Beth took her usual place at the table. Within a few minutes, Craig and Nicole entered and sat next to Beth. Carla knew that Agents Donnie Slack and Scott Carlson were already in the station meeting with Chief Evans.

Finally, with everyone seated at the table, Carla took control of the meeting, passing out the documents. She urged them to keep an open mind while she explained each item in the folder. One thing she left out was the letter from John Dickerson because she knew it was human nature for people to thumb through the material while someone was talking.

"Before I go through each document in the file folder,

I feel it's prudent I read a letter I received from John Dickerson today." That drew some comments, especially from Agent Slack. "Please bear with me as I read it. It was dropped off by a young lady this morning. I watched the video segment, and I believe this person had nothing to do with our case. He likely paid her to drop it off. Please listen closely; I'll pass out a copy to each of you at the end of my comments. However, after hearing the letter, there may not be any reason to go through the material because it will seem pointless. After all, John has confessed to everything."

While hiding her emotions, Carla handled herself professionally as she read the letter aloud. She paused momentarily and glanced around the table to gauge the atmosphere in the room. When she came to the part about Penny, Carla glanced at Agent Scott Carlson since he grew up with her, and according to Beth, had a crush on her early on in his childhood. Carla could see the concern and a high level of interest in his eyes. Returning her focus to the letter, she continued reading it. Commanding their attention, she finished reading the letter. While passing a copy of it around the table, she waited for comments and questions to fly her way.

Moments of silence sent her pulse racing all the more. Agent Carlson was the first to speak up. "Carla, do you honestly believe Penny is alive after all these years? Do you believe John?"

"Umm, yeah, I do. He wants to be with his wife and son again. They are still in a federal witness protection program, correct, Agent Slack?"

"Correct, but I don't know where she is."

"Well, Agent Slack, you may not like what I'm about to tell you, and please don't jump to any conclusions, but

I know where she is. During a difficult time in my life recently, a friend took me away to relax. While there, I thought a lady at a hotel looked familiar. It bothered me so much when I returned; I had forensics help me determine if my hunch was right. Through facial recognition programs and our sketch artist's creation, I discovered her. I won't tell you where because we will need her to catch John and get Penny back. We both want that, right, Agent Slack?"

"Right."

"Great, John will make a move like he did when he kidnapped my best friend, Laura Watson. Then he'll call to make a deal for whoever he decides to take or kidnap. He knows I know where his wife and son are, so he'll do something. I don't know what or when, but he will, trust me on this."

Craig asked, "What about Hawk and Paul? Do you think they are still around to carry out his plan?"

"Honestly, I think we will find them dead somewhere. That's how John works. Every member of Alpha Tango is deceased. He had them all eliminated except one, and John took care of that himself. He leaves no one that can tie anything back to him. So, yeah, they're dead. Maybe we find them; maybe we don't. Any other questions before we go through the material that may be meaningless now that I have this letter. John told us everything we wanted to know, that's how he plays the game."

Silence and shock bounced off the walls of the conference room. Everyone around the table glanced at each other, wondering who was going to make the next move. John's letter still shocked everyone, but she continued presenting the rest of the material. After a lengthy review of all the documents and notes, she asked for questions.

Up to now, Chief Evans had been quiet and finally broke the stalemated silence in the room. "Carla, let me get this straight. You believe Jackson Walker kidnapped Penny Miracle fifteen years ago and delivered her to a sex-trafficker. He moved to Ohio, abducted two girls, and then moved on and ends up in Lexington, where another girl ends up missing. To date, no bodies have ever surfaced in any of these cases. You build a financial footprint of Jackson Walker, and red flags pop up everywhere. You joined forces with Lexington police, and they eventually bring him in for questioning. Now, he and his girlfriend are dead. Then, you receive this letter from John Dickerson this morning, and all of this adds up to what conclusion?"

"It's all tied to sex or human trafficking, and John Dickerson is connected."

Chief Evans responded, "Really, these are young girls, way too young."

"My research shows twelve to fourteen-year-old girls are prime targets, right Agent Slack?"

"Right, sex-trafficking is big business and young girls, yes even twelve years old, are selected based on physical appearance. They're brainwashed, treated well to gain trust, and eventually placed into the pipeline here or abroad as sex slaves. Fear for their life, and fear for their family is the driving factor that keeps them alive and cooperating."

Chief Evans interjected, "Okay, say you are right. What's next?"

"We need our FBI friends to review and investigate possible sex-trafficking rings in cities fed by the interstate highway system; you know I-64, 65, 70, and 75. I'm talking about Atlanta, Tampa, Miami, or St. Louis. Agent Slack, wouldn't Atlanta or St. Louis make the most sense given the proximity to where these girls went missing."

Agent Slack replied, "You've done your homework. Sex-traffickers need quick access to interstates to deliver their score. We will start with both locations and see what we can uncover. There is no guarantee that any of these girls ended up in either city or even alive. I also remind you that our goal is to catch John Dickerson first, then find these missing girls, if they're alive."

Chief Evans once again interjected, "Carla, how do we find John?"

"We don't have to. He found us, and unfortunately, we must wait until he makes a move. That's the hard part because someone could get hurt or even die."

Agent Slack asked, "Detective McBride, you mentioned you know where his wife is, and she is important to catching him; how?"

Carla responded with a defiant attitude, "I won't play all of my cards today, you'll have to trust me. She needs to stay put for now, and that will be very important in catching John. We need you to do your part. If somehow his wife is moved, or she bolts, we may never catch him or find Penny and solve these abductions. That's why it is important that you not pursue her whereabouts."

Agent Slack vehemently responded, "All due respect Detective McBride, you don't tell us what to do or how to do our job, as I said, our goal is to capture John Dickerson, and don't forget that."

Agent Carlson recognizing the points Carla made, chimed in. "Donnie, think about it. The key to capturing John Dickerson is through his wife. That's why he is doing all of this. So, don't be a jackass about this, we all want the same thing." Agent Slack didn't like his new partner embarrassing him and flashed a stern stare his way. Agent Carlson grimaced, but continued, "We need to do our part and investigate possible sex-trafficking rings as Detective McBride requested."

Agent Slack, still showing some resistance, responded, "I'll think about it, but I still don't like being told how to do my job."

Carla wanted to cram her fist down his throat, but she knew that would be the end of her career and likely put her in a federal prison. Instead, she took a few deep breaths and responded, "Agent Slack, thank you for being so cooperative and considerate. Can we move on to forming a plan once John contacts me, and he will, trust me?"

Carla finished her explanation and asked if there were any questions. She glanced around the table, waiting for a response, but all she saw were heads moving back-and-forth. She ended the meeting with one final statement, "Remember, we are all on the same team, I'll keep you informed of any changes in our plans. As soon as John contacts me, you'll be the first to know, okay?" Everyone in the room nodded and gathered their documents, ready to leave when, unexpectedly, there was a knock on the door. Carla got up to open the door and stepped outside for a moment. After about a minute, she returned with a deeply concerned look sprawled all over her face.

She took a seat and said, "We have the body of a young female found in the brush at Lake Catalpa. According to the description, it appears to be the young lady that delivered the letter for John. It appears he has already struck to get our attention and prove he was serious. The game has started, and unfortunately, we may have to play it his way. Unless there are any further questions, we need to get to work because he will contact me soon."

A somber atmosphere followed everyone out of the conference room. Carla and Beth left to visit the crime scene; however, before leaving the police station, they passed Bernie walking toward Chief Evans' office. There wasn't any time for chit-chat; they would catch up with him later and find out why he was here today.

Arriving at the crime scene, they immediately walked to where the coroner, DJ, covered up the body. Carla said, "Pull it back. Let me see her." DJ pulled the white sheet of death away, revealing the victim. Carla grimaced at the blood that saturated her neck. "Okay, you can cover her up, it's the lady on the video I reviewed this morning."

"Carla, this was left on the body." He handed her a black rose with a note attached to it. She read it to herself and grumbled vulgarities under her breath. "What did you say, Carla?"

"Nothing. Who called it in?"

"All I know is some passerby, a man I believe, called 9-1-1, left no name, and the caller ID was unknown."

"Probably John Dickerson himself. He wanted us to find it right away."

On the way back to Carla's car, Beth asked, "What did the note say?"

"Game on, detective, are you up to it?"

Returning to the police station, Carla went directly to Chief Evans' office to find out why Bernie was meeting with him. With the door closed, she knocked. Within a minute, the door opened, and she entered. She sat down beside Bernie and smiled.

"What are you doing here, dickhead?"

"Umm, Lydia is driving me crazy. I needed to come back to work and finish what I didn't do fifteen years ago, and help you solve the disappearance of Penny Miracle. Unless you have a problem, bring me up to speed and let's get to work."

CHAPTER 31

The next morning as Carla approached her car, something white, maybe an envelope, was under her wiper. The sight of it sent her pulse raging. After removing it, she turned it over. Not being sealed, she pulled out the flap, a piece of folded copier paper glared at her. With heightened anxiety in her soul, she removed it. After unfolding it, she read it to herself; four-letter vulgarities disturbed the morning serenity. She knew someone had recently placed it there because the envelope was dry. It appeared whoever put it there, wiped away the morning dew. Looking up and down the street, most people were still dreaming of a better day. Putting the letter back in the envelope, Carla headed for the police station.

Beth was already at her desk with her laptop open. Carla walked toward her and motioned her to follow her to the interrogation room. Bernie, who was at his work-station, saw the look on Carla's face and got up and walked toward the room as well. After they were in the conference room, the slamming of the door described

Carla's explosive demeanor. Beth and Bernie knew what was next.

"That son-of-a-bitch John Dickerson…if I get the chance, I'll blow his freaking brains out this time. It's not a threat, it's a promise."

"Whoa, partner, calm down. What's going on?" She pulled out an envelope and took out the letter. Next, she pulled out a black rose and put both on the table. Carla strained to keep her composure. Bernie replied, "Yeah, you're right. This is not good."

"Damn straight, dickhead. It's not good." Picking up the letter and unfolding it, she read what John had written aloud.

"Dear Carla, I see you found her. She was a druggie. I probably did the world a favor by getting rid of her. Now you know I'm dead serious about being reunited with my wife and son, and we will play the game my way this time, or many more people will die. I will stop at nothing, and I think you know that. I will call you tomorrow with a deal and how it will go down. Game on, bitch."

Eerie silence swarmed the room, and Carla sat down as did Beth and Bernie. Carla was concerned that this was unfolding too quickly. She doubted that the FBI were anywhere close to investigating any sex-trafficking rings, leaving her no choice but to let it play out on his terms. After a lengthy discussion, there was only one choice, and that was to play defense and protect the people that he may go after.

"Bernie, go home and help Lydia pack to leave town. Have her go visit some relatives. I'll call Chris and tell him to do the same. I don't think either Laura or Walt are in jeopardy." Suddenly, her phone rang. She answered, "Sam, are you okay?"

Putting the call on speaker, Sam's voice filled the room. "Yeah, I reviewed the video and then remembered that someone I served specifically mentioned your name. I'm emailing you a still shot of the man."

"That's great, but you need to pack some belongings and get out of town. Your life may be in danger once more. Do it now, and call me once you're safe, okay?"

The call ended, and Bernie left to help his wife find a safe-haven. Once she was on her way, he would return to the police station where he, Beth, and Carla would camp out until this ordeal was finally over. Carla contacted Craig and Nicole and informed them of the change in plans and to sit tight in Lexington. Carla called Agent Slack, telling him of what was happening. She requested they join them at command central at the police station. Finally, Carla had to inform Chief Evans of their defensive game plan. After completing it, they waited for John to make his move.

Agents Slack and Carlson arrived about two hours later and brought everyone up to speed on what they had discovered. All locations were possible where Penny could be; that's if she was even alive. Command central was set up with all the equipment to record any call from John. Carla had set up her iPhone to forward all calls to the number for command central. Carla had received the still shot of the man that mentioned her name. It wasn't a great photo, but better than nothing. The man looked nothing like the John Dickerson she knew; he had disguised himself well. All law enforcement in the region received a copy of it, and put out a BOLO on John. They were ready to bring down him for good. Unfortunately, it was a waiting game and he was in control, just how he liked it.

By four o'clock in the afternoon, Bernie's wife had arrived at a relative's in Dayton, Ohio. Sam had made it to Ashville, North Carolina, while Chris stayed with Walt and Laura secured by a strong police presence. With everyone safe, Carla was relieved John wouldn't be able to harm any of them, but that's the only thing she felt good about. Well into the evening, there was not a peep from John. Pizza boxes scattered the table with empty cans of soda. Notes and documents filled the walls. John's photo took center stage in the middle of everything.

A knock on the door startled everyone. Carla opened it. Sherry asked for Beth, and she followed her back to her office. A file folder lying on the desk seized Beth's attention. Fixated on the file, Beth's moment of truth had arrived. She would learn if Penny Miracle, her childhood friend, was her twin sister or not. Sherry handed Beth two printouts, and she studied them as Sherry explained the results. All during Sherry's explanation, Beth sat still and showed no emotion of any kind. After asking Sherry a few questions, she handed the results back to her.

After Beth got up to return to the conference room, Sherry rose from her chair to walk with her. While mixed emotions were building inside Beth, she remained calm until she reached the door of the department. Sherry noticed a few tears trickling down Beth's cheeks, then a subtle smile found Beth's face. As she wiped the tears away and opened the door, Sherry grabbed Beth's hand, squeezed it, and then gave her a short, compassionate hug. Beth wiped away a few more tears and took two deep breaths to calm herself down. She returned to the conference room where everyone waited for a call from John.

Carla could easily see that Beth had shed a few tears in her meeting with Sherry. Carla wondered whether the tears were ones of joy or sadness or both. Under this situation, the conference room was not where Beth wanted to show her vulnerability. Approaching Carla, Beth took a few deep breaths, and asked, "Anything new going on?"

"Agent Slack received a call from the St. Louis regional detachment indicating the abandonment of one sex-trafficking location and removing one individual. I guess they had an informant on the inside, not sure what that was all about. What went on back there?"

Beth knew that this was not the time or place to inform Carla about what she just learned and ignored her endless questions. Beth was to the point of giving in when the phone in the conference room rang, rescuing her. Carla walked over to the phone and stared at the caller ID as it continued to ring. The caller ID read unknown. She said, "Showtime everyone, are we ready?" The tech guru gave her a thumbs-up gesture, and Carla put the call on speaker.

"This is Detective Carla McBride."

"Listen carefully, bitch. You have six hours to deliver my wife and son to me, and I mean only you, or more people will die."

Hoping to buy some time, Carla paused before replying, "John, nice to hear your voice. I need more than six hours. How about eight?"

"Let's not fool around. Six hours, or the people I'm holding hostage will die."

"Who are you holding captive? How do I know you are even holding anyone?"

The line went dead, and everyone in the room collectively held their breath. The phone rang again, and Carla immediately answered.

"Don't screw with me. Six hours, you got it?"

"Got it. Prove to me you are holding someone first."

"I'll text you a picture in about an hour."

The call ended, and the tech guru shook his head back and forth. After about an hour, Carla's iPhone chimed. Her screen lit up. A photo of an elderly couple filled the screen. A man and a woman, blindfolded, gagged, and tied up, sat on a sofa. In the text message, John wrote *six hours, or they die*.

Minutes later, the phone rang again. Carla answered and listened. "You get the picture?"

"Yes, what about Penny?"

"Her name is Delilah now. I'll text you a photo in about two hours once she has joined this party."

The line went dead. Carla glanced at the tech guru, and as before, he shook his head back-and-forth. A warm glow captured Carla's face. "Come on, guys, tell me we have something we can use."

The tech guru replied, "He's obviously using an untraceable burner phone and moving away from his current location to make the calls, sorry."

"Okay, guys, we have to put our plan into action now. Agent Slack, are we ready?"

"Ready. Here's the plan. We have two FBI agents in Lewisburg ready to extract John's wife and son. We will tell her that John escaped and discovered her location. To protect her, they must move them immediately to an undisclosed safe house until a new location is selected, and a new identity is created. If she resists, our agents on the ground will call me, and hopefully Carla can convince her. I'll make the call now."

About ten minutes later, Agent Slack's phone rang. He answered and then handed it to Carla. "Gina, listen to me. John escaped several weeks ago and had already killed one young woman. Through his vast array of contacts, he traced my boyfriend's credit card receipts back to Lewisburg. We can't take any chances. He may be on his way to find you; we need to get you to another safe house immediately. We have a helicopter ready at the airport. For your safety, don't fight me on this." A moment of silence and the call ended. She handed the phone back to Agent Slack. "She bought it. She should be in Oakmont in about two hours. Once they land, they will be held at the airport until we are ready. Now, we wait for John to call back."

The tension in the room was sticky and tense; each person showed signs of stress and nervousness. A glance at the clock indicated an hour had passed since John's last call. Another hour to go. Carla grabbed Beth and took her outside the room for some fresh air and to find out what she and Sherry discussed.

"Okay, Beth, how did it go? Is Penny your sister?"

Beth reluctantly replied, "The DNA analysis shows that…"

As the conference room door opened again, it interrupted Beth's response. Agent Slack appeared, motioning them back in the room. Beth and Carla entered to a phone ringing. After Carla noticed the caller ID, she picked up the call and listened. On the other end, John spoke. She listened intently without interrupting him. Everyone heard her say, "Okay, got it." She put the receiver down, knowing there was no use asking the tech guru about a trace. "We have to play his game. I'll receive a photo of Penny with instructions and directions where this will all go down. I will be on my own. Anything else, and three more people will die. I know none of you like how this will go down, but we have no choice. John instructed me to leave my phone here and turn it off. As of now, all calls or texts will go directly to my phone which will be silenced. Any questions?"

Agent Slack asked, "How do we know this is not a setup? How do we know that photo he sends is Penny? I don't like how this is going down."

Carla replied, "Listen, guys, once we get the photo, we'll match it to the image that Sherry has already created using the facial reconstruction program, but honestly, until a DNA analysis, we can't be certain. We have to trust John because the one thing he wants back in this entire world is his wife and son."

The silence in the room broke as Agent Slack's phone rang. He answered, listened, and ended the call. He announced that the helicopter carrying Gina and Landon Dickerson had landed at the county airport.

CHAPTER 32

A n hour had passed, and Carla wondered what took John so long to send her a photo of Penny, the instructions, and directions for the switch. A knock on the door startled everyone. The door opened, and Officer Pete Wiesmann entered. Everyone focused on him; he coughed to clear his throat and then addressed the room. "Listen, everyone; we just got word that two men matching the descriptions of Nathan Moribito and Paul Francisco were found in some thick brush just north of town. From the information I have, it was an execution-style hit."

Carla said, "Bernie, you and Officer Wiesmann investigate that crime scene and confirm that it is them. That way, I'll know I'll only be dealing with John and not any of his pawns. Make it quick. I don't want to stall him when his text comes."

After they left, everyone waited for the text from John. Carla noticed the clock in the conference room and realized that it had been well over an hour since John last called. Thoughts of concern were running rampant through her mind. They were close to solving the disappearance of Penny and, hopefully, in the process, taking John down for good. In her mind, he had destroyed so many lives that she would get pleasure from putting a bullet in his brain. Another glance at the clock, ninety minutes had passed, the tension and stress were unbearable.

The ringing of Carla's phone broke the muffled silence in the room. She answered, "Bernie, is it Nathan Moribito and Paul Francisco?" Pausing for a moment, she then responded, "Okay, that's what they get for doing business with John Dickerson."

The call ended. She announced to everyone that it was them, and she would be dealing with only John as far as she knew. Everyone continued to wait and pass the time with some informal chatting. Carla walked outside the conference room for a moment to send a text to Bernie. As she returned, her phone screen lit up. False alarm, it was Bernie's reply.

With patience wearing thin, more time ticked away, increasing the tension in the room. It had been almost two hours since John made the last call, and everyone was on pins and needles. Casual chatter was drowning out the silence smothering the room. Carla asked Beth to step outside the room again to question her about the DNA testing. Once outside the room, Carla asked, "Okay, Beth, what were you going to say earlier?" Beth was trying to avoid answering the question but knew Carla would hound her until she got her way. She hoped that Carla's phone would beep any minute. "Beth, just tell me. Is Penny your sister?"

Beth giving in, began to speak, "Carla, the DNA analysis indicated…"

The beep on Carla's phone saved Beth again. The screen lit up, and the photo of Penny loaded. The instructions and directions followed. They both re-entered the conference room.

"Okay, folks. It's showtime. I'm printing the picture John sent now; we'll make a quick comparison before I leave."

Walking to the printer, Carla picked the picture up along with her instructions and directions to John's location. She took the image back to the table and placed it beside the one created by the facial reconstruction software. Everyone carefully studied the two pictures.

Looking at Beth, Carla asked, "Could this be Penny?"

Studying the image, Beth wiped away tears in her eyes. In a slightly broken voice, she replied, "Yeah, it could be. You can never forget someone's eyes."

Carla responded, "Agent Carlson, your thoughts?"

"Other than the hair, it looks like it could be her."

"I concur, but to be certain, we'll perform DNA analysis before making any announcements. Until then, everything is under wraps, understand?" Carla glanced at everyone, and nods met her gaze. "Great, it's time. As John instructed, I'll turn off my phone now. Wish me luck."

Carla left the police station on her way to the county airport, where she will team up with the FBI agents guarding Gina and Landon. From then, she would travel to where John is holding Penny and the couple in the photo John sent. Carla had specific instructions to follow when approaching the house.

The airport was a twenty-minute ride under normal circumstances; however, this situation was not normal, and she arrived there under fifteen minutes and pulled up to the idle helicopter. After waiting in her car for a few minutes, another car pulled up beside her and lowered the window. She smiled at the individual and said, "What took you so long, dickhead?" Bernie flashed her the bird, and that's all she needed to know before it was game time as John called it.

Carla and Bernie flashed their badges and introduced themselves to the two FBI agents guarding the helicopter. After some casual chit-chat, the agents left. The pilot helped Gina and Landon out of the chopper. After greeting them, she introduced them to Bernie. For a few moments, they just stared at each other, and Carla could see a deep concern painted on Gina's face. On the other hand, Landon was grinning ear-to-ear. Realizing that look, Bernie said, "So, Landon, flying in that bird was pretty cool, right?"

"Yeah, man, that was rad, super cool, right, mom?"

"Yeah, Landon."

"Bernie, why don't you show Landon around the airport while I talk to his mother?"

"Sure. Landon, come with me. See that jet over there? Let's walk toward it, okay?"

"Yeah, this is so, so cool."

Carla informed Gina they would travel to a safe house soon. She and Bernie would stay with them until US Marshals took them to a new location tomorrow. All the time Carla was explaining all of this, concern and disbelief painted Gina's face. Carla hoped and prayed this would all turn out well for everyone except John.

However, she knew that she had never been in this situation before, and there were so many things that could go wrong. Bernie returned with Landon, who ran to his mother, talking a mile a minute about what he had seen. Meanwhile, a few feet away from them, Carla and Bernie confirmed their game plan.

They joined Gina and Landon and walked away from the helicopter. Within a few minutes, the blades rotated, and they watched the chopper disappear into the night sky. With Gina riding shotgun, Bernie and Landon sat in the back. The engine growled, and they left the airport hoping for the best.

CHAPTER 33

Twenty minutes away, Detective Carla McBride versus psychotic John Dickerson would play out, and hopefully, closure would come for the Penny Miracle saga. Reverent silence gripped the inside of the car as Carla questioned her game plan over and over. It was risky and dangerous, and she hoped God would answer her prayers.

By the time they arrived, the night sky would give way to a transparent backdrop with twinkling stars and a bright crescent moon. A peaceful summer night, usually meant to be enjoyed, was different for them. Tonight, lives were at stake, making this tranquil setting into a darkened quagmire. Inside the car, hearts pounded furiously for various reasons.

According to the navigation screen, the address was just five-hundred feet ahead. Approaching it, Carla slowly pulled off the road. As beams of light faded away, darkness surrounded the car. As the car idled softly, Carla turned to Bernie. Raw fear met his eyes for the first time since becoming partners, sending his pulse higher.

"Umm, I'll see you inside in about five minutes. We all good, partner?"

"Yeah. When it's safe to proceed, I'll signal you like always. We okay on this?"

Carla swallowed hard and nodded. After a thumbs-up gesture, he exited the car disappearing into the shadows of an uncertain outcome. Five minutes seemed like ten, but a brief flash from Bernie's phone meant it was time to wear her game face and sell her risky plan to Gina. Turning toward her, "Bernie just signaled me, we are safe to proceed. A US Marshal is already in the house, so don't be alarmed if we don't see one outside when we reach the house, okay?" Gina reluctantly nodded. "As an extra precaution, I will stop along the driveway and flash my lights, letting them know it is us. When we get to the house, he will come out and greet us, okay?"

Gina nodded once more, and beams of light illuminated the driveway entrance fifty-yards ahead. The car crept forward and turned right onto a gravel driveway. Straight ahead, a dark vehicle, parked in front of the dimly lit house, sent Carla's pulse racing. This showdown just got real. In John's email, he had instructed her to stop at the first tree on the left side of the driveway and flash her lights three times very quickly. She was to travel to the next tree on the left, about thirty yards from the last one. Reaching it, following John's instructions, she was to flash her lights three times, pausing five seconds in between each flash. Once completed, she was to park on the right side of the car, quickly flashing her lights twice, then killing them.

Finally reaching the house, she parked beside the dark sedan with tinted windows, flashed her lights twice, and the engine grew silent. A glance at the dark vehicle, it appeared empty as far as she could tell. According to Craig Bjornson, Jared Lester, aka Corey Hawthorne, left the Lexington Police Station in a black sedan with tinted windows. She surmised that John took it after he killed Hawk and Paul. Time seemed to stand still, and Carla's moment of truth was upon her. She had no idea what she would find inside the house, that's if she even made it inside. Her instructions were to remain in the car until he appeared on the porch, then she was to exit the vehicle.

A soft light emanated from somewhere inside the white-frame house, muted shades of pitch-black blanketed the outside, and that's what she wanted. Gina recognizing John right away would be disastrous. Up to this point, Carla convinced her she was going to a safe house, and not a lion's den where her ex-husband held three people hostage. Thus far, Carla felt good about her plan, but now that the moment of truth would soon open the door, a different type of anxiety never experienced before punished her soul. However, it was too late to worry about it. Once inside, she hoped her instincts would take over, and her anxiety would crash and burn.

Suddenly the door opened, and a man stepped out on the porch. Unable to see his face clearly, she assumed it was John. As instructed, she exited the car remaining behind the driver's door for safety. With her service weapon tucked in her waist, it was ready if needed. Seeing John standing there, shooting him crossed her mind, but that wouldn't be prudent. The last thing she wanted was to endanger the lives of everyone. There was no choice but to play this out his way, regardless of the outcome. Closing the car door, she hoped Gina would not be able to hear their conversation.

After a brief exchange, John turned around and re-entered the house. Walking around to the passenger side, Carla opened the door, and Gina got out. Opening the rear passenger door, Landon got out and grabbed his mother's waist. "Okay, Gina, we're going to go inside now. The US Marshal said everything was safe. I want you to hold Landon's hand while you open the door and enter. I will follow you in, okay? Listen carefully. Everything will be okay, got it?"

Gina just nodded as her heartstrings welled up into her throat, and swallowing hard, her heart began to pound furiously. After a few steps on the small porch, the door was in front of them. She turned the doorknob and opened the door. While remaining behind them, Gina's body shielded Carla's gun in her right hand. Carla thought she'd never use anyone for a human shield; however, this situation gave her no choice. Although she knew John would never harm them, it didn't make her feel any better about it.

Entering the room, John stood tall with his back toward them, Carla's pulse was now into overdrive. He turned around facing them, a gun in his right hand stopped Gina in her tracks. Immediately recognizing her ex-husband, Gina said, "Detective McBride, what is going on? How could you do this to me? I told you before that I never wanted to see him ever again."

John, in a caring tone, said, "Honey, please don't feel that way. I've been waiting a long time for us to be together again, to be a family, to watch my son grow up. Everything I've done has been for you...you have to believe that, Gina."

Landon, oblivious to what was happening, blurted out, "Is that you, daddy?"

"Yeah, son. Come over and give me a big hug."

While holding on to Landon's hand tightly, Gina responded, "No, Landon. Your dad is not a nice man, he's sick."

Scanning the room, Carla didn't see anyone. Angry butterflies fluttered, sending nauseating bile upward, and she felt her heart jumping out of her chest.

"John, where are they?"

Gina said, "What is she talking about, John? What's the gun for, and what have you done, you monster?"

"Oh, honey, it's nothing to worry about. Carla, they're safe for now in the room to the right. I know you have your service weapon drawn. Put it on the floor, and slide it over to me."

With no choice but to do as he told her, she met his demands. While squatting down, his eyes remained on Carla. After retrieving it, he stood up, and tucked it in the rear of his pants. This situation was not playing out as Carla planned, and she hoped that Bernie had found a way into the house, or the end was near for her and the hostages. Erratically waving his gun, John motioned them into the other room.

As soon as Carla entered the room, a temporary sigh of relief gave her hope. Everyone was still alive. Sitting side by side, bound, gagged, and blindfolded, they resembled people ready to face a firing squad. Seeing this, she felt better about her chances, although the odds of surviving weren't in her favor just yet.

While flabbergasted at the people on the sofa, Gina lashed out at John. "What is going on here? You going to kill everyone, you sick bastard?"

Amazed by Gina's demeanor, Carla let her instincts take over. "Yeah, John, are you going to kill these innocent people? Talking about innocent people, I can't believe you were responsible for abducting Penny when she was only twelve-years-old for sex-trafficking. Yeah, tell your wife and son all about that, why don't you?"

Waving his gun erratically at her, he shouted, "Shut up, bitch."

Even more furious, Gina's barrage continued, "You're disgusting, you know. Put that gun away."

"Yeah, John, put that gun away before you hurt yourself. And what about the other three girls we know about, twelve-year-old girls for sex-trafficking. Abbie, Melody, and Natalie. Remember them?"

"I told you to shut up."

Pressing on, Carla went for his trigger button. "Yeah, John, do you want your son to see you kill all of us and have that emblazoned in his mind forever?"

Continuing to wave the gun at Carla, his anger reached the point of no return. Walking over to Carla, he pressed the barrel of the gun against her forehead, and she winced. "You should know how this feels. Remember you did this to me the last time we met. Do you feel its coldness, its deadly power? You didn't have the guts to pull the trigger when you had the chance, but not me. Remember, I was trained to kill. I said I would get you in the end, and that time has now come. Goodbye, Detective McBride."

Seeing this would not end well. Gina sent Landon to the other room. She didn't want him to witness whatever was going to happen. Fixated on Carla, John was oblivious to Gina as she moved slowly towards him. Hiding in the darkness of the hallway leading to the room where Landon stood, Bernie crept slowly toward the room. Unfortunately, Landon saw him. Putting his finger to his lips, Bernie hoped that Landon would remain quiet. As

Bernie crept softly toward him, Landon looked at Bernie, then back at his daddy. An air of uncertainty filled Landon's eyes. He screamed, "Daddy, daddy!"

Keeping the gun pressed to Carla's forehead as his trigger finger twitched, he said. "What, son, what is it?"

"Daddy, daddy, there is a man…"

With John momentarily distracted, Gina lunged at him, knocking his arm upward. A shot rang out, grazing Carla's scalp. After touching her scalp, her eyes met a crimson smear on her fingers. Gina grabbed onto his wrist as they wrestled for control of the gun. Another shot rang out. Instinctively, John grabbed for his right buttocks, where Bernie's bullet entered.

While Gina continued to wrestle the gun away from John, another errant shot rang out. Bernie noticed a firearm protruding from John's waist. Like a defensive end rushing the quarterback from his blind side, an explosive driving blow sent John and Gina to the floor, dislodging the gun from his hand. On top of John, Bernie yanked Carla's weapon from John's backside tossing it aside.

Meanwhile, Carla grabbed her gun from the floor, immediately taking aim at John. Immobilized by Bernie's weight, John winced from the wound on his backside. With his knee digging into John's back, Bernie grabbed the right arm, then the left arm, cuffing him. Pulling John up, Carla helped Gina up from the floor. Glaring into Carla's eyes, John felt her uncontrollable, revengeful anger as his head snapped violently backward, and he fell to the floor.

As soon as Bernie entered the house before all this melee took place, he called for back-up, EMS, forensics, and the coroner, not knowing how this would play out. In the distance, sirens blared louder and louder as they approached the driveway to the house. With Bernie freeing the couple on the sofa, Carla did the same for Penny, if indeed, she was Penny. Within minutes, the sirens stopped, as multi-colored flashing lights lit up the pristine summer sky.

Multiple footsteps approached the house; Beth was the first one through the door, immediately locking eyes with Penny or whoever she was. Approaching her, she called out her name. The frazzled and torn young woman stared deep into Beth's soul and showed no emotion. Beth called out her name again. A whimpered response met her ears, "Delilah, my name is Delilah."

Glistening eyes on eyes, Beth knew in her soul, it was Penny. She remembered those eyes as though it was the night before she disappeared. "Penny, I'm Zoe, remember me?"

Those unforgettable eyes remained stoic and silent until a fifteen-year-old tattered photo of them filled Penny's soul. Gently taking it, she turned it over, reading the message written on the back. Fifteen years of separation and loneliness exploded in their souls. Tears of endearment flowed down their cheeks. Beth whispered, "I promised I would find you, and you're safe now." As she continued to console Penny, a flashback appeared in Beth's repressed memory; their last embrace the night before that fateful day fifteen years ago. Penny hung on tight as her sobbing turned into soft whimpering.

Bernie joined Carla outside, where she had calmed down Gina and Landon for the moment. They were sitting in the back seat of her car, where Landon had cried himself to sleep while Gina held him tight. Gina realized she was stronger than she could have ever imagined. For them, the ordeal was over for now. While Carla arranged their transport to an official safe house, EMS brought John out on a stretcher.

Emotions were controlling her thoughts, and she walked over to John. Staring deep into his eyes, she fired an imaginary bullet into his brain. After walking over to Bernie, her emotions finally came crashing down. Throwing her arms around him, she sobbed tears of relief and happiness. Releasing her embrace, she gazed deep into his glistening eyes.

"Thank you, why didn't you just kill him, dickhead? It would have been justifiable, you know?"

"Yeah, I thought about that, but that would have been too easy on him. He destroyed so many lives and deserved to rot in prison with all that blood on his hands. Plus, the realization of never seeing his wife and son ever again, well, that's the living hell he will have to endure the rest of his life."

"Umm, I guess so, you know, I'm so thankful Chief Evans made us partners, how about you?"

Grinning ear-to-ear, he nodded as his arms swallowed up her exploding emotions, soaking his big broad shoulders with tears of redemption.

CHAPTER 34

Beth was sure that the young woman she showed the picture to was indeed Penny Miracle; however, the only thing that could prove it was a DNA test. Given the emotions running rampant inside each of them, that could wait until tomorrow. EMS transported Penny, accompanied by Beth, to the regional center for women's domestic violence in Oakmont. Although Beth was a psychologist, treating her would be too personal, and an on-site psychologist would coordinate the recovery process.

Arriving late at night, the center processed Penny and assigned a room. Even though Beth spent the night with her, Penny resembled someone in a catatonic state of mind. Beth wanted to show her that she was safe. Eventually, Penny crashed from exhaustion. At four in the morning, Penny screamed, startling Beth. She immediately approached the bed and sat on the side, hugging Penny, reassuring her everything was going to be fine. However, it didn't help much as she kept mumbling,

"Please don't hurt me, don't hurt me, please, don't hurt my parents."

Morning finally broke as slivers of sunlight sneaked through the partially closed window blinds. It had been a rough night. Beth knew there would be many more to come before Penny would fully recover if that were possible. The smell of fresh coffee permeated throughout the facility. Although Beth wasn't sure if Penny liked coffee, she fixed two coffees, cream and sugar, just in case. After returning to the room, Beth noticed Penny was sitting up in the bed with her knees drawn close to her chest. Even though Penny still looked tired and frazzled, a genuine smile met Beth's beaming face.

"I assume you like coffee by that smile. Cream and sugar, I assume?" Penny nodded. She added sugar and creamer, stirred it, and handed it to her. She took a sip and set it on the nightstand. While smiling at Beth, joyous tears crowded her eyes. "It's going to be okay, Penny. It's just going to take time to adjust and catch up on the life stolen from you."

Penny nodded and picked up her coffee and smelled the aroma. Out of the blue, she said, "Thank you for not giving up; thank you for finding me like you promised you would."

"How did you know that?"

"Doesn't matter, umm, thank you."

"You're welcome. Now drink your coffee and get your rest. Later this morning, a medical doctor will examine you, and then in the afternoon, a psychologist will be in to talk with you about your recovery process, okay?" Penny nodded and put the cup of coffee to her lips and savored it for a few seconds. "The center has provided you some undergarments and a lounging suit. Why don't you take a hot shower and get cleaned up before the doctor arrives? You appear to be in great shape; however, it's normal operating procedure that you be examined by a medical doctor as long as you remain here. Same goes with the psychologist."

Penny nodded and finished her coffee. Getting out of bed, she stood up. Being a little shaky, she started to fall. Beth grabbed onto her arm, pulling her close to her body, hugging her.

Penny smiled, and said, "Thanks." She walked gingerly to the bathroom and closed the door. Beth sat in the lounge chair, and her emotions got the best of her. The toll of the last several days was surfacing; Beth was glad that Penny was in the shower and couldn't witness her emotions erupting. Beth knew she had to be very strong for Penny and couldn't imagine what she had been through the past fifteen years; what thoughts she had about her parents. About ten minutes later, the door opened, and Penny came out refreshed and smiling. However, her outward appearance was just a masquerade; inside, she was still a broken soul with nightmares and fears to conquer. She walked over to Beth hugging her as tears dotted her cheeks.

A little startled, Beth said, "What was that for?"

"It's been fifteen years since we shared a hug like that. I miss that, I miss you."

Tears began streaming down Beth's cheeks. She wiped them away and returned the hug and said, "Hmm, I missed that, too."

A woman dressed in a white lab coat appeared in the doorway and gently knocked on the door. Beth turned in that direction and walked toward her extending her hand, "Hi, I'm Beth Pendergast with the Oakmont

Police Department. I was Penny's best friend growing up."

"Nice to meet you. I'm Dr. Jill Shriver. I assume this is Penny Miracle."

Beth nodded as Dr. Shriver approached the bed. Holding Penny's hand, Beth introduced her to Penny, assuring her that Dr. Shriver would take good care of her. Penny nodded and stood up to greet her, extending her hand. Dr. Shriver took Penny's hand in hers and gave it a gentle squeeze. "Nice to meet you, Penny. You may sit back on the bed while I check your vitals and, as Beth explained, take a DNA swab. After I leave, an on-site nurse will be in to draw a blood sample, and that should do it for now. Are you okay with all of this?"

Penny nodded, and the examination began. During it, Penny remained extremely quiet, which was understandable given the last twenty-four hours. Dr. Shriver explained she would check with her tomorrow to see if she needed anything. A few minutes later, a nurse arrived to draw a blood sample. As the nurse left, an eerie quietness filled the room. Although the temperature in the room was a balmy seventy-two degrees, Penny pulled the covers up over her to keep warm. Noticing Penny's actions, Beth inquired if there was anything she could get her. Penny shook her head back-and-forth and smiled at her. "Okay, lunch should be ready. I'll go pick it up and bring it back here. Normally, everyone eats in the small cafeteria, but we will have a private lunch here, okay? You remember when we picnicked under the big tree in your backyard." She nodded and smiled, tears of joy surfaced in her eyes once more.

Beth left and returned with a tray containing two sandwiches, chips, and iced tea. After a quiet lunch, Beth explained that the staff psychologist would arrive soon, and she would have to leave. Again, Penny wasn't much for words other than acknowledging her and cracking a smile. Heather McAdams, the staff psychologist, arrived at two o'clock as planned. After introductions, Beth left as Heather began talking with Penny.

Beth wanted to be back at the center by four o'clock and stopped by her apartment to check on Aliyah and freshen up. After that, she stopped by the police station to speak with Carla about finding Penny's parents. Beth returned to the center just as the psychologist was leaving. Heather provided her with an update on Penny's mental state; that Penny's prognosis was favorable for a full recovery.

It didn't take Carla long to track down Penny's parents. As it turned out, they were living in Altmont. Sandy Miracle had landed a part-time job with the local newspaper as a feature writer. Through the many options available on the internet to find out personal information, she secured her address. Jack and Sandy Miracle lived in the county just outside the city limits.

CHAPTER 35

A week later, Dr. Shriver met with Beth to reveal the results of Penny's DNA analysis. As Beth surmised, she confirmed the previous DNA analysis matched the DNA swab she performed on Penny. A sigh of relief filled Beth's soul. Penny's parents would finally find out the truth of their daughter's disappearance and have closure.

Beth felt it would be safe for her and Carla to make the two-hour drive to visit Penny's parents in a few days and tell them Penny was alive and, for the most part, doing well considering the circumstances of the past fifteen years. Beth felt it best not to call them about finding Penny. She knew it would not be easy to deliver what should be great news because no one knows how it will be received. Until Penny's parents agreed to DNA testing, they couldn't be sure that Penny was their biological daughter.

Beth wasn't sure how she could even bring it up, inform Jack and Sandy that their daughter was alive. Over the past several days, Penny had inquired on her own about her parents. Beth showed her the picture of her and Penny with their mothers. However, because of all the mental trauma she had been through, Beth felt it was not registering with her. She hoped that when her mom visited her, the past would click in for her.

After calling the newspaper in Altmont, Beth found out that Sandy Miracle was off today, and hoped she would be home when they arrived. The staff psychologist, Heather McAdams, was making significant progress with Penny. Beth had spent much time with Penny and agreed that every day was getting better for her. Heather had gained Penny's trust, and that was so important in continuing her progress.

Beth and Carla had planned to arrive at Jack and Sandy Miracle's house around eleven o'clock. In the first part of the drive, personal chit-chat dominated their conversation along with periods of silence. They had been through a lot and didn't want to relive it. With their conversation over, Carla turned the radio on. Tim McGraw's *Live Like You Were Dying* blared from the speaker. She smiled and joined in.

Once the lyrics faded away, Carla muted the volume and said, "So, we definitely know that Penny is Penny. You've been avoiding telling me whether you and Penny are sisters. It's time to fess up." Beth knew she couldn't keep it from her because Carla was relentless, just like her mother. Carla interjected, "Don't hold out on me any longer. Once you get it off your chest, you will feel better, so what is it?"

With disappointment in her voice, she sighed and replied, "She's not my sister. We're not even related, period. Even though we had the same birthdate, she is one year older than me. End of story, okay?"

"Whoa. I'm sorry because I know you hoped that she was your twin sister."

"Don't be sorry. I'm disappointed, but it's not the end of the world. We found Penny, and she is safe and alive. That's all that is important. She was always like a sister to me, and that will never change. Hopefully, in the future, we can have that sisterly relationship we both had growing up."

"So, what's next? You still going to continue searching?"

"Yeah, this was just a minor bump in the road."

"What about Nicole? You even mentioned it to me?"

"I believe when the time is right or when I don't expect it, I will find my sister, or maybe she will find me. I believe it's our fate, and we will be together if it's meant to be. I believe God will help us find each other."

"Uh, do you have a dedicated line to the man above?"

"I pray to him a lot, and one day he will answer my special prayer, just you wait and see."

Silence encompassed the car for the rest of the drive. Carla slowed the vehicle down, coming to a full stop in front of a modest ranch-style home. A white sedan was in the driveway, and they could see into the house through a full-length storm door. It appeared they were in luck, and Sandy Miracle was likely home, or it could be Jack or maybe both. The best-case scenario was that both were home. Carla pulled into the driveway behind a Nissan Altima. She shut off the car and turned to Beth, "It's showtime partner, you ready?"

"Partner, I like the sound of that, yeah, I'm ready as I'll ever be. Let's do it."

After exiting the car, they walked up to the front door and rang the doorbell. They could hear it bounce off the walls inside the house. Patience was something neither one of them had a lot of these days. Just as Beth was going to push the doorbell again, her second mom as a child approached the door. Both recognized her immediately, and other than fifteen years taking its toll on her, Sandy Miracle was as she remembered her. Sandy pushed open the door and addressed them. Pulse racing like a roaring locomotive, Beth took a deep breath and replied, "Mrs. Miracle?"

"Yes, how may I help you?" By then, Jack appeared.

Beth got what she was hoping for and asked, "Do you all remember me, remember her?"

A dumbfounded expression-filled their faces. Beth, her heart racing and respiration fast and furious, said, "I'm Zoe Pendergast, and my partner is Detective Carla McBride of the Oakmont Police Department. Here are our ID badges. We have news about Penny. May we come in?"

Shock and disbelief gave way to tears as Sandy and Jack embraced each other. Sobbing uncontrollably, they comforted each other, not knowing what they would hear. In many ways, whatever the news was, it was going to give them closure. Sandy opened the door and let them in, motioning them to sit on a worn sofa. Before sitting down, Beth shared a hug with them. Jack and Sandy sat across from them, anxiously waiting for closure.

Beth thought she had prepared for this moment; however, although the words were happy ones, they were still difficult to say. After taking a deep breath, she said, "We've found Penny, and she is alive. I know after all of these years that's hard to believe, but we confirmed it through DNA. Your daughter is alive and recovering at a facility in Oakmont. I can't go into detail about how this all came about or when you will be able to see her. She has a long road ahead of her, but in my heart, I believe she will fully recover with your love and support."

Overcome with emotions, Jack and Sandy sat crying in each other's arms. After they were composed, Beth explained that they needed a DNA sample from each of them, standard procedures she told them. After things had calmed down and many questions answered to the best of their ability, they left with two DNA swabs.

Before heading back to Oakmont, Beth needed to make one more stop. She was hoping to see Pastor Terry Clark, who arranged her adoption. In the papers that her mom left her, she found his name and knew that if anyone knew where her sister was, he would know. According to the Boyd County Fellowship Baptist Church website, he lived in the rectory beside the church.

After getting lost on a county road, they finally found the quaint little church. The rectory, a red brick house showing its age, was beside the church as the website indicated. A Kentucky Blue Honda Civic sat in the driveway. Exiting the car, they walked up the steps leading to a massive wooden door. Beth rang the doorbell. A minute or so had passed, and she rang it again but never heard footsteps. The door had an old brass door-knocker, using it, she hoped it would work, and someone would answer the door. Several doses of that classic dull metal thud clanged out. About ready to give up and walk down the concrete steps, a young girl, about sixteen years old, answered the door carrying a young child.

Through the screened door, she asked, "May I help you?"

"I'm Beth Pendergast. Is Pastor Terry Clark at home?"

"No, ma'am, he is not. I'm just the babysitter."

"When do you expect him home?"

"Ma'am, I don't know. He's very sick and in the hospital. May I give his wife a message from you?"

"Yes, have him call me. Sorry to intrude on you. I will keep him in my prayers." Before handing the babysitter her business card, she turned it over and wrote something on the back. Taking the business card, the babysitter looked it over front and back, then closed the door.

Beth and Carla walked down the concrete steps showing disappointment. After entering the car, Carla started it and headed back to Oakmont. Beth broke the silence raining down on them as Carla took the entrance ramp onto the interstate. "Oh, well, I was hoping for some better news there, but maybe someone will eventually call me back."

"So, what now?"

"All I know is that God will eventually answer my prayers; he has no choice in this matter."

The rest of the drive was solemn. Jack and Sandy got the good news they had been waiting for fifteen years to hear. Beth, unfortunately, struck out with Pastor Terry Clark, who held the key to finding her twin sister and biological mother.

CHAPTER 36

Several weeks had passed since Beth had received the news that Jack and Sandy Miracle's DNA analysis confirmed what she already knew. Penny was Penny, and she was their biological daughter. Beth's mom got that all wrong, and Beth let her know when she spoke to her ashes from time to time. Penny had made enough progress to warrant a visit from her parents. After the first visit, the psychologist recommended by-weekly appointments.

Beth and Nicole had become terrific friends; they were more like sisters than good friends and colleagues. Unbeknownst to Beth, Nicole had a DNA analysis performed after that one night they were together talking about finding their biological mother. Recently after a bottle of Pinot Grigio, Nicole confessed to her. They compared reports and laughed about it. They weren't sisters or even remotely related, but they didn't care because, in their minds, their relationship had grown much more than a sisterly one. It also made her forget that she had a real sister somewhere. Initially disappointed that neither Penny nor Nicole were her twin sister, Beth knew one day God would answer her prayers.

Beth had heard nothing from her visit to Pastor Terry Clark's home several weeks ago, and honestly, she hadn't expected a call from him. There was no time to worry about it because Chief Evans had handed her the next cold case. Feeling good about attacking it, she liked working with Carla because, in many ways, she had become her big sister, but more like a motherly figure. Beth knew Carla had her own life, but she was a person she could turn to for some motherly advice. Also, distracting her away from finding her twin sister was Agent Scott Carlson. After Beth and Scott reunited, they were together every night, and he wanted to move in with her. However, she wasn't ready because she didn't want to suffer the heartache he caused before.

Another reason she put the search for her twin sister on hiatus, she was trying to find her mother's birth mother. Given the likely age of her mother's biological mother, it was more important to find her. According to her mother's letter, she had already did some research and at least knew the birth mother's name or at least what she went by, and that was Lilly. That wasn't much to go on, but at least it was something. She had the adoption papers, but knew, getting information from the adoption agency was next to impossible. Making several calls and leaving messages, none were returned. She had even sent letters hoping she would get a response, but that never happened as well. Remembering what Charlene Anderson said to her and Carla after they intruded on them several weeks ago, maybe it was better to leave well enough alone, she thought.

When Chief Evans assigned Beth Penny's case, her

confidence in solving it wasn't high. Since her hunch that Jackson Walker turned out to break the case wide open, her spirit was sky-high. She was eager and excited to begin her next case. Beth knew it involved the murder of a seventeen-year-old girl named Angel Hardesty, whose mutilated body was discovered in a ditch by the road leading to the local cemetery. At first, she wasn't sure about this particular case, but helping to find justice for a human that had her life stolen from them was enough to give it all she could.

A meeting with Carla, Chief Evans, and other individuals that worked on the case over the past thirteen years was to begin at eleven o'clock. Glancing at the big-round-clock on the wall, it read 10:30 AM. With thirty minutes to go, anxiousness filled Beth's soul. Glancing at Carla, she could see that she was engrossed in something. "Hey, you ready for the meeting?"

"Of course, are you?"

"You bet, always ready." Carla rolled her eyes and got up from her chair to walk away. "Where are you going?"

"Get my mail."

"Well, get mine, if I have any, which I probably won't."

A few minutes later, Carla returned and sat down in her chair. Beth noticed she had several pieces of mail, but probably none for her. Since beginning her job, her mailbox never received a single piece of mail, not even junk. In some ways, she felt disappointed because not receiving any mail gave her the feeling that nobody cared. She glanced at Carla, and jokingly said, "Do you have a letter for me from my secret admirer?"

Carla rolled her eyes and, in a flick of a moment,

tossed an envelope toward her landing face up. Beth's eyes flew open as she stared at her first piece of mail. The white number-ten envelope glared back at her. Immediately, she noticed it didn't have a return address on it. She turned it over. There wasn't any return address on the back either, and with the flap sealed with tape, she needed a letter opener. After borrowing Carla's letter opener, Beth slid it under the flap, being very careful not to damage whatever was inside. She pulled out a one-page letter. Reading it carefully, she didn't hear Carla speaking to her. "Hey, it's time for our meeting, whatever you are so engrossed in will have to wait, gather your stuff and high-tail it to the conference room, okay?" Beth nodded and gently put the one-page letter back in the envelope and put it in her purse. She gathered her information and walked to the conference room.

After two hours of intense discussion, they adjourned for lunch. During the entire meeting, Carla noticed Beth was preoccupied. Walking out of the conference room, Carla said, "Lunch at McGruder's?"

In a very monotone voice, she responded, "Yeah, sure."

Carla recognized that Beth was disturbed by something, maybe the piece of mail she had received, and inquired, "Is everything okay? You were very quiet in the meeting, and you look visibly disturbed. Did you get some bad news in that piece of mail?"

"Umm, a friend of mine died unexpectedly, I'll be okay."

"I'm sorry to hear that."

"Thanks."

All during lunch, Beth did her best to be friendly; however, the disturbing news in the letter took center stage in her mind. They returned to the police station and reconvened their meeting. Again, Beth seemed distant and uninterested about anything. After the meeting was over, she returned to her desk and opened her laptop. Keying in Pastor Terry Clark, she waited for the most recent information to load. Beth's disposition turned even sourer as his obituary glared at her. Carla continued staring at her knowing whatever was in the letter had put her into a sour mood.

"Beth, snap out of it, I don't mean to pry, but whatever is in that letter has profoundly affected you. Talk to me. I can help you get through this."

"Let's get out of here and get a drink somewhere. Whisman's should be very quiet this time of the day."

"Hmm, it's early, but if that will bring you out of this funk, I'm all for it. I'll drive because you are clearly in no frame of mind."

Beth nodded and grabbed her purse. It was a very silent ride to Whisman's. Carla didn't dare press her any further about the contents of the letter. If Beth wanted her to know, she would tell her. As predicted, Whisman's was empty. Gabe wasn't there; even Rufus was not sitting at the bar as usual. They sat in a booth near the front of the building. Within minutes, a young lady came and took their drink order—a double shot of Jameson on the rocks for both. After the barmaid delivered their drinks, they informed her they didn't want to be bothered, and she walked away.

Beth raised her glassed, motioning Carla to do the same. It was a customary cheer; both took a drink and put down their glass. The silence in the empty bar was intense; the only sound came from a neon sign in the window that read "Open." Carla was just about ready to give Beth some tough love when she pulled the envelope out of her purse. Taking the letter out, she read it silently and handed it to Carla. After reading it quietly, she gave it back to Beth. Tears trickled down Carla's cheeks but quickly wiped them away. Beth was fighting back the tears as well.

"Beth, this is good news. What are you going to do?"

"I don't know. I thought I could handle it, but I'm just not sure now. Before we left, I Googled Pastor Terry Clark, and his obituary popped up. I guess the name of my twin sister and biological mother went with him to his grave."

Beth wiped away her tears and downed her drink. She raised it toward the bar capturing the attention of the barmaid. Within minutes, the second round of drinks arrived. Beth raised her glass, and Carla did the same, clinking their glasses together one more time. An eerie silence took over the booth; the annoying neon light buzzing in the window seemed louder than ever.

CHAPTER 37

Through the window blinds, slivers of sunlight warmed Beth's face as she cherished the remnants of the best sleep she'd had in a long time. While lying in bed, she recalled the past several weeks of her emotional roller coaster journey. Keeping her promise to Penny made her smile as she was recovering remarkably well. John Dickerson was finally apprehended and would spend the rest of his life in maximum security or, better yet, solitary confinement. "Yes," she whispered aloud as her right arm flew into a victory pump.

Carla had become her surrogate mother, while Bernie did his best as a father figure. Beth was thrilled to have both of them watching out for her. Scott re-entered her life, giving her hope that a long-term commitment was in the near future. Life was good. However, finding her twin sister and biological mother would replace the emptiness burning in her soul.

While standing in front of the bathroom mirror, her

reflection looked happy, the happiest it had been in a long time. The ghosts of her past had vanished, and sanity replaced the voices in her head. A renewed confidence replaced her self-doubt.

After showering and dressing for work, a quick cup of coffee and yogurt warmed her soul. A meow startled her; Aliyah rubbed her leg affectionately. Reaching down to pet her, she purred, nuzzling her hand. Placing her favorite cat treats on the floor, she attacked them with a vengeance. "Hey, hey, slow down, you are about out of these treats. I'll stop at the store before work and buy you a new stash, okay?" Looking up at Beth with a myste- rious wink and winkling of the nose, Aliyah sauntered off to her favorite place.

While visiting the grocery store to pick up the cat treats, Beth noticed someone she hadn't seen in a while and approached the individual.

"Mrs. Sandy, how are you doing?"

"Fine. Beth Pendergast, right?"

"Yeah, that's right."

"Nice to see you again. You know, seeing one of my books on sale still sends chills throughout my body. I heard about you solving the Penny Miracle case. That's an amazing story that would probably make a great novel one day."

Beth nodded. "Yeah, I'm sure it would. You know, I listened to your book, *Last Breath*, and enjoyed it. I have to be honest. I didn't like the ending even though it was a big surprise."

"Well, then I accomplished what I set out to do. Thank you for taking the time to listen to it."

"You're welcome. Are you working on a new book that you can talk about?"

"Umm, yeah. It's about a lady in her forties who's dying from an inoperable brain tumor. As a young teenager, she gave birth to a baby boy, and after an agonizing decision, she put him up for adoption. She wasn't ready to be a full-time mother then. Now that she has about a year to live, she wants to find him and ease the guilt she has been living with for the past twenty-five years. We'll see how it goes."

"Umm, sounds interesting, good luck."

"Thank you. You know, my cat, Fiver loves those treats, eats them like candy. Maybe that's why he is so plump and happy all the time."

"Hmm, you know, maybe we should have coffee or tea sometime. I'll just stop by, and you can tell me more about your book, would you like that?"

"Of course, that would be nice. Here's my business card. Call me sometime. Maybe we can meet at Parsons' Coffee Emporium. I love the place."

"Yeah, me too, see you soon."

Beth entered the police station in a much better frame of mind than yesterday. Running into Ali Sandy this morning affected her in unexplainable ways as though fate had brought them together for some strange reason.

Carla was already hard at work, researching another cold case. Beth sat down at her desk, and Carla glanced at her with an affectionate motherly smile. Smiling back, Beth immediately opened the file and reviewed her new cold case. Time flew by, and Carla inquired about taking an early lunch. Beth nodded, and Carla suggested McGruder's. However, on this day, Beth preferred Apollo Café for a change. It was busy, which Beth wanted because she didn't need Carla hounding her about the personal letter she received yesterday, and what she was going to do about it.

After a quick and quiet lunch, it was back to the grind researching her new cold case. While still feeling the effects of Jameson in her soul, the day couldn't end soon enough for her. Even after a quiet and filling lunch, her energy level was still low, and she was quickly running out of gas. The big clock on the wall glared back at her with more vengeance than ever before. Practically willing it to move faster, she wanted to go home and crash to the soothing sounds of Aliyah and the tender touch of Scott. The hands of the clock appeared to stand still, reminding her of the big clock on the wall in the hospital waiting room the day her mother died. That clock was still an unrelenting hell in her mind.

Out of her peripheral vision, a young woman about her age was standing at the information desk talking to the receptionist, Darlene Morrison. Within a minute, Darlene was standing at Beth's desk.

"Beth, you have a visitor. Says she must meet with you today."

"I'm not up to any visitors right now. Tell her to make an appointment."

Darlene left, and after what seemed like a minute had passed, she returned. In an apologetic gruff, Beth asked, "Now what?" Darlene handed her a business card. Beth looked at it and turned it over, then sent a curious glance in the young woman's direction. "Tell her I'll be there in a minute."

Beth watched Darlene tell the young lady to take a seat. Beth eyed the young woman as she nervously glanced around the common area waiting for her. After smiling at Carla, Beth went to greet the young woman.

Carla watched them and wondered who the young woman was. Carla turned her head for just a brief moment, and when she returned her gaze toward them, Beth and the young woman were gone. Walking over to Darlene, Carla inquired where they went. Darlene informed her that Beth would be out the rest of the day, and not attempt to contact her.

Twenty minutes later, Beth opened the door to her apartment and motioned the young woman to sit on the sofa. Aliyah came running and greeted them as Beth's phone rang. She glanced at the screen and let the call go to voicemail. Beth rolled her eyes as Carla never followed instructions. The young woman pulled a DVD out of her purse and handed it to Beth. Taking the DVD, Beth inserted it into the video player, turned on the television, and hit the play arrow.

On the screen, a man, Beth had never met, spoke with a raspy, weakened voice. After a half-hour, the video ended. Watching this life-altering moment together, it didn't take long for twin sisters to embrace and share their tears of joy. For the next hour or so, they laughed and cried after viewing a compassionate video by Jaymie's adopted father, Pastor Terry Clark. Going to the kitchen, Beth gave Aliyah her favorite treats. Opening the refrigerator, a bottle of Pinot Grigio stood tall and ready for a celebration. She returned to the living room with the bottle of wine and two glasses.

"Hope you like Pinot Grigio, sis?"

"My favorite, but you already knew that, didn't you?"

Nodding, Beth handed Jaymie a full glass and smiled. Beth held her glass toward her sister. "Here's to us." Jaymie followed her lead and repeated it. For a while, a peaceful silence blessed them, and the destined union of two separated souls was complete. After Beth finished her wine, she gently squeezed Jaymie's hand.

"What!"

"We better cool it with the wine. Besides, I want to take you somewhere."

"Where?"

"You'll understand once we get there. It's not far from here."

Ten minutes later, Beth and Jaymie entered Parsons' Coffee Emporium. Beth led Jaymie to the back of the café to her favorite table. In the hallway, Beth showed Jaymie a picture of Alicia Williams-Parsons from her basketball playing days at Western Kentucky University. It wasn't long before Mrs. Parsons approached them.

"Beth Pendergast, right?"

"Right, Mrs. Parsons. I want you to meet my twin sister, Jaymie Saunders."

As Mrs. Parsons shook hands with Jaymie, a strange sensation moved up her arm.

"Nice to meet you, Jaymie."

Giving her a brief smile, Jaymie replied, "Likewise, Mrs. Parsons. You have a very nice place here."

"Thank you, but please call me, Ally, okay?"

Jaymie acknowledged her, and they ordered two small coffees with cream and sugar. Ally left and promptly returned with their coffees. "Remember, these are on the house, enjoy." She returned to the counter to wait on another customer that had just entered the café.

Jaymie took a sip of the steaming coffee, letting it warm her soul. "Ally is our mother, right?"

Reaching across the table, Beth gave Jaymie's hand a gentle squeeze. Smiling at her, Beth nodded. "Umm, unless your dad, uh, just made all that stuff up."

"My dad never made anything up or ever lied; he always told the truth no matter how much it would hurt."

"Well, then, sis, umm, she is our mother, and we've got a lifetime together to get to know her. Now is not the time nor place, we'll both know when it's right if you know what I mean?"

Jaymie acknowledged her, and they continued to enjoy the coffee and their long-awaited and destined reunion. After the last sip of coffee. "Sis, I want you to meet somebody else."

After finishing their coffee, they stopped by the counter to say goodbye to Ally and thank her for everything. As they left, Ally felt a strange-like-happiness invade her soul and couldn't take her eyes off them.

Ten minutes later, Beth pulled in front of 411 Washington Avenue in the west end of Oakmont. After turning off the car, Beth continued to stare at the house. As a woman in a wooden rocker moved back and forth, she enjoyed a glass of lemonade as she glared at them.

"Beth, what are we doing here? Do you know her?"

"Yeah, follow me, and I will introduce you to her." The woman noticed them approaching and stood up to greet them. "Mrs. Anderson, do you remember me, Beth Pendergast, I grew up in this house?"

"Oh yeah, I recall you were looking for something. Did you find it?"

"Yeah, and so much more. I'd like you to meet my twin sister, Jamie Saunders."

"I can see the resemblance. Would you two like a glass of lemonade and sit for a spell? I could use the company. Harold is out golfing with the guys, and who knows when he'll be home. You know, I've never quite figured out how the nineteenth hole last so long or why he even plays that silly game."

"Umm, I know nothing about that, but lemonade sounds great, thank you."

After one glass of lemonade and casual conversation, Beth returned to the police station to drop off Jaymie as she had to drive back to Boyd County, where her mom was taking care of her two-year-old son, Joshua Clark. Beth made plans to get together over the weekend to meet her nephew and Jaymie's adopted mother. After a long sisterly hug and warm tears of endearment, Jaymie left.

Beth entered the police station, where Carla was still hard at work on their new case. Walking over to one pissed-off smile, she addressed Carla. "You got an hour or two, let's go to my place. I have something you need to watch. Then, you can help me celebrate. I won't take no for an answer, so let's go."

Twenty minutes later, Beth fixed them a very generous Jameson on the rocks. In the living room, she motioned for Carla to sit on the sofa. Handing her the Jameson, Beth sat hers on the coffee table. Turning on the television, she pushed the play arrow on the video player. Pastor Terry Clark appeared and started his confession.

A half-hour later, Pastor Clark gave way to an annoying buzz and a fuzziness that filled the screen. Carla stared at the screen for a moment, then back at Beth in amazement as the annoying buzz and the speckled screen disappeared.

Finishing Jameson in one swallow, Carla took a deep breath and silently mouthed, "No way!"

With a beaming smile and a few more tears, Beth nodded, and downed the remainder of her Jameson.

"Wow! Umm…you know, this might seem extremely crazy or far-fetched, umm, but you definitely have his eyes and nose…he's your…umm…father, isn't he?"

"Yeah. Yeah…he is. Umm…another Jameson?"

EPILOGUE

Several weeks before cancer took over his mind, Pastor Terry Clark created a DVD for his daughter. He told the incredible story of how he helped a young troubled girl twenty-five years ago find peace. That girl, Alicia Williams, gave birth to a set of twin girls. She entrusted him with finding a loving home for them. She insisted they never be separated, and he tried his best to honor that request.

He knew Brian and Judy Pendergast were desperate to have a family after a miscarriage destroyed that possibility. He knew the twins would be in good hands with them and did his best to convince them to take both girls. However, as much as they wanted to, it would be a financial hardship for them, especially with a new job in a new community. After exhausting all options and talking with God, he came up with a plan. He gave in, and Brian and Judy adopted Elizabeth Annie and changed her name to Zoe Elizabeth.

Pastor Terry Clark and his wife, Patty, couldn't conceive and adopted the other girl named Jaymie Linley.

In the video, he told his daughter he made that decision because it was the best way he could honor the young mother's wish of keeping them together in his out-of-the-box way. He had talked with God many times about his dilemma; never once did God give him a signal he disapproved of his actions.

Over the years, he kept a diary of Zoe's movements. He knew exactly where she was and what she was doing. That was his way of keeping them together, and he always knew he would reunite them when the time was right. He believed it was God's will, and he kept them safe until that day arrived. He also kept tabs on the biological mother, Alicia Williams, because he knew one day, God would reunite them as well.

Originally, Alicia and her father moved for his job in the western part of the state. Beth's mom thought it was Bowling Green; however, she found the wrong Alicia Williams as did Beth. The correct Alicia Williams grew up in Glasgow, Kentucky, and was a star in basketball at Western Kentucky University. After graduating with a degree in business management, she married Larry Parsons, a lawyer in Lexington. Eventually, she found her way to Oakmont and established Parsons' Coffee Emporium, finally realizing her lifelong dream of owning a business. Because there were complications with delivering a set of twins at age seventeen, Alicia lost her ability to conceive. She and her husband discussed and considered adoption many times; however, the timing was never right because of their careers.

Beth's mom Judy, in her own written confession to her daughter, asked that she find her birthmother. After repeated attempts to get information from the adoption agency, it looked like Beth would never honor that request until she received a letter one day, her first piece of mail at work. It turned out the adoption agency was closing its doors after being in business for over fifty years.

Janice Parish, an employee with the agency for forty of those years, was upset at the agency for closing, and she would lose the job she loved so much. She was overwhelmed with emotion after reading Beth's second letter, a compassionate plea for information. Adopted herself and knowing her biological mother and the bond they had, Janice knew how much it would mean to Beth to honor her mother's wishes. Janice drafted a letter providing the details of Judy Pendergast's adoption. It was her last good deed before the agency closed.

With all that information and the internet, it wasn't long until Beth connected the dots finding her mother's birth mother. Charlene Lillian-Edwards, known as Lilly, encountered a date rape, a he said-she-said incident, in her sophomore year of high school. Embarrassment tortured her soul, and she dropped out of school to have the baby girl. After giving birth, she promptly gave it up for adoption. Janice Parish handled that adoption, her first case. Charlene went on to a successful career in accounting, finishing her career in Oakmont at one of the city's leading industries. She is living in what was once her daughter's house.

Beth never told Charlene what she knew because the time wasn't right, and understanding the circumstances behind her mother's conception, she felt it was better to leave well enough alone, her mother's advice, and Charlene's as well. Beth continued to visit Charlene regularly and share a glass of lemonade on the porch telling her all about her adopted mother, Judy. One day Beth showed

Charlene a picture of her. Charlene studied it for a long time, focusing on the eyes. Even though there were tears in her eyes, she never gave Beth any sign she knew that Beth's adopted mother was her daughter.

Carolyn Alison Sandy, aka Annie Nicole, published her latest novel, *Unforgettable Eyes*. Eventually, Beth met her for coffee at Parsons' Coffee Emporium. She gave her a signed copy of the book, and they agreed to meet again after she had read it. For some unexplained reason, something was drawing them to each other.

Before leaving the café that day, Ali dropped off a copy of her book on the counter for Ally. Later that day, she opened it—Ali's sincere message took her breath away.

Ally, it's never too late to find your daughters and forgive yourself for the years of guilt you've endured. They're closer than you think. All the best...your faithful sorority sister...Ali.

Eyes glistening, tears of guilt and forgiveness splashed on the counter. Ally remembered the night her sorority sister, Ali Sandy and she had too much to drink. On that night, Ally confessed her deepest and darkest secrets, and how much she regretted giving up her twin daughters.

ACKNOWLEDGMENTS

My wife, Bonnie, was instrumental in contributing to this novel. In the early stages of writing this story, she provided me with crucial information. It helped move the story along in the direction it should have gone in the first place. At that time, she didn't know how much she helped me in creating this story. A big thanks goes to my wife, whom I love very much.

A LOOK AT BOOK FOUR:
QUANDARY

Incumbent City Commissioner Bryan A. Walters just lost his re-election bid after seven consecutive terms in office. Now, he's missing. Not only one of the most powerful former city officials, Bryan is also CEO of Oakmont Trust and Savings—the largest bank in the community.

Hired to investigate his disappearance, Detectives Carla McBride and Bernie Kowalski start by searching his home. Shocked at the discovery they find inside, the case quickly becomes their most challenging and bizarre one yet.

Reaching an impasse in the investigation, they take a calculated risk by hiring Beth Pendergast, the police department's forensic psychologist and profiler.

Justice for all is the end goal. But will Carla, Bernie, and Beth be able to take down a devious criminal who enjoys playing mind games?

AVAILABLE FEBRUARY 2023

ABOUT THE AUTHOR

Author Nick Lewis lives in Richmond, Kentucky, with his wife, Bonnie. He graduated from Marshall University in the fall of 1970. Upon graduating, he taught school and coached football for one year at Eidson Elementary. He then switched directions and began a forty-year newspaper career. He held circulation and marketing positions at four different newspapers in Ohio, West Virginia, and Kentucky. In 2004, he was appointed publisher of *The Richmond Register* in Richmond, Kentucky. He retired from that position in June 2013 and began his quest to become a full-time author.

In January 2014, Nick created The Detective Carla McBride Chronicles. The first book in the series, *The Gold Fedora*, debuted in October 2019. *The Black Rose, Chasing Truth and Redemption,* and *Quandary* completes the series to date. Book five in the series, *Enigma*, is forthcoming. He has another published novel, *When Eagles Soared*.

When Nick is not writing and revising manuscripts, he enjoys golf, gardening, and creating new adventures with his wife of fifty years. Bonnie plays an essential role in his journey of writing novels. He is an avid Marshall University football fan with three grown children, three grandchildren, and two cats named Zorro and Ziva.

www.ingramcontent.com/pod-product-compliance
Lightning Source LLC
Chambersburg PA
CBHW011450170626
46816CB00009B/2606